EVEN MONEY

All In Duet

EVEN MONEY

All In Duet

Copyright © 2018 by Alessandra Torre All rights reserved.

No part of this book may be reproduced or transmitted in any form or by any means, electronic or mechanical, including photocopying, recording, or by information storage and retrieval system, without written permission of the Publisher, except where permitted by law.

This book is a work of fiction. Names, places, characters, and incidents are the product of the author's imagination or are used fictitiously.

ISBN-13: 9780999784143

Digital ISBN: 9780999784129

Editors: Madison Seidler, Marion Archer, Natasha Tomic

Proofreaders: Angie Owens, Perla Calas, Erik Gevers

Front Cover Design: Najla Qamber Designs

Front Cover Photography: Sean Nel, Shutterstock

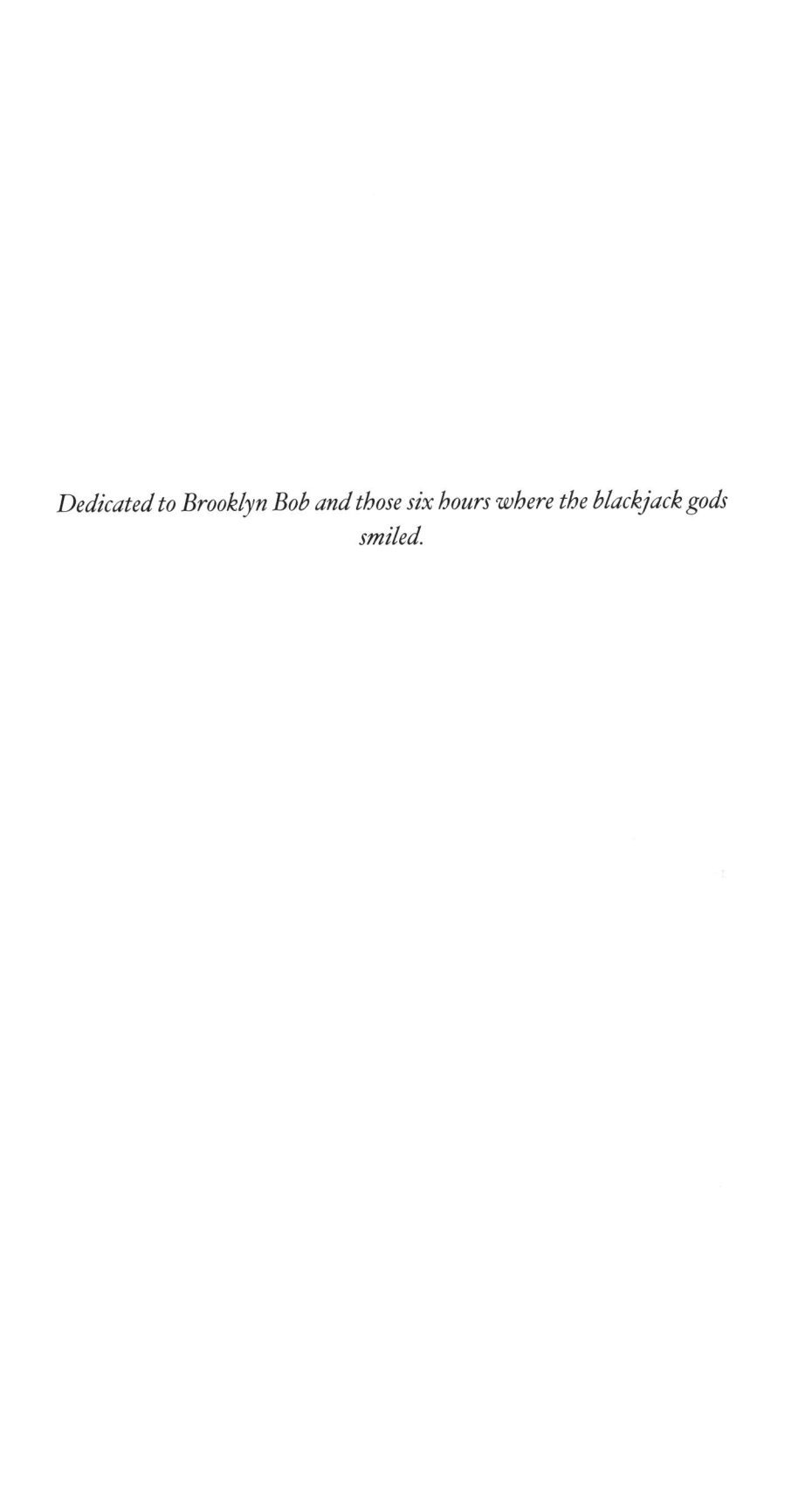

Dedicated to Brooklyn Bob and those six hours where the blackjack gods smiled.

ONE

e·ven mon·ey (*noun*)

odds offering an equal chance of winning or losing, with the amount won being the same as the stake.

The guy in the bumblebee suit was going to walk out of here a millionaire, assuming he didn't get his fingers cut off by Big Don. I carefully balanced six shot glasses on the glass tray, Maker's Mark swaying as I moved toward the top table, ignoring a few blatant looks and the hand that found my ass and squeezed it.

I climbed the steps, waited for the tuxedoed protection to move aside, and approached the top table. There were four men left at the felt, all of them silent, their eyes on the flop. I stopped next to the Iranian and carefully deposited the first shot on the green surface, lining up all six in a straight line. He passed me a black chip, and I pocketed it. "Thank you, sir."

He nodded, and I drifted my gaze over the table to see if anyone else needed anything. There was a flip of cards and the upward drift of cigar smoke. None of the men moved and I stepped back, my attention returning to the game as Bumblebee pushed a tall stack of black and pink chips forward.

Big Don called the bet, and I held my breath as the fourth card unfolded. It was an ace, the second one on the table. I watched Big Don and he leaned forward and smiled. I knew his tells. He had jack shit. I saw a line of sweat drip down Bumblebee's face and mentally urged him to bet.

He didn't. He tapped, Big Don tapped, and I turned before I saw fifth street. Nodding to the heavy, I took the steps to the main level and walked through the tables, glancing up at the gold clock above the bar. Almost one, still three hours left in my shift. I moved to the cage and slipped the black chip into the copper box with my name stamped into the top.

I stepped into the dark confines of the back room, the small place dominated by the grid of video feeds that showed every inch of the adjacent room.

"Hey, beautiful." Lance leaned back in an office chair, his hands linked behind his neck, his eyes flitting over the screens.

"Hey." I nodded to the screens. "I've got the yellow and black suit on the top table. A hundred says he cleans out Don and Mattis."

"You're not stealing from me."

"Give me two-to-one odds, and I'm in." Rick spun his chair toward me and spoke through a mouthful of Cheetos, a pair of huge headphones half-cocked on his head.

"Done. I got chips in the box." I didn't need proof of his ability to cover a hundred-dollar bet. I made pennies compared to the dollars that Rick and Lance brought in. For two Stanford drop-outs, they had done all right, operating the most successful underground house in Vegas.

We watched in silence as the hand ended, a fat stack of chips pushed toward my player, who carefully rearranged his winnings before pushing in the next blind.

"What the fuck is he wearing?" Lance asked.

"I don't know." I reached forward and stole a bright orange Cheeto from Rick. "He thinks he looks cool." The striped yellow and black suit might not have been so bad if the material wasn't so shiny, the resulting effect that of a psychedelic bumblebee.

"He's distracting. That might be helping his game," Rick commented.

"Lloyd shouldn't have let him in the door. Bell, would you grab me a soda?"

"You got it." I stepped back and pulled at the handle of the mini fridge, pushing aside beers and finding one of his Sprites. Outside of this room, the place was a palace, but in here, it felt like home. Worn furniture, the guys in sweats and t-shirts, two of the monitors on ESPN, the others on the cameras. There was almost as much gambling in this room as on the floor, and I was as guilty as them, all of us players, our industry the same as our addiction. They stayed in here and kept their money between them, but I'd heard the stories. Lance once bet a stripper she couldn't fit his cock down her throat. Rick bet ten strangers at the Bellagio that he could swim across the fountains ass naked and escape without being arrested. And those had been the bets *outside* the casinos. Inside, there were rumors that Lance took the Mirage for three million and used that windfall to open this place. Rick apparently came from money, and lost it all, including his watch, on a bad run of blackjack four years ago. He screwed a drunk Chinese princess for ten grand and built it up to two hundred thousand the next day.

Or, so the stories went. Outside this room, they were Vegas legends. In here, they were two guys on a few hours of sleep, who hadn't had a real meal in weeks. Lance ran his hand over his face, pulling down on his cheeks before reaching out and taking the Sprite. He didn't thank me, and I didn't expect it, but I still poked his arm when I headed back out the door.

"Thanks," he mumbled.

"You know it." I nodded at Britni and met the eye of a man on table four, watching as he tapped his fingers on the top of his beer. I moved behind the bar and grabbed a fresh one for him, along with a few waters, and stepped back on the floor.

A groan went up at the top table, and I glanced over, watching as Bumblebee stretched his hands forward, gathering more chips. I grinned.

Three hours later, I leaned against the building and checked my phone. According to the app, my ride was nine minutes away, which is what it had said for the last six minutes. I sighed.

The back door opened, and Lance stepped out, his head down, attention on his cell. He glanced to the side, saw me, and paused. "What are you still doing here?"

I pocketed my phone. "My car's in the shop. I'm waiting on a ride."

"And you're out here alone? You trying to get snatched?"

I smiled. "I'm fine."

"Fuck that. We pay security for a reason, B." Lance pressed a button on his keys, and his Viper flashed in the dark. "Cancel the car. You can sit on Rick's lap."

"The driver's only a few minutes away."

I watched him turn as the door opened and Rick stepped out. I listened to Lance update him on my car, and I rolled my eyes, refreshing my screen, the vehicle's dot moving closer.

"Lloyd's gonna wait with you," Rick decided. "You shouldn't be out here alone."

I shrugged. "Fine. Will that make you guys happy?"

"I'm happy." Rick glanced at Lance, who spun the key ring on his finger and strolled toward the car. "You happy?"

Lance sighed. "Ecstatic. One less dead employee." He leaned back, stretching.

I moved aside to make room for Lloyd, who lumbered outside with the athletic prowess of a garbage truck. "Sorry, Lloyd. The boys are paranoid."

"You kidding?" He settled against the brick and rummaged in his pocket for his cigarettes. "Best looking part of my night."

I smiled and watched the pair climb into the Viper, the engine revving, the top lowering, baseball caps pulled on. They were closer than brothers and felt like family to me. I'd been a waitress at a truck-stop diner when the pair of them had wandered in, two years ago. They'd been drunk and almost got killed by two bikers on the wrong end of a meth high. I'd stepped into the argument and gotten fired for it, but my intervention had kept their pretty faces intact and won their eternal loyalty in the process. The next night, they'd offered me a job, one that paid enough to get me out of my trailer and into the city limits, with enough left over to allow me to think about college.

Speaking of which... I smiled at the thought of tomorrow's statistics class and its delicious professor. If I got in bed by five-thirty, I could get in five hours of sleep and still have time to hit his office before my afternoon class.

Headlights swept over the lot, and I straightened when I saw the vehicle turn in.

Lloyd followed my gaze. "That yours?"

"Yep." I reached out my fist and bumped it against his. "Thanks."

"Stay safe, B."

"Always." I opened the door and tossed my purse inside, ducking in and confirming my address with the driver. Closing the door, I settled into the seat and fought a yawn. The car pulled forward and the neon signs of The Strip came into view.

Vegas is shaped like a caterpillar, the Strip its body, the casinos its legs. Lance and Rick's place was on the ass end, far enough off the strip to avoid tourists, but close enough to allow the big boys to swing by without being too far from home.

In a city filled with tables, we fit the unique need of the elite—a place for the gods to play. Steve Wynn couldn't play at his own house, and couldn't be seen at a competitor's table, so he came here. All of them did. It was a place where they could discreetly talk shop, play big, and loosen their ties.

Granted, not all of the clients were casino heads. Celebrities came to lay low and Vegas's hoteliers, restaurant owners, and politicians—anyone who didn't want to show favor with any particular casino, or who wanted their gambling habits kept quiet—also came to us.

"Which house is yours?" The driver glanced in the rearview mirror.

I sat forward, my hand gripping the headrest before me and trying to see the dark street. "It's the second one. Right there."

He stopped in front of the driveway and I grabbed my purse, sweeping a hand over the seat to make sure I had everything. I thanked the driver and stepped out, turning to the dark, ranch-style home.

I frowned, a prickle of unease tiptoeing up my back. I almost reached back to catch the driver's attention and ask him to wait.

But he pulled forward, his tail lights glowing as he took a right at the stop sign and was gone.

My house shouldn't be dark. I lived with three women, all who worked hard, partied harder, slept with their TVs on, and didn't know how to turn out a light to save their life. There was a reason our electricity bill never dropped below three hundred bucks, and it was primarily because our house was *never* dark.

I walked up to the porch and paused on the stoop, my eye on the knob. The unease inside grew, morphed. It had me sliding my hand into my purse and wrapping my fingers around the small handgun I kept there. I forced my arms to relax until the tremor in my grip stopped.

I'd had this feeling before.

TWO

Eight years ago. The horse limped, favoring its front hoof in an exaggerated motion that gave me pain just to watch it. I walked slowly, guiding it to the stall and unclipping the lead rope, patting the mare's neck as she passed me by and headed for the feed bucket.

"Good girl."

I pulled the door shut. There was the contented quiet of the barn, the soft nicker of horses, the sound of buckets bumping against stalls, of crickets outside. Peaceful, yet something was off. I glanced at the open doors at the end of the aisle, at the dark fields behind them. Nothing out there but a thousand acres of fields, the dotted black of the timber forests barely visible in the dusk. My unease grew, and I watched the mare eat and willed her to hurry up.

Headlights cut across the stalls, and the growl of an engine hummed through the quiet. Relief came and I pushed off the stall gate, heading to the front of the barn. Mom probably got off work early and swung by to save me the walk home. I paused at the sight of the truck. The driver's side door opened and I raised a hand to shield my eyes from the headlights, watching as the passenger door also opened.

"Bell?" The voice was gruff and deep, an unfamiliar one.

I took a step back. "Yes?"

"It's John." He shut off the lights, and I could see Mr. Wright, the owner of the barn, a man I'd only seen a few times before. I typically dealt with his son. Johnny was a few years older than me and had the twitchy muscles of a drug user and the sort of wandering eyes that caused me to wear jeans and long-sleeve shirts in the dead of summer.

From the passenger side, Johnny stepped out. He flung the door closed and I flinched at the sound. He came closer and I watched a smile slowly stretch over his thin face.

I shifted my weight, uneasy. "I just finished feeding the horses. I'm headed home now."

"Well, don't run off so soon," Johnny called. "We'd like to talk to you first."

They came closer and I forced myself to stay in place.

It was a mistake.

I stepped back from the front door and weighed my options, trying to push back the old memory, the clench of their grip around my arms as they'd dragged me back into the barn. I should have run. The moment they'd stepped from the truck, the second I'd felt that spark of fear ... I should have taken off. They wouldn't have caught me. Not that stiff man with his big gut. Not Johnny, with alcohol on his breath and that pack of cigarettes in his shirt pocket. He'd started panting before they'd been half done with me. There was no way he could have caught me in a sprint.

But I hadn't run. I had stood there because I didn't want to be rude, because I didn't know what else to do.

Now, I wasn't a scared fifteen-year-old girl. I had my handgun and a phone. I could get another taxi or try the police. I could call one of my roommates and find out what the hell is going on. I took the third option and dialed Jackie.

It rang, and I took a deep breath and eyed the other houses in the neighborhood. Everything looked normal, each home well-tended and still. It was the sort of neighborhood where the houses were stacked on top of each other, the front-facing garages all blocked by minivans and SUVs. Jackie's car was in our spot, and I spotted Meredith's Camry two spots down and Lydia's Jeep just behind it.

"Hello?"

"Where are you?" I stepped closer to the house.

"Home. By the way, don't turn on the lights when you get here." She sounded annoyed and I relaxed, pulling my hand from my bag and moving toward the house.

"Why?"

There was a rustle of background noise, and she cursed. "Fucking Lydia. She had a bunch of lightning bug larva in her room, and they hatched. We're trying to catch them now, and we can't find them in the—oh! I got one!"

"Why don't you just open the door and let them out?"

"I tried. She needs them for a project. She wants them alive and it's a *total* pain in the ass. When are you getting home?"

I laughed, relief sweeping through me. Nothing was wrong. They weren't dead. There was no one inside, waiting to cut my throat. "I'm outside." I pushed a hand through my hair and vowed to watch less true crime documentaries.

Jackie hollered loud enough that I could hear her through the brick walls. "Bell is OUTSIDE! Someone block the front door!"

She refocused on our conversation, her voice at a more normal level. "Come in quick. And for God's sake, if you see a lightning bug, catch it."

Nine hours later, lightning bugs were the last thing on my mind. I gripped the edge of the desk and closed my eyes, enjoying the bite of fingers into my skin, my panties yanked down, my skirt up.

ULV had a few shortcomings, but statistics professors who knew how to fuck wasn't one of them. Dr. Ian Clarke swore, running his long fingers down my inner thigh and in between my legs, rubbing them along the sensitive area. I opened my thighs, propping myself up on an elbow and watching him. "Stop teasing me."

"Tell me about linear regression." He growled out the order as he leaned forward and kissed me. "And pull up your shirt and show me those sweet nipples."

"I can't think about linear regression right now." I yanked up my tank top, bringing it over my breasts, his eyes focusing on them, and I stretched down the lace cups of my bra, letting my breasts fall loose atop them. He dove in, running his tongue over my right nipple and sucking on it gently before kissing his way over to the left, his two fingers sliding in and out, a steady rhythm that caused my bottom lip to hang, my eyes beginning to close.

"Are you going to fuck me, Dr. Clarke?" I arched my back and pressed against his hand, his thumb taking the hint and rubbing a gentle circle around my clit. He bit carefully down on my breast, and I moaned in protest.

"Not yet. First, I'm going to make you come all over my fingers, and then I'm going to send you into class. I want to spend the next hour thinking about bending you over my desk as soon as the bell rings."

I laughed. "We don't have bells."

"Shh... You're ruining the fantasy." He withdrew his fingers and slapped my ass hard enough to make me yelp. Straightening, he braced one hand on the desk and looked down on me.

"Lay flat. Close your eyes. You're about to drip that sweet little pussy all over my papers."

I obeyed, letting my legs open wider, his fingers talented in their smooth dip, in and out of me, a slick friction that increased in speed as he applied careful and deliberate attention to my clit. First his hand, then his tongue, the hot and wet sensation causing me to thrash against the desk, my thighs trembling, my hands clawing for a handhold before I bucked off his desk and came.

He lifted me off his desk, pulling me against his body and letting me feel the hard ridge of his arousal. "I'm not going to be able to move from behind the podium today. I'm going to be hard as a rock for the next hour, thinking about your perfect pussy wrapped around my cock. Stay in the room after class."

"Yes, Dr. Clarke." I bit my bottom lip and slid my teeth over it, letting it pop free and enjoying the way his eyes darkened as a result.

He smiled, his hand tightening on my ass. "God, you're perfect."

"Not yet." I pulled away from him and fixed my skirt, gathering my hair and twisting it into a loose ponytail. "But I plan to be soon." I bent at the waist and reached for my bag, letting him get an eyeful before I straightened.

His lips twitched into a smile, and he ran a hand over his mouth, nodding to the door of his office. "Get to class before you drive me mad."

I turned to leave, grinning as I opened his office door and stepped into the hall. He was filthy in the best way possible. God didn't put a man like that in front of twenty thousand coeds and expect him to behave. Just like he didn't put Ian in front of me, have him invite me to office hours, and expect me to keep my clothes on.

Granted, that first tutoring session we didn't do anything. Ian sat on his side of the desk, I sat on mine, and we discussed binomial and normal distributions like two perfectly responsible adults. But on the way out, he walked me to the door, his hand on the small of my back, his fingers drifting a hair lower than was proper, the gentle caress before release telling me all I needed to know.

The next session, he suggested we block out an hour instead of thirty minutes. We got through confidence intervals before he told me to sit on his desk, that he wanted to taste me before he went fucking insane.

In fifteen minutes, I learned that the statistical probability of an orgasm from his mouth was one hundred gazillion percent.

And Mom said college wouldn't teach me anything.

THREE

I woke up to an orgy. I blinked, fuzzy images coming into focus. Two men on one girl. Two different girls, on their knees. There was some whipped cream action and an old guy with nipple rings. I closed my eyes. "Can't you watch that somewhere else?"

I heard a loud snap of gum and pictured it, bright pink and showing with every smack of Meredith's jaws.

"The Wi-Fi isn't working in my room. I keep telling you guys, we need to move the router to the kitchen."

I rolled over on the couch and folded the pillow in half, stuffing it under my head. "I thought porn came on DVDs."

"Are you kidding? Nobody does that anymore." The sounds of fuckery paused as she fast-forwarded the scene, then pressed play. I watched as the old guy moved toward a cluster of plaid-skirted blondes. Meredith mumbled something about production value, and I snorted out a laugh.

"I'm almost done. I got one more video after this."

I closed my eyes and groped around for an extra pillow, pulling it over my head. "Turn it down a little."

"Fine."

The sounds diminished, and I kicked a foot free of the blanket and tried to fall back asleep. Maybe it was time for me to move into my own place. One free of roommates, especially ones whose class projects involved the analysis of the adult film industry and its moral evolution.

She poked my foot. "Look at this guy really quick, B. He's got a freaking *hose*."

I growled and considered getting up and moving to my bedroom. It was my own fault. That's what I got for bingeing on reality TV and falling asleep on the couch. Gangbangs for breakfast.

I squeezed the pillow tighter and managed, despite the moans and slaps, to fall back asleep.

I was scrubbing vomit off the toe of my heels when Britni burst in.

"Dario *Fucking* Capece is here."

It was an announcement that caught all of our attention, Lance and Rick slowly easing upright, our gazes moving from Britni to the monitors.

"Where?" Lance asked.

"Outside. I saw him getting out of his car when I was out for a smoke."

Rick scowled at the activity, but let it slide, his interest more focused on the city's biggest whale, one we'd never had. He turned to Lance. "What the fuck's he doing here?"

Lance shrugged. "Maybe he's playing."

"He doesn't play. Everyone knows that."

Lance caught my eye. "Bell. Go out and welcome him. Find out what's what."

I looked down at my shoe, the gold silk ruined, thanks to a mixture of liquor and what looked like fettuccine alfredo. I worked it onto my foot and winced at the ugly result. "Okay. I'll do my best."

He nodded, leaning forward in his seat, the urgency clear in the air. Britni let out an annoyed huff, moving aside when I passed. I ignored her bullshit performance. This particular job was one neither of us wanted. Vegas was full of sharks, but Dario Capece was a killer whale, the kind you only saw right before you got eaten. Britni didn't want anything more to do with him than I did.

Lance looked up from the monitors. "Hurry. He's almost through security."

I stepped out the door and onto the floor, moving quickly toward the entry.

The entry space was our most boring room, one decked out with industrial gray carpet, a metal detector, a bank of lockboxes, and the main attractions—Tim and Jim. Those weren't their real names, but they refused to make small talk with anyone, so that's what we had coined them. Where Lloyd was the friendly big guy, they were the ex-Special Forces assholes everyone hated. I stepped into the room, nodded to the closest one, then turned to Dario Capece with a smile.

I should have checked the monitors first. Peeked through the security window. Done something to give me more warning.

I'd expected a dozen things. A suit. A scowl. A bodyguard. An expensive watch. Closed lips and wandering eyes. A sexist remark or friendly hands.

I hadn't been expecting something in me to yank when our eyes met, a pull of need that occurred before his mouth even opened. He paused, and the wary look in his eyes matched everything I was feeling.

He was handsome, but it wasn't even his looks. There was something between us, and I stepped back in hopes it would fade. It didn't.

"Mr. Capece." I managed the greeting with a calm and professional tone. "Welcome to The House."

His mouth curled into a smile, but his eyes didn't. He glanced at Tim. "Watch your fucking hands."

Tim moved carefully, patting down his legs, then his arms. He nodded to the metal detector, and Mr. Capece walked through, then collected his phone and wallet.

"Will your men be playing also?" I rested a hand on the door, wondering if we should wait for them to be checked.

"No." His first word to me, and it was muttered as he looked over his shoulder to his security. "Wait in the car."

There was a small and silent battle, one where they questioned his decision with a subtle tilt of their heads. He turned back to me, and the battle ended. I pressed on the door, and we entered the hall.

"We have blackjack and poker on the floor."

I walked slightly ahead of him, the hallway too narrow to allow anything else. He was tall, my shoulders the height of his chest, and I lifted my chin to make sure he heard me as we entered the main room.

"There are only six slot machines, but they are all high limit. The cage allows markers of up to a million dollars, but exceptions are common. Depending on the night, we have different specialty games, and craps on the weekend."

I motioned toward the cage. "Should I have chips pulled for you?"

He let his eyes move over the room, and I followed his lead, wondering what his impression was of the space. The House was a converted warehouse with floor-to-ceiling curtains around its perimeter, crystal chandeliers hanging from its faux ceiling, marble floors, and enough opulence to hold its own with any high-roller room in town, his included. Granted, we didn't have the largest hotel in Vegas behind it, or his fifty thousand square feet of tables, but we had bigger names in this room than anywhere.

"There's a bar in the next room if you are just here to socialize. It's an invitation-only space."

There was no need to mention his standing invite. Dario Capece, the poor kid from Louisiana, had been given the keys to the city when he'd married Gwen Hawk, the heiress to the Majestic Casino. He'd turned those city keys into golden handcuffs when he'd transformed the struggling Majestic into the hottest address on the Strip. Now Vegas was his playground, his kingdom, his supermarket. In the ten years since he'd married into money, he'd bought three more casinos, and his legend had grown legs and done the tango.

"I'd like to speak to your boss." His words were quiet, but I knew they were being picked up by the hidden mics, set into every seam of this building. He turned to me, and in the direct eye contact, I felt unstable, a scrap of paper loose in a hurricane.

Did everyone feel this way? Was this how he'd captured our city so easily, how he'd filled thousands of hotel rooms and seduced the best talent into his workforce? I reached out, resting my hand on the railing and forced myself not to grip it for dear life. "I'm afraid that isn't possible. The owners aren't here tonight."

"Ah." He nodded and stepped closer. I forced myself not to move. This close to him, I could smell his cologne. I could feel the edge of his pants as they brushed against my bare legs.

"I don't believe you," he said quietly.

I lifted one shoulder in the most casual way I could and shrugged. "Sometimes people don't."

It was a risky move, and I thought of all the stories I'd heard, men who had lost body parts or disappeared, all for playing the wrong way, counting the wrong cards, or saying the wrong things. I met his eyes, tightened my gut, and prepared for the worst.

Then, he laughed, turning back to the floor, his hands resting on the railing, the edge of a grin visible on that handsome face. He was beautiful, in a fierce, wild way. Short dark hair, littered with silver. Big, strong features, a once-broken nose, but handsome lines. He looked like a pretty boy who grew into a man and beat the shit out of the kid he'd once been. He looked like a night full of filthy, delicious sex, and a string of orgasms that would leave you panting and delirious. He looked untouchable.

He looked back at me, and the hint of a smile still touched his lips. "Ballsy. I like that."

There was a soft touch at my elbow, and I turned and saw Lance, his hoodie and workout shorts replaced with dress slacks and a button-up shirt. I raised my eyebrows, and he leaned forward, kissing me on the cheek.

"I'll take it from here, B."

"Nice outfit," I said quietly before he pulled away. I gave him a small smile and stepped away from the railing, nodding to the visitor. "Would you care for a drink?"

"A Coke, if you have it," Dario responded.

"Certainly."

I turned from them, moving down the steps and to the main floor, bee-lining for the bar, and shaking my head when Britni shot me a quizzical look. I grabbed a tumbler and fixed Lance's usual, then grabbed a glass and filled it with ice, opening one of the small bottles of Coke and pouring it in.

I glanced up at the entrance balcony where I'd left the men. Dario Capece rested his forearms on the railing. They looked friendly, and I wondered what they were discussing. His gaze connected with mine and I turned away, stacking the items on the tray and adding the dark purple House napkins. I stalled for a moment, taking a steadying breath before I hoisted the tray on my shoulder and headed for the stairs. Delivering drinks wasn't exactly groundbreaking stuff, something I could do blindfolded and one-handed. I had no reason to be nervous.

But something about him, something about that short exchange and the way his face had pulled into a smile... I felt unsure and exhilarated, all at the same time—a dangerous combination around a man like him.

FOUR

I knew what to do. I'd served princes and presidents, celebrities and mobsters. I was to deliver drinks and disappear. I didn't hear anything and I didn't speak unless spoken to. If flirted with, I politely evaded. If yelled at, I retreated and let security deal with it. The rules weren't taught to me, but learned from two years in this building, two years of mistakes and lessons, hundred-dollar tips and occasional scorn.

I'd been proposed to and propositioned. Groped and flipped off. Cursed out and courted. Everyone who had the means to walk in these doors was entitled, and that made for a volatile cocktail, one contained by distractions. Women. Alcohol. Risks. Possibilities.

I walked toward Lance and Dario Capece and wondered what Capece's distractions were. Certainly not alcohol, not with the Coca-Cola he'd ordered. Not cards, since he hadn't stepped toward a table or glanced at a chip stack. Maybe risk. Maybe women. I slowed as I approached, and his gaze slid from Lance to me, his eyes starting at the bottom, at my vomit-stained heels, and moved up my bare legs, lingering across the sequined shorts and the black halter top. The action was so obvious that Lance turned, his eyes darkening as he saw me, the apologetic look in them almost laughable. I reassured him with a smile and took the final steps toward them.

I served Lance first, then tucked the tray under my arm, passing the glass of soda to Mr. Capece. I didn't meet his eyes and stepped back to allow them privacy. Escaping down the back stairs, I let out a long breath.

He had checked me out. Held my gaze longer than necessary. Two things that happened a dozen times a night. That was half of our purpose here, being eye candy. Britni and I got more attractive the more they drank, the more they won. It wasn't the first time that evening a man had blatantly swept his gaze over me.

I shouldn't have been trembling, not just from a brief moment of interaction. And I definitely shouldn't be smiling. I fought to swallow the expression and wondered what the hell was wrong with me.

I entered the control room and shut the door. Rick glanced over and held up a hand for silence.

"--and that's how we plan to keep it," Lance finished.

I watched the monitor, saw Dario's mouth move, the sound of his voice a bit delayed. "What do you do when you get hit hard? Too hard?"

"We have cash reserves to cover up to twenty mill."

Dario's quiet chuckle came over the speaker. "Twenty mill? Come on. That's one winning streak for these players."

"It hasn't been a problem yet. You know what it's like. No one walks away on top."

"Still…"

There was a break in conversation as someone walked by, words of greeting exchanged, a restless moment where Rick stretched his legs and I watched the monitors. I needed to get back to my tables, yet I couldn't move from this spot.

Quiet fell.

Dario spoke first. "I'd like to invest in your operation if you aren't interested in an outright purchase."

Rick leaned forward, his fingertips pressing together as if in prayer.

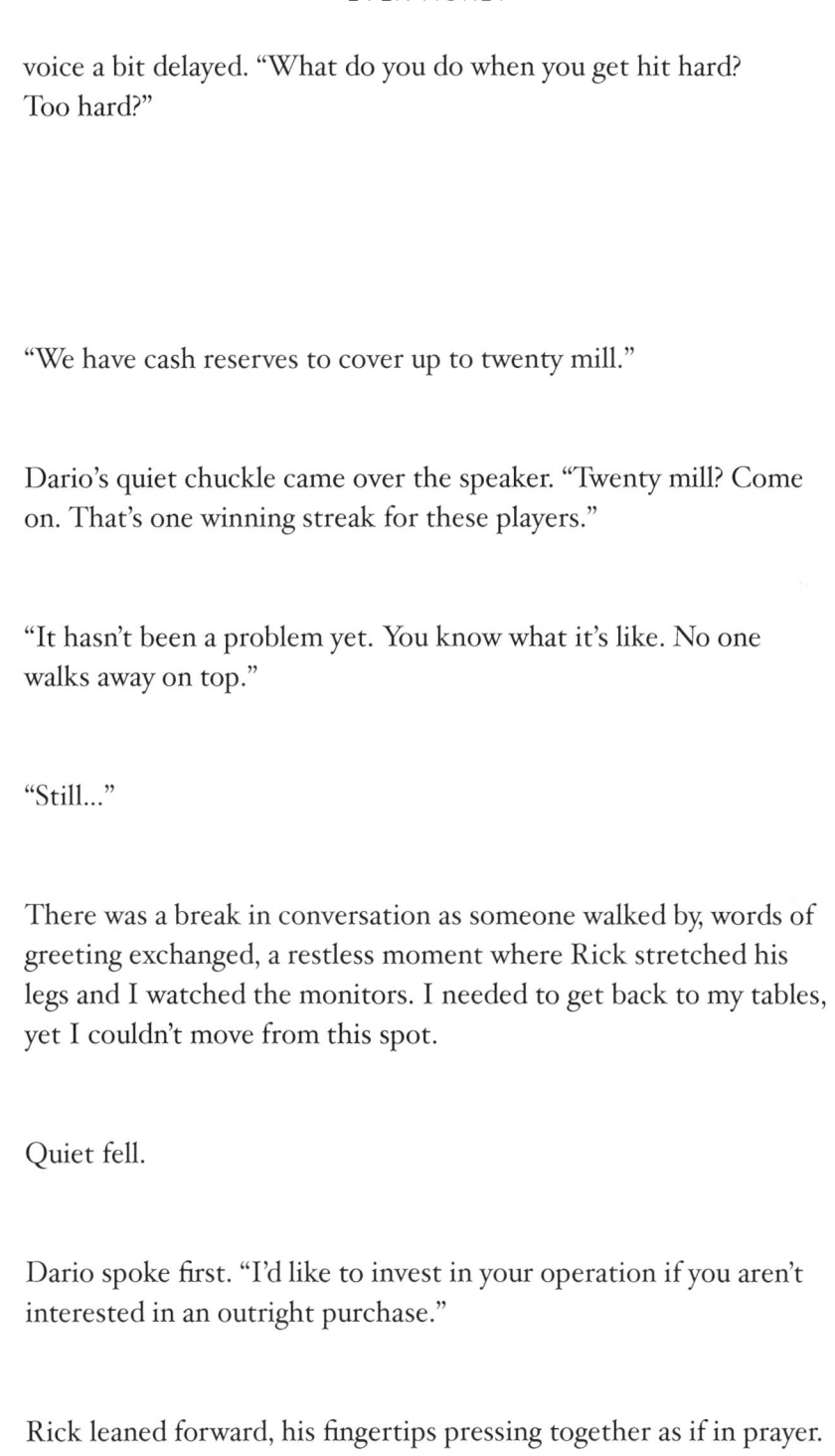

"We aren't interested in selling. Besides, the reason we work is because we are a neutral location, with neutral ownership. You don't want to be seen at Bellagio, and they don't want to be seen at your place."

I watched the monitors as Lance spread his arms, encompassing the place.

"Here, you can all gamble in private and without padding any of your competitors' pockets."

"A good point." Dario nodded. "But I could be a silent owner or investor."

Lance shook his head. "We aren't looking for either. Still, I appreciate the offer."

"You'll need a bigger bankroll. Who you going to call when you are in the red? The Italians?"

"I was under the impression that *you* were the Italians."

There was a smile in Lance's voice, but I still stiffened. In this town, success didn't come to the innocent, and there were few men as successful as Dario Capece.

The devil smiled. "Everyone in this town is, in some way or manner,

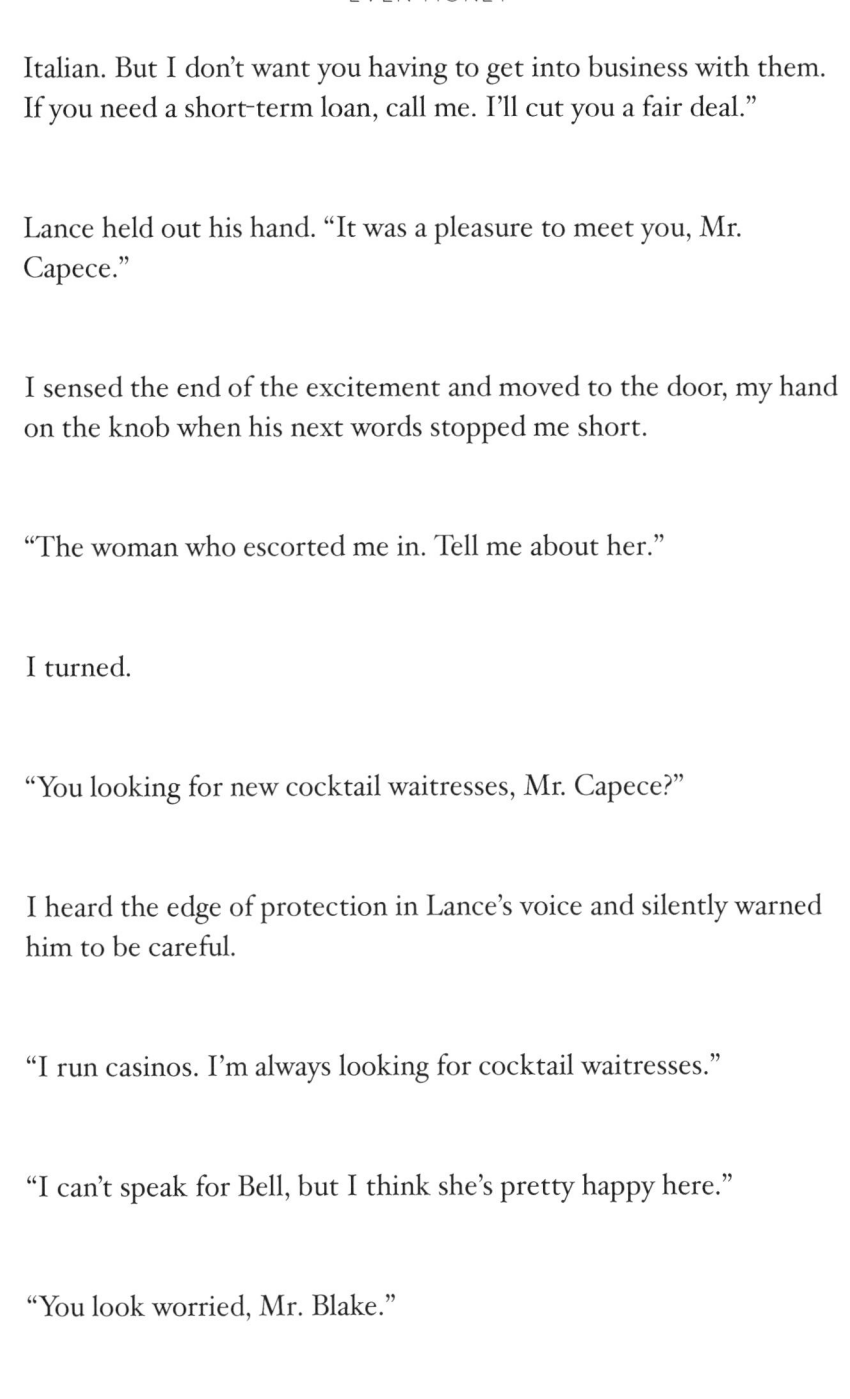

Italian. But I don't want you having to get into business with them. If you need a short-term loan, call me. I'll cut you a fair deal."

Lance held out his hand. "It was a pleasure to meet you, Mr. Capece."

I sensed the end of the excitement and moved to the door, my hand on the knob when his next words stopped me short.

"The woman who escorted me in. Tell me about her."

I turned.

"You looking for new cocktail waitresses, Mr. Capece?"

I heard the edge of protection in Lance's voice and silently warned him to be careful.

"I run casinos. I'm always looking for cocktail waitresses."

"I can't speak for Bell, but I think she's pretty happy here."

"You look worried, Mr. Blake."

I turned to watch the monitor. On it, Lance's arms were crossed over his chest, his imposing stance diminished by Capece's powerful build.

"I'm concerned any time a stranger asks about someone I care for."

"It's just curiosity. I'm a man. She's a beautiful woman. You understand."

Lance shifted. "As I said, she's happy here."

"Noted."

I watched the monitors as the two men shook hands.

"Call me if you ever need funds, or anything else."

"Thank you."

They turned, making their way back to the front room, and I looked away from the monitors, Rick's gaze dead on mine, stopping me in my exit. "What?" I asked.

Rick spoke slowly, as if I might have trouble understanding him. "Dario Capece is bad news."

"Yeah. Got it." I tilted my head toward the gaming floor. "So are pretty much every one of those assholes out there. Don't worry about me."

"I saw you two. Whatever *moment* that was?" He flicked his index finger back and forth, between me and an imaginary Dario. "You're a tiny minnow in this town, B. Sexy and smart as hell ... but still a minnow. And he's—"

I interrupted him before he got fully into the lecture. "I KNOW. He's a whale. Or a shark. Or a killer whale, or whatever freaking ocean reference you're about to make. I get it. Focus on your own shit, because he came in here after your business, not my ass."

I yanked the door open and didn't miss the twitch that broke his stern expression into a smile.

"I got you peanuts."

Meredith held out the bag, and I grabbed it, moving my feet and giving her room to pass. She juggled two beers and almost spilled both of them by the time she settled into the seat next to me. "God, it's hot."

I stole the second beer and lifted it to my lips, nodding in agreement. "Miserably."

There was the crack of a bat, and we shifted out of the way as everyone around us rose to their feet, then moaned in disappointment and settled back down.

"Foul. I knew the minute I heard it," Meredith said.

"Sure."

"I'm serious. You can hear when they hit the right spot."

I smirked, my mind taking the words in a dirty light, and she rolled her eyes.

"Stop."

"You're the one playing porn in our house all hours of the day. How are we supposed to keep our minds clean with all that?"

She sniffed. "I'm almost done with the project. Then, I swear, I'm done with glory holes and gangbangs for life."

The soccer mom ahead of us turned, glared, and covered the ears of her teenage son, as if he'd never heard those words before. Meredith stifled a laugh, and I elbowed her with a smile. The kiss cam came on the scoreboard, and the crowd started to cheer.

"So … tell me about this man." She leaned in, raising her voice to be heard over the crowd.

I sighed, tipping back the beer and looking out at the stands. "You know. Another guy."

Meredith scoffed. "*Another* guy? I don't know anything about casino stuff, and even I know *Dario Capece*."

"I shouldn't have mentioned him. He checked me out. He was hot." I pulled open the peanuts and shook a few out, offering the bag to her. "And he's married."

She nodded in the annoying way that typically precluded idiocy. "Uh-huh. Forbidden love."

"Forbidden *love*? You're so dramatic. Love and I aren't even in the same hemisphere right now."

"Not even with the sexy professor?" She put her beer in the cup holder and settled back in the plastic seat.

"*Especially* not with Ian."

"Yeah … A hot, smart guy with a job and a delicious Irish accent. I agree. Worthless. I can't believe you're even wasting your orgasms on him."

I hid behind my beer as the mom ahead of us turned around again. I swear, we weren't even talking loudly. And her son had to be fifteen. Too old to have his ears covered. Meredith was right. On paper, Ian was pretty damn awesome. Naked, his stock was even better. But other than having fun with him, there were no feelings involved, no fluttery emotions, or breathless anticipation of our next meeting. "I'm pretty sure our thing is going to end with the semester."

"That sucks."

"Not really."

Meredith fished in her purse and held out a bottle of sunscreen. "Here, I brought this for you. Cover that pasty white-girl skin of yours."

I took it without argument, and squeezed out a generous glob in my hand, eyeing her ebony complexion. "You need some?"

"Nah. Already got it on." She settled back in her seat. "So, let's get back to forbidden love. You think this guy's gonna come back in The House?"

I sighed. "I don't know."

I'm a man. She's a beautiful woman. I thought of the way he'd shrugged, as if because he was male, and I was female, that it was done. "He asked about me, said he needed cocktail waitresses."

She asked where I'd make more money, and I mulled over the question.

"Probably staying where I'm at. Besides, I can't leave Lance and Rick."

It was the truth. They were too good to me, and they were like family. The thought of leaving them, of working at one of Capece's giant supermarket-sized casinos—it was of no interest to me. *Especially* if it was one he owned. I didn't need to work for a man like that.

I passed back the bottle. "And, I don't think it was a legitimate job offer. He was just fishing." *Fishing to find out more about me.* The thought shouldn't have caused a reaction in me, but a spark of excitement still occurred.

Meredith dropped the lotion into her purse. "You're not changing jobs, your lovefest with professor Hot Pants is ending in five weeks, and you're basically the most boring person I know. That sum everything up?"

Damn, I loved this girl. From the moment she'd sat down next to me in a freshman orientation session, we had clicked. And friendship—true friendship—was hard to find in this town of users. Which was another reason why I loved Rick and Lance so much.

I smiled and pulled my sunglasses back down, shielding my eyes. "Nailed it."

Number 8, the shortstop with the great ass, walked up to bat, and we started paying attention to the game.

FIVE

The man, sitting at the first spot on one of the main tables, looked like a model and reeked of suspicion. I watched him carefully through his first few hands, delivered his drinks and stiffened when he reached out to tap me.

"A cigar, please." He smiled, and I nodded, stepping away.

He was hot, whatever he was. Clean cut. Pretty eyes. An expensive suit that didn't quite fit him right, like he'd borrowed it from someone or stole it off their dead body. In this city, either was possible. But a guy betting a thousand bucks a hand ... I eyed his chip count with increased suspicion. His suit should fit.

I took three more orders on the way to the bar and forgot him amid getting drinks, cigars, and a bottle of champagne for the chubby guy at table two. An hour later, I was on my way to the bathroom when the pretty boy stepped in my way, blocking the hall.

"I'm Chris." He reached out a hand and I shook it. It was the sort of handshake that involved an object, though I couldn't tell if it was cash or a note. I pocketed the item without looking.

"I haven't seen you before." He leaned one hand on the wall and his suit bunched around the shoulder.

I smiled politely. "Well, you haven't been here before."

He laughed, and I'm not that funny. I stepped to the left to see if he would move. He didn't.

"I meant, I haven't seen you around town."

My bladder was close to breaking, and I lied through a pained smile. "My boyfriend keeps me busy."

He winced. "Ouch. I was hoping that maybe ... you work outside of here."

He tucked his hands in his pocket, a casual gesture that didn't soften the sting of the words. *You work outside of here*. He was asking if I was an escort. If he flashed five thousand bucks, would I suck his dick? If he promised ten, would I go back to his suite and spread my legs?

I shook my head. "I don't have any side jobs. Just drink delivery and good luck carrier." I patted his arm and squeezed around him, making enough of a production about it that he stepped out of the way.

"I'll pay anything." He followed me, reaching into his pocket and pulling out a purple chip. A purple chip that could cover my bills for an entire year. Or even better, the remaining mortgage on my parents' house.

He held it out. "Come on. Just a few hours."

Just a few hours. It had taken less than one for Johnny and his father to ruin my innocence. This boy with the handsome smile wouldn't —couldn't—do anything worse. He'd probably want anal. A blowjob. Me to call him Daddy and let him fuck me against a Vegas window. It didn't matter.

I took another step away. "I appreciate the offer, but I don't do that. The terms don't matter." I moved further and wondered if he'd follow. Wondered if those eyes would turn hard, his grin morphing into a sneer.

"Good luck," I called the words over my shoulder and pushed open the ladies room door. I stepped into the empty space and reached into my pocket as soon as the door shut behind me, looking to see what he'd slipped me.

It wasn't cash, and I pouted a bit at that. It was just a piece of paper, his first name and phone number scrawled across its front as if we were fifteen years old. I tore the paper into pieces and dropped them into the toilet, unzipping quickly and handling my own business. A purple chip. *Fifty grand.* My first week at this job, I would have been tempted, even knowing the risks. Back then, I was still living at home, watching illegal cable, and living off fast food and diner leftovers. Now, I had no excuse. I made good money, and becoming a prostitute was absolutely not part of my future plans. I flushed his number, washed my hands, and reentered the floor, my mind going over the interaction, my early suspicions about him growing.

He hadn't just been a john looking for love. Who had he been with? Las Vegas PD? A competitor or a human trafficker? Had he come specifically for me, or had I just been an attractive opportunity?

I stepped back on the main floor and glanced over the open tables, but whoever Chris was, he was gone.

DARIO

The door to the limo opened, and the Chippendale dancer folded himself into the backseat.

Dario looked up from his phone. "Well?"

"I don't know." The man stretched out his legs and reached into his pocket, pulling out a wad of cash and handing it over. "Here's your change."

"*I don't know* isn't an answer."

"She's not a prostitute." Chris watched as Dario took the cash.

"Are you certain?"

"Short of her slapping me in the face? Yeah. She mentioned a boyfriend, but that seemed bogus. Either way, I gave her the number you gave me. So maybe she'll change her mind and call."

Dario finished counting the cash and looked up. "Are you sure you had the right girl?"

"The brunette with the great ass?" The kid grinned, and Dario wanted to punch the expression off his face. "Yeah. Her name is Bree or Bee, or something like that?"

"Bell."

"Right. Anyway, it was her." Chris leaned forward, rubbing his hands and eyeing the roll of money. "So, we done here?"

Dario nodded, his eyes lingering on the casino's dark entrance, the dim lighting that gave little hint as to what was inside. He'd heard rumors of the place for years, and had felt a pull of nostalgia at the idea of a small house casino, something built by kids, a business model that reminded him of late night games on back porches in Louisiana. The rumors had persisted, and he had grown to want it: the building, the business, the clients. Bell Hartley had been a surprise, one that had stuck. But he needed to refocus on the task at hand—acquiring The House. A cocktail waitress shouldn't matter in this equation. She couldn't.

Which was all easy to say, but he was still sitting in a limo, looking at a stripper in a rented suit. All for what? To find out if this potential acquisition also dabbled in illegal prostitution? Or to see if a prospective cocktail waitress would moonlight as an escort?

It was all a complete waste of time. It didn't matter if The House had hookers; that was an issue that could always be fixed. And it didn't matter if Bell Hartley fucked strangers for money. She wasn't looking for a job, and hiring waitresses was about a dozen levels beneath him. Not to mention, if escorting was an eliminator for employment, half of his floor staff should probably turn in their resignations.

There was no plausible scenario to explain why he was here, yet he was. Dario pulled five bills off the stack and passed them to the model.

"Thanks." The man pocketed the cash and cracked open the door. "Appreciate it."

Dario nodded and waited until the door was shut, the locks engaged, before he unbuttoned his jacket and reached for the bottle of ice water. Unscrewing the lid, he poured it over ice.

"What's going on?" The question came from the man next to him, the bodyguard who had been at his side for the last decade. Dario ignored the question.

"You fuck this chick somewhere? Is that why you're interested in this place?"

"No." Dario tilted back the water glass, taking a long sip. "I met her here the other night."

His man stayed silent, letting him collect his thought. It was a courtesy Dario appreciated, and he leaned back in the seat, thinking about the girl, the way her eyes had held his without fear. The way the corner of her mouth had twitched with the hint of a smile. The way she had flowed when she'd walked. He lived in a world of beautiful women, a constant buffet of sex and temptation, yet … ever since he'd met *this* woman … he couldn't get her out of his head. When he had first looked up, mid-frisk from a security guard, and saw her—he'd had to force himself to look away, force his breath to even, his heart to calm.

One look and she'd had some sort of a hold on him.

One conversation, a few lines about drinks and business, and he was obsessed.

Obsessed was probably the wrong word, but intrigued was far too pale. And everything he'd done since—running background checks, going through this dog and pony show with the Chippendale model ... it fit into the obsessive mold as cleanly as a dollar bill was eaten by an Amatic slot machine.

He didn't have time for this. He had casinos to run and millions to make. He sighed. "Screw this. Let's end this hell of a day."

In the condo, he undid his watch and slid it off his wrist, setting it in the black velvet drawer, next to the others. Working on the sleeves of his shirt, he glanced up, into the mirror. His father's face stared back at him, lined with stress, his eyes tired, the silver in his hair more prominent at times like this, when it needed a cut.

"Let me get that." Gwen approached, her slender fingers tugging his sleeve, deftly undoing the cufflinks and dropping them into their place. She reached for the other one, and he watched her work, glancing at her face. Her hair fell down, a dark curtain of sheen hiding the delicate features. She was a beautiful woman, and he lifted his hand, pushing the hair gently out of the way, the action causing her to look up, her mouth curving into a smile.

"Thank you." She raised on her toes and pressed her lips against his cheek. "I'm heading to bed."

"Goodnight," Dario said, emptying his pockets. He set the thick wad of cash on the counter, followed by his keycard and phone.

"Everything okay?" She paused at the entrance to his closet, leaning her cheek against the doorframe, her eyes on his. That was the problem with being married to your best friend. They knew everything without asking. Still, her face held the question.

"It's nothing." He shook his head, sitting on the bench and working the knot of his laces. "A non-issue."

She studied him for a long moment, one he avoided by removing his left shoe, then his right. He inserted the shoe tongues in each, then looked up at her. "Just one of those long days."

She smiled and raised her hands in surrender. "Okay. Mope on your own. I'll be in bed if you need anything."

He watched her leave, the satin slip clinging to her curves as she walked to her bedroom. She was one of the most powerful women in Vegas. In her day, she'd also been one of the most beautiful, a beauty that had refined and matured as she'd aged. For one brief and early moment in their marriage, they'd tried a physical relationship. It hadn't done anything for either of them and now, ten years later, they had settled in the comfortable roles that worked for them. She handled the hotels, the food and beverage, the events.

He handled the casinos, the finances, their umbrella corporations, and any dirty work that crossed their golden plates.

Dario changed into workout shorts, then took the staircase down to their private gym. Hitting the treadmill first, he put on music and ramped up the incline and speed until he was jogging.

Their marriage was anything but normal—a business relationship solidified by friendship and respect. He fucked a dancer named Meghan on a regular basis, along with Laney, a waitress from the Marlin Club. Gwen had her own lover—Nick, their foreman at the ranch. Out of mutual respect, they kept their affairs hidden from each other, the public, and from Gwen's father. But things were observed between them and mistakes were sometimes made. They were both intelligent adults with a clear understanding of their marriage and the unbreakable friendship at its core.

But this waitress from The House ... out of every woman he'd met in Vegas, she had the potential to be trouble. He should walk away. Never enter that place again and drop any continued efforts to buy it. Stay in his life of power and away from the exotic brunette with the legs he wanted to bury his mouth between. He needed to forget everything about her and continue forward on his golden path with Gwen.

He increased the speed until he was sprinting, his heart hammering in his chest, his Nikes pounding the treadmill, his breath coming hard, sweat dripping down his chest.

It had been sixty seconds of interaction. Less than a commercial break. As short as a hand of blackjack. Forgetting her should be easy.

But in sixty seconds, a gun could be fired. A knife thrust. A bomb ignited. Sixty seconds could be nothing, or it could destroy a man.

He stumbled on the treadmill, against the furious pace, and felt his life veer off track.

SIX

BELL

Naked, I walked down the hall and into the kitchen, leaning on the island with a lazy groan. "I can't find my dress."

Ian turned away from the stove, a piece of toast in hand. "Look on the balcony."

Ah. I had a vague recollection of straddling him on the chaise lounge, and it coming off. I snapped my fingers and pointed at him. "Good thinking."

He smirked, ripping off a bite of toast. "I never forget my best work."

"And *that* was your best work?" I raised my eyebrows. "Maybe you need some tutoring."

He laughed, not at all concerned with my critique. "Your orgasms didn't seem to mind it."

"Yeah, they aren't very picky. But, I'll probably keep you around a little longer. As a charity project, of course." I grinned at him and walked around the counter, stealing a crumb of his toast and popping it into my mouth. "Please say that you have more than burnt bread to woo me with."

"There's yogurt in the fridge."

"Oooh. Sexy. You're like a hot Emeril Lagasse."

He spun slightly on the stool. "At the risk of getting you all hot and bothered, I've also got cereal in the cabinet."

I made a face. "I think I'll just grab something on the way to work."

"Your loss. I've got to get back to the university anyway."

He grabbed a shirt off the floor and pulled it over his head. Pushing open the balcony slider, I saw my sundress puddled on the deck.

"Need help?" He stuck his head out the door, a baseball cap now pulled on, and *damn*, he was pretty. Five o'clock shadow, T-shirt snug over his lean muscular build, and enough height to make me look up into his eyes.

Tugging it up my body, I started on the side zipper. "Nah, I'm good."

He hesitated in the doorway as if he had something to say.

I finished getting the dress into place. "What?"

"Speaking of keeping me around a little longer, I was wondering if you might want to go out to dinner tomorrow night."

"Dinner?" I hesitated. "You mean, like a date?"

He chuckled. "Yeah, Bell. Like a date."

Alarm bells sounded at full strength. Dating wasn't what I was looking for. While sizzling hot sex with a consistent guy was right up my alley, thoughts of emotional attachment gave me hives. Not that he was proposing emotional attachment. But that's what dates led to, right? Relationships. *Real* relationships, not the fuck-buddy stints of my past.

I shook my head. "I can't."

"Because you're working, or because you don't want to?"

"Both." I met his eyes. "I thought we were on the same page with what this was."

This wasn't his fault. My steadfast commitment to emotion-free sex wasn't normal. Losing my virginity to two assholes who left me bleeding on a barn floor had certainly affected my viewpoint and left me with deep emotional scars. For the first two years after that night, I had nightmares. I'd been terrified of men and avoided any interaction with them. Long talks with my mother had helped. She taught me that I couldn't be a victim. She's the one who took me to the gun range on weekends and gave me the confidence to believe I was no longer vulnerable. Counseling, a year later, had cleared several more hurdles. But Elliot Wilton was the one who did the heavy lifting in my emotional healing. Sweet, terrified of me, Elliot Wilton had done the impossible and calmed my fear of men. We'd had a semester-long history project together, a project that led to a dozen late nights alone together in the dark recesses of the library. He'd all but quaked when my hand had brushed against his leg. Three weeks later, I'd kissed him with the hesitancy of an alley cat and he'd blushed bright red. I'd felt power in that kiss, had felt the way his skin had heated with the touch, had seen the way his eyes had shone with worship when I'd pulled away and wiped my wet mouth. With Elliot, I wasn't the victim, I was the aggressor. Slowly, I learned that I could do anything I wanted—or didn't want—and he'd let me.

Elliot gave me a taste of the power of my own sexuality. And with that taste, I was addicted.

The project ended, Elliot graduated, and I moved on to a foreign exchange student who barely spoke English but introduced me to the beauty of his mouth in between my legs. After my own high school graduation, I grew bolder, testing the waters with an electrician five years older than me, one who could spit game like a pro but was putty in the bedroom.

With each male, I grew stronger, less affected by the events of my past and more detached from the act of sex. I didn't want a relationship. I wanted pleasure. I wanted control. I wanted the ability to walk away without a thought, pain or heartache.

Which is why this Irish sex god and I couldn't go on a date. This needed to stay like every other physical relationship I'd ever had—a mutually beneficial arrangement set up with clear ground rules. They needed to treat me with respect. Sex wasn't ever a guarantee. Condoms would be used. And no emotions needed to be involved, other than friendship.

Initially, I avoided emotional attachment because of the potential risk. Not so much to my body—that had already been run through the gamut of abuse—but to my heart. I was terrified that, after surviving the emotional train-wreck caused by the rape, heartbreak would be another burden I wouldn't be able to handle.

Those worries had been unnecessary. Far from heartbroken, I

seemed to be an emotional cactus, dry and parched of any of the emotions that led to love. With the first few guys I messed around with, I'd nervously waited, in the quiet moments after sex, for the feelings to come. The rush and exhilaration. The high. The butterflies. The endorphins that turned ordinary people into lovesick idiots. None had ever come. Eventually, I'd stopped worrying and gave up on the feeling altogether, accepting that that part of me might have broken that night in the barn.

Ian flipped his keys in his hand and scowled at me. "It's just a date, Bell. I'm not proposing."

"Oh, I know. I just ... I'm not looking for anything serious." I stood on my tiptoes and pressed a quick kiss on his lips. "Are you okay with that?"

"I guess I'll have to be." He frowned. "Since the burnt toast didn't appeal to you, want to go grab something quick. Subs?"

I pretended to swoon. "Subs? Like, with meat AND bread?" I fluttered my eyelashes. "You are an Adonis of sexual temptation."

"So I've been told. I also issue A's for exemplary blow jobs."

"I already earned my A." I stuck out my tongue. "And ... I'm going to pass on your gourmet lunch offer. But after class next week, I'll let you spell out my homework assignment with your tongue."

Still smiling, I wiggled my fingers at him and pulled the door shut, jogging down the steps and into the warm Nevada sunshine. I let out a hard breath. Prior to his date night invite, I had liked the ease of Ian and assumed he was hooking up with several other coeds. But maybe I'd read him wrong. Maybe he wasn't a man whore wanting a casual lay. Which sucked, because Meredith had been right, Ian checked off all the boxes in an ideal man. He'd be an ideal boyfriend, if I was looking for that. But... I checked my feelings. Nope, still repelled by the idea of love.

Pulling my sunglasses from my bag, I headed for my car, grateful for the newly-fixed air conditioning. Glancing at my watch, I quickened my pace. I didn't have much time to get home, shower and change before work.

I pulled out of the complex and was halfway to the main road before I realized I'd forgotten my phone. I pulled a quick U-turn and almost hit a black Tahoe, also on its way out. I kept going, seeing Ian's Jeep, and slowed down when I saw his hand reaching out, waving at me.

"Forget this?" He held my cell out, and I shifted into park and half crawled out of the window to grab it.

"Yep. Thanks." I worked my way back in and waved. "See you in class."

He nodded, and his Jeep bounced a little on its shocks as he bumped it into drive.

EVEN MONEY

Fifteen minutes later, I juggled a giant Styrofoam cup in one hand and eased my car out of the McDonald's drive-thru, the nose of it almost clipped by some prick in a Tesla. I craned my head forward, looking down the road, and noticed the dark SUV, two cars down, parallel parked under a tree. There was an opening in the traffic, and I pulled out in a screech of almost-bald tires. Settling into my lane, I glanced back at the SUV. As I watched, it pulled out into traffic, four cars back.

I set down the cup and put both hands on the wheel, darting my gaze between the road ahead and the rearview mirror.

It was ridiculous to think it was the *same* Tahoe from Ian's neighborhood, ridiculous to think that it had sat and waited for me to finish my fast food order, and *extra* ridiculous for me to think that it was now following me.

I got in the left lane and it did nothing. I waited until the last possible moment, then switched back to the right lane and whipped off on the exit ramp.

The Tahoe continued straight, and I let out a hard breath. *See? Nothing. I was being an idiot.*

I was humming down the road when I spotted it again, materializing out of nowhere as if I hadn't just shot off in a different direction, not three miles ago.

I reached for my phone, driving with my knees as I dialed the number and put the cell on speakerphone.

Rick answered on the fifth ring. "Hey."

I blew out a frustrated breath. "This is probably nothing, but you were the only person I knew to call."

"Got a body that needs burying?"

I smiled despite my nerves. "With your puny arms? Please. I'd call Lloyd for that."

"Hey, I devote serious time to these biceps. Want to insult my calves, go for it."

Traffic opened up a bit, and I pressed the accelerator a bit. "I'm probably being paranoid, but I think someone's following me."

"Where are you?" The laughter was gone from Rick's voice.

"Umm... Martin Street, by that Chipotle. He's been behind me about ten minutes."

"Come to our house. Lance is home now. I'll have him grab the Hummer and hem him in."

Hem him in? The idea sounded reckless. I chewed on the inside of my cheek. "Maybe I should just drive to a police station."

"And the minute you turn in, he'll drive away and we won't know anything about him." I heard muffled talking, his hand probably held over the receiver. "Lance is getting the H1 now."

I could hear the excitement in his voice, the increased pitch as he called out something. I told him so, and he let out a long puff of air.

"I am not, in any way shape or form, excited by the prospect of kicking some creep's ass." He spoke the words in a dead monotone. "I promise," he added.

"Whatever. Just don't be stupid about it."

"I'm going to open the garage door and move my Benz. Just pull in and go in the house. We'll handle the guy."

We'll handle the guy... With someone else, I would have been afraid. But Rick and Lance had managed to survive situations a hundred times hairier than this. Still, he sounded too cocky to be safe and too confident to be cautious. I turned into the entrance of his neighborhood and started to second-guess my decision.

"I don't know..."

"STOP worrying. And drive normally. I don't want him to suspect anything."

"I just pulled into your neighborhood. Please be careful."

I turned down his road, noticed the black grill of Lance's H1 idling on a side street, and pressed the gas a little bit harder, passing their neighborhood's 23 MPH speed limit sign like a badass doing thirty.

Rick and Lance lived in one of those neighborhoods that didn't quite know its place. It was a cluster of overpriced mansions built during the real estate heyday, back when ordinary people got loans on million-dollar mansions they couldn't afford, then defaulted nine months later. Half the houses had overgrown lawns and For Sale signs in the yard. Their house sat at the end of the cul-de-sac and was a three-story frat house, disguised in respectability and brick. From the street, you couldn't see the six-car garage that stretched along its back, nor the pool with the grotto waterfall and Slip 'N Slide.

I didn't know the rules of following someone, but I assumed this guy's vehicle had a navigation system, one that would tell him, as I approached Rick's house, that it was a dead-end. I approached the cul-de-sac and Rick's Mercedes SUV rolled across the width of the turn-off road, the door opening as I passed. He lifted a hand to me and I focused on his driveway, hitting it at a brisk ten miles per hour and pulling around to the back, the last garage door open and waiting for me.

I pulled in, jerked the car into park and turned off the key. I cracked open my door and waited for the sounds of disaster.

SEVEN

My engine had no concept of danger. It ticked as it cooled, and when I pushed the car door open, it creaked. I crept out of the car and around its hood, moving carefully down the long garage, past the vintage Mustang, the Range Rover, jet skis, and motorcycles. I tried the door to the house, found it unlocked, and stepped inside.

The interior smelled like pizza and Pledge. The television in the living room was on, and I moved through the kitchen and to the front windows. Light streamed through the open curtains, and I sidled up to them and peeked out.

The Tahoe was parked at an angle, too far away for me to see or hear anything. I saw a blob of person move, and they could have been a sumo wrestler or a six-year-old kid. I gave up my attempt to hide behind the window and just pressed my face to the glass, cupping my hands to shield the sun.

Nope. Still couldn't see anything. I hesitated, then moved to the front door. I gave myself a moment to consider the first option—staying inside like a good little girl. I tossed that to the side and turned the knob, stepping outside and into the situation.

It turns out that the "situation" was waaaay back where Rick had parked his Mercedes. That was where the Tahoe had gotten wise of the situation, attempted to turn around, and got stopped by the front bumper of Lance's Hummer. I headed toward their cars and made it two houses down before my feet started sweating in my heels. Another house further, I decided to pull them off and go barefoot. Another six steps and I realized the sidewalk was hotter than a skillet. I hopped to the side and put them back on. I continued, sweating through my sundress, and was practically wheezing by the time I approached the confrontation, one that had both of my boys out in the middle of the street, arms folded across their chests, a scrawny little white-haired guy between them. My fear took a nose-dive. *This* was the guy following me?

I limped up to the threesome and Lance glanced at me. "God, woman, you are out of shape."

I ignored him and made eye contact with Rick, who nodded at the stranger. "He's a private eye. Won't say who he works for."

"It's not against the law to follow someone." The old guy spit on the ground, then looked at me as if *I* was the criminal.

Lance stepped closer to the vehicle. "I've got his name and tag number. I'll make some calls." He yawned, obviously disappointed.

No doubt he'd wanted a fight, a chance to liven up his Wednesday with something more than a senior citizen with a saliva problem. He opened the Tahoe's passenger door and the old guy whirled around.

"Hey!"

"Easy." Rick caught the man's arm and held him in place, his fingers biting into the man's leathery flesh. "Just stay right there."

Lance leaned inside the vehicle. When he straightened, he held an insurance card in his hand, satisfaction stamped on his face. "MJS Holdings owns this car."

The name meant nothing to me. I turned to Rick, who still had one hand clamped around the man, the other on his phone, his thumb working over the display. "Give me a minute… Got it."

He looked up. "MJS Holdings is an asset management company."

Lance shut the car door, the insurance card still in hand. "What assets do they manage?"

"Looks like real estate across the state and casinos." Rick's last word caught my attention, the tightness on his face held it. "They own The Majestic."

"The Majestic," Lance repeated. "So… Dario Capece."

Rick nodded. "Dario Capece. Or maybe… his wife?"

They turned to me, their eyebrows lifted in question. Between them, the old geezer smirked.

Rick put his hands on his hips and looked at me as if I had the key to the Dario Capece vault of understanding. "This is fucking bullshit. Following you? What the fuck for?"

Lance ran a rough hand through his hair. "You think this is about us? Or her?"

I sank into Rick's couch. "It can't be about me. I walked him in and brought him a drink. That was it."

"He hasn't contacted you since?"

I frowned. "Since a couple of *days* ago? No."

"You *are* pretty sexy." Rick leaned against the stone column that helped divide the living and dining room. "Maybe he's smitten."

I coughed out a laugh. "Smitten? What are we, in eighteenth-century England? No. But thank you for the compliment." I blew him a kiss and he tipped an imaginary cap in response. Prying off my sweaty heels, I flopped my bare feet up on the couch. "Is this a valid excuse to be late to work? Because I still need to eat and shower."

Lance frowned and completely ignored me. "Maybe he's trying to get dirt on us. Maybe we're all being followed."

The room fell silent in the face of this new possibility. I shifted against the leather, half-pleased at the possibility that I wasn't the main target. I was also half-disappointed, which made no sense, as there was no good situation that involved me being the sole focus of a surveillance operation.

Rick shifted his attention back to me. "Bell, you said you were coming from a friend's house, right? Who, specifically?"

I lifted one shoulder and freed my hair, which had gotten pinned underneath me. "A guy I'm sleeping with. My stats professor."

"Wow." Lance looked down at his hands. "We just dived right into that."

I shrugged. "It's the age of sexual empowerment, Lance. I'm not ashamed of it."

Rick shook his head. "Dario Capece doesn't care about a college professor, so it's not about that."

In the back of my mind, something nagged at me. I tried to capture it, but Lance's phone rang, and it was gone.

⁂

I laid in bed, my hair still damp from my shower, wide awake at four a.m. Somewhere else in the house, I heard the quiet sounds of a sitcom, one which would probably play all night.

It had been a good shift at work. Some big winners, the sort who tipped heavy and laughed a lot. Some big losers, but the kind who didn't bitch about it and could afford the loss. I'd earned just over three hundred bucks and had forgotten—for those ten hours—the creepy smile of the private investigator. *Dario Capece. Or maybe... his wife?* When the PI had smirked, I'd wanted to shove him against the car, wrap my hands around his neck, and force him to tell me everything. I'd almost lost control and ignored the fact that I was such a tiny, vulnerable kitten in a city full of beasts.

I thought of Dario Capece's loose and confident stance, the way he had stood at that railing and watched me approach, his eyes moving over me and stopping at my eyes, holding his gaze there. I couldn't get that look out of my head, the moment between us, the pull of that contact.

I'd met and served a thousand powerful men and been attracted to plenty of them. There had been sparks, flirtations, and chemistry, but none of which compared to that moment.

There had never been *anything* like the way that connection had filled the air with heat, nor the way my breath had caught in my throat. I saw him and understood why Vegas had fallen at his feet, why the city's heiress had married *him* out of all the possibilities. He had been magnetic and I had been almost helpless in the face of it. I had walked away and assumed he hadn't felt the same, assumed he affected every woman in that way. I had continued with my life and pushed aside any other thoughts of him.

But I couldn't ignore him any longer. Not when someone from his company had followed me. Was it because of his interest in purchasing The House? Or was it a specific interest in me?

Could he have felt the same connection I did and was now ... *stalking* me? I frowned at the thought.

My phone buzzed on the bedside table, and I rolled over, glancing at the clock. Almost five in the morning. A little late, or early, for anyone to be up. The text notification was from an unfamiliar number, and I unlocked my phone.

—Bell, this is Dario Capece. I just found out what happened yesterday and would like to apologize. I hope he didn't scare you.

What the hell? I read it a few times, trying to understand it. *How did he even get my number?* I typed out a quick response.

why was he following me?

The minutes stretched along with no response and I reread his text, my initial surprise fading, curiosity taking its place. My phone lit up.

—*I needed to know more about you.*

I rolled onto my side, and repositioned the pillow, struggling with the emotions the text was enticing. I shouldn't read that text and feel a burst of butterflies. I should be filing a restraining order and double-checking my locks. I should be blocking him on social media. I shouldn't feel *excited* that a married man wanted to know more about me. I'd told Lance earlier that it's the age of sexual empowerment. But a married man was a different animal, one I'd never wrestled with before and had no interest in tangling with now.

I selected his phone number and scrolled through the options until I got to the "block number" selection. It would be so simple. One tap of the finger and no more texts, no chance of a phone call. It'd be the easiest way to send him a clear message.

I backed out of the menu and went to his text.

I hit *reply* and tried to find the strength to tell him off.

EIGHT

I didn't return his text. I let it hang, the words taunting me as I fell asleep and dreamed of his eyes, the way they had feasted on me. In my dream, I had a long and twisted affair with the man, and woke up with my heart pounding, the high of our interactions still filling my chest with a dreamy, perfect sensation.

I closed my eyes and tried to find it again, wanting to resurrect the feeling. Instead, I woke up three hours later, my mouth cottony, my heart empty, mind blank.

I found my phone in the sheets and pulled up the text conversation. Nothing new had come in since I fell asleep, the ending note still his.

—*I needed to know more about you.*

Maybe I was reading it all wrong. Maybe this wasn't a sexual, or even romantic, thing. Maybe Dario Capece needed to *know more about me* for a strictly business reason. I rolled onto my back and kicked the covers loose, my body suddenly warm.

Dario Capece was trouble, I reminded myself. MARRIED trouble. Getting involved with him would be a disaster. I thought of the moment he had laughed, the flex of his hand on the railing, the way he'd peeked at me out of the corner of his eye ... I pushed it all from my head and forced myself to get out of bed.

DARIO

Dario carefully folded his shirt in half and laid it over the metal folding chair. He walked forward and the man before him winced at his approach. Dario was a man of habit and dedication. Two hours each night in their personal gym. Four hours on Saturday and Sundays with the boxing bag and jump rope. As a result, he had the body of a twenty-five-year-old, one without an ounce of fat, the large build one that came from weights and genetics, his muscles properly proportioned without the side effects of steroids and supplements.

He stopped in front of him and the man's eyes darted to Dario's, a plea babbling from his lips. His apologies were too late. The asshole should have thought about this outcome before he manufactured poker chips in his garage, then tried to toss them on a table and play.

Dario closed his eyes, blocking out the sound of the man and taking a moment to picture a different man—someone older, his shock of white hair giving him an air of wisdom that almost hid his psychosis. *Gwen's father.*

He opened his eyes. When he swung his fist, it carried the impact of the two hundred and forty pounds of muscle behind it. The man's head snapped backward and the crunch of teeth was strangely satisfying in their vulnerability.

BELL

"The Palms sucks. And that bouncer will be there. The one we hate." Meredith leaned against the bathroom counter, her face close to the mirror. "Help me with these fake lashes. I watched that YouTube video four times and I still can't do it."

I gestured her toward me and she turned, the bits of fake eyelashes clumped together in a delicate pile on her palm. I pulled out a cluster of them and took the glue from her hand, squeezing a tiny drop on the end of one before leaning forward and carefully pressing it against her top lash. "Come on. It's Ladies Night at The Palms. It'll be fun."

"Right. Ladies night. An ovary-fest. Just what my libido needs." Jackie spoke from her place on the bed, where she sat cross-legged, a bowl of cereal in hand. "B, see if you can call your sexy bosses and get them to go out with us."

"Hey, Lance and Rick are off-limits." I untangled another clump of fake black curls and got them gluey. "We've discussed this. At length."

I decided eons ago that mixing my male friends and my roommates was a recipe for hell. I loved the three of them, but their relationships tended toward the dramatic and short-lived. If Lance and Rick ever decided to settle down, it needed to be with girls who could handle their lifestyle, personalities and sex drives. After living with these three for the last eighteen months, I could safely say that none of them qualified.

"Yeah, B is keeping them as her backup plan." Lydia spoke through a toothbrush, leaning forward and spitting in the sink before returning to her dental process—one that qualified as OCD to anyone who paid attention to it.

I made a face at my least favorite roommate. "*Another* conversation we've had a million times."

"So, the Palms is out," Meredith decides. "And Bell gets no votes because she's got more men than she knows what to do with right now." She met my eyes and winked.

"You do know that your eyelash-batting future is in my hands, right?" I pressed on her next batch a little more aggressively than necessary.

"Ouch. Stop."

"If not the Palms, then where are we going?" Jackie looked down, fishing out a spoonful of Fruit Loops and lifting them to her mouth.

"What about the Gold Room?" Lydia piped in the suggestion while opening a new container of floss. "This girl at work said it's amazing."

My body tensed at the mention of The Majestic's latest club. It was the new hot spot among tourists and locals alike. Meredith's eyes studied mine, and I looked away, focusing on the application of super glue to the end of false eyelashes. The sure-fire way to have a conversation I didn't want, or guarantee our presence at the Gold Room, was to nix it as an idea. I stayed quiet and motioned for Meredith to turn and give me her other eye.

"Yes!" Jackie hopped up from the bed, her bowl in hand, and headed to the kitchen. "I've been wanting to go there."

"I don't think they have any drink specials..." Meredith ventured.

I gave her a small smile in appreciation and, behind me, Lydia snorted. "Drink specials? I'm wearing my push-up bra. Tonight, drinks are on *these* babies."

Despite my silence, and Meredith's casual attempts to save my ass, forty-five minutes later we were packed into Lydia's car and headed north, toward Dario Capece's newest crown jewel.

It'd be fine. It was one club out of a dozen he owned, and the chances of him being there were slim to none. I put my phone on silent and slipped it into my clutch, fastening the clasp and leaning forward, turning the radio up, and belting out the lyrics to the song, hoping I was right.

DARIO

The lobster was sweet and tender, the steak a little overdone. Dario cut into it and moved it to the side, the waiter instantly beside their table, removing the tenderloin and apologizing.

"Let Robbie know."

His reference to the chef was met with a quick nod. "I'll bring another one right out, sir."

"And another bottle."

"Certainly."

The man escaped, and Dario met Gwen's eyes across the candlelit table, noting the tired way she rubbed the back of her neck. "Long day?"

"God, they all are lately." She held her hand over her mouth in an attempt to cover up a yawn. "When did we get so old?"

He chuckled. "I think about five years ago."

"Maybe we should just give up on everything." She stole a piece of his lobster and dipped it into the drawn butter. "Sell it all and move to Tahiti."

"Tahiti?" He smiled. "You'd be bored stiff."

"Well then, maybe we just need a week there. Long enough to appreciate our busy lives a little more."

He raised the wine bottle, refilling her glass, and she smiled in appreciation, bringing it to her lips once he'd finished.

"Give me your foot."

She obliged, lifting one of her heels into his lap and he undid the strap, dropping the thousand-dollar stiletto onto the floor and running his hands over her sole, working the tired muscles, the arch of her foot flexing under his fingers.

"God..." She closed her eyes, settling back in the chair. "That's entirely inappropriate, but it feels glorious."

"We own the place. I don't think management will say anything."

She laughed, a quick and delicate trill of pleasure, and pulled her foot free, replacing it with the other. "In that case, do this one too."

"Yes, ma'am." He looked down at her foot, exquisitely wrapped in delicate ropes of leather and gold. "You should get into the spa tomorrow. I can handle your meetings. Take a day and let Vincent pamper you."

"Now see, I *knew* there was a reason I married you." She smiled at him over her wine glass. "Sexy *and* brilliant."

He nodded at the waiter as he returned with a new steak. She pulled back her foot and there were a few minutes of companionable silence as they finished eating.

As their plates were cleared, his phone buzzed, and he glanced at the text notification.

—*Bell Hartley is in the Gold Room. Upper level, with three other girls.*

He closed the text.

"Everything okay?" She bent forward, fastening her heels.

"Yeah. I've got to go up to the Gold Room."

She stood, reaching for her purse and putting the thin strap over one shoulder. "I think I'll stay at the ranch this weekend. I haven't worked the horses in weeks."

"You should." He leaned forward, giving her a kiss. "And go to the spa tomorrow. I'm forcing you to."

"Yes, sir." She mocked his serious tone and squeezed his arm. "Don't work too hard. I'm going to head up. I'm about fifteen minutes from falling asleep."

"Sleep well." He kissed the top of her head. "See you in the morning. I'll get the tip."

He watched her weave through the tables, waving to a few of their regulars. Reaching into his pocket and pulling out a wad of cash, he peeled off a few bills and set them on the table. Before leaving, he picked up his cell and texted his head of security back.

headed there now

He avoided the front entrance and went through the kitchen, taking the service elevator and pressing the button for the seventh floor.

This morning, he had hesitated before texting Bell, unsure if an apology was appropriate via text. There was the chance it would only freak her out more, the knowledge that he had hunted down her number. His need to reach out had won out over his hesitation, and she hadn't responded to his final text—an unfinished conversation that had left him unsettled, a feeling he didn't like. A feeling he wasn't used to.

The elevator doors opened, and he stepped into the Gold Room's kitchen, nodding to familiar faces as he moved through the space. Everyone thought his domination of Vegas had been luck, fueled with Gwen's bankroll and his security team, one that bent rules and broke unfriendly arms. But his employees knew the truth—it was hard work behind his success. Nineteen-hour-days. Knowing employees and systems in every restaurant, every division. Remembering names, favors, clients, and whales. Continually being present, staying on top of things. Working his ass off.

He stepped into the club and looked up to the second level, glad he'd had the foresight to have Vince send her image to all of his doormen. It had been a longshot, but out of a hundred nightclubs in the city, she was here.

It couldn't be a coincidence.

NINE

BELL

Take away the fact that my new stress point owned the Gold Room, you had one badass club. A hot band was playing, the drinks were fantastic, and it was full but not stifling, the doorman carefully cherry-picking the line and controlling the crowd. We were lucky to be in, our odds artificially inflated by the fact that Lydia had recognized a bouncer and flirted our way to the front of the line.

A group of guys approached our table, the typical tourist sort. Black pants. Stiff shirts. Freshly shaved, with gelled hair and probably wives and kids back in Florida. They reeked of bachelor-party recklessness and—after introductions and handshakes—invited us to dance. Meredith bowed out, saying she'd watch our purses and drinks, and Jackie grabbed my hand, pulling me onto the floor. A fast beat thumped, and the crowd roared to life, the energy contagious. I laughed, my nerves relaxing, and let the tallest guy in the bunch pull me against him. His shirt smelled faintly of aftershave, and I felt his hand wander, settling on the curve of my ass, and I avoided his kiss when he tried to get one, spinning out of his arms and laughing.

He called after me and I shook my head, turning to the band and lifting my hands, swaying to the beat and singing along with the words. He came up behind me, his body fitting against mine, and I allowed it. I turned my head, watching a display of lasers dance across the club, and saw *him*.

On the raised ledge that surrounded the floor, his weight against the rail, in a suit that looked like a million dollars, Dario Capece watched me. Our eyes connected, and my thought process stalled, my body stuttering mid-sway. The guy behind me pulled at my hip, and I pushed away, coming to stand on an empty spot, holding the gaze of Vegas's most powerful man.

He was here. I'd known it before we left the house, had expected it at the coat check, the bar, the moment we'd sat down at the high top. I'd looked for him in every crowd and expected him with every breath. Still, I was surprised. I hadn't properly remembered the crush of my lungs, skip of my heart, the sheer *force* of his eye contact. He tilted his head toward the spot beside him and I didn't even hesitate.

DARIO

She was beautiful. Eyes closed, body moving. When he watched her dance, he wanted her underneath his body. Needed to feel those movements against his cock. Craved that smile, that laugh, that mouth. He watched her and didn't think about their loan refinance, or the ADR decline at the Palace, or Cirque du Soleil's contract renewal. He watched her and felt something he didn't understand. Vulnerability with a side of fear. Want eclipsed by need. Intrigue overshadowed by jealousy.

She finally looked up and saw him. Her hips slowed and she came to a stop in the middle of the dance floor, the man behind her ignored, the beat forgotten. There was nothing, in that moment, but the two of them. And in the connection of their eyes, everything inside of him intensified.

This girl would be the death of him.

THE BABYSITTER

Claudia was bored with watching Dario Capece. The damn man didn't know a woman he didn't want to pursue. It was a full-time job, keeping up with his revolving door of pussy. She watched the pretty brunette make eye contact with Dario and wondered if *this* would be the one that was a problem.

Eventually, one of them would be. At some point, the impenetrable Dario Capece would go too far and fall in love. And when he did, *if* he did, Claudia would be there. And that girl wouldn't be like the others, the mistresses that she hid from Hawk and kept safe, unbeknownst to their pretty little heads. That girl, the one who finally snags Dario Capece's heart?

Claudia would have to tell Robert Hawk about her.

And she... she would have to die.

◆

BELL

"Where are you going?" Jackie grabbed my arm.

"I'm taking a break," I called out over the music, and she flashed a thumbs-up in response. I turned, working my way through the crowd, and found a small staircase to the side that led to his level. There was a guard, a huge man who opened the rope without a word and nodded to me with respect.

Surprised, I thanked him and made my way along the railing. As I approached, Dario turned to watch. Unlike last time, his eyes didn't take a tour of my body, something that almost disappointed me. Despite my best intentions, I'd chosen this dress—an attention-grabbing gold number that showed off my legs—for him. Instead, his gaze locked on mine, a small smile pulling at his mouth.

"Of all the gin joints in all the towns..."

"I didn't plan to walk into yours," I interrupted. "I blame it solely on the three women who dragged me here." I smiled to soften the words.

"Ouch." He winced. "I'll have to see what I can do to persuade you to come back, since a three-million-dollar renovation hasn't done its job."

I joined him at the railing, looking down on the crowd, grateful for the excuse to break eye contact. "The club is great. That wasn't the reason for my trepidation." I forced myself to turn to him, hyper-aware of how close we were. My arm brushed his and I felt the current all the way to my toes. I couldn't believe I was having this conversation with him. Dario Capece, a man who created millionaires and paupers every day, and he was focused on me as if he had all the time and interest in the world.

"You don't need to be afraid of me, Bell."

"I'm not afraid of you." It was the truth. Maybe I should have been. But the only thing I feared was the pull I felt toward him. It was dizzying, the loss of control, the struggle to keep my attraction in check. No wonder he owned this town. I bet there wasn't a person in town, male or female, that he couldn't persuade into doing his bidding. I wet my lips. "I just think you need to learn boundaries."

He smiled broadly, and the sight of it almost knocked me over. It creased his whole face, twinkled through his eyes and exposed a full set of perfect teeth. In The House, I'd gotten just a tease of the gesture. Getting it head-on was another level altogether, one I wanted to experience again as soon as it dropped from his face.

"I think you might be the first person to ever tell me that."

"Really? How do the other people you stalk handle it? They write thank you letters?"

He attempted to scowl, but I could see the amusement still present in his eyes. "I wasn't stalking you. I was doing research."

"Research on what?" I crossed my arms over my chest, and it wasn't my fault the action pushed up my cleavage a little. His attention strayed for the briefest of moments, then returned to my eyes. "You said that you *needed to know more about me*. Why?"

Maybe it was good we came here. Fueled by the two vodka martinis I'd downed just after walking in, my tongue was spitting out all of the things I couldn't seem to text him and say.

He studied me for a long moment before he responded. "I don't dive into relationships without properly vetting someone."

It was such a ridiculous statement that it took a moment to process. When I managed to speak, my words stuttered on their way out. "Dive into *relationships*? What makes you think I *want* a relationship with you?" That question wasn't that difficult to answer. Most women would claw their way through insulation for a chance at this man, assuming they were willing to overlook the gold band on his ring finger.

My monologue gained traction. "And aren't you forgetting the fairly major detail that you're married?"

He watched me calmly, as if I hadn't just presented him with an impossible equation. When I stopped talking, he raised one eyebrow. "You finished?"

"Yeah," I snapped.

"You probably don't want a *relationship* with me. But I'd be willing to bet the title of this club that you want me to fuck you. And I don't fuck strange women that I know nothing about. As you pointed out, I am—on paper and for appearances' sake—married. I can't risk that union for flings with unstable or talkative women. And I don't step into *any* situation without knowing what is potentially at stake, both for me and for them." He nodded at me. "You're single. Intelligent. Not interested in monogamy. Hardworking. And—"

"Yeah, I'm awesome." I interrupted. "I know."

"And humble." He smirked.

His confidence irritated me, mostly because that smirk seemed to cause my lady parts to clench and pant. I lied to cover the reaction. "Despite what you may think, I'm not interested in you *fucking* me."

He shrugged. "I don't like to waste my time, Bell. If you don't want me to chase you, I won't."

It was a question and a statement, all at the same time. Did I *want* him to chase me? Did I *want* Dario Capece's attention?

I didn't. *I did.*

I wanted to step away and return to my friends.

I wanted to move closer and feel his hands against me, his mouth on mine. The idea that this man had thought about me, had taken steps toward a physical or emotional relationship ... it took my lust of sexual power to an entirely new level. I'd seduced boys like Elliot and men like Ian. I'd never come close to someone like Dario. A man who could have any woman of his choosing yet was fixating on me.

I wanted him to take me away from the crowds and do even more.

I swallowed and evaded the question. "So, your marriage is fake? That's what you're saying?"

"I'm not saying anything. My relationship with Gwen isn't your business, not at this point. If you're struggling with a moral line caused by my wedding ring, I can assure you that my wife doesn't care who I fuck, only that any indiscretions are kept secret."

I didn't know how to respond to that, hated that I believed his words, the calm look in his eyes giving me a feeling of security that was foreign to me. I glanced away. "You seem complicated. And I ... I like my life as it is right now."

"I liked things how they were last week. But then I met you, and now, things are different."

I shook my head, my hands tightening on the railing. "We spoke for a minute, and I served you a drink. That was it."

"I am a man of a million interactions a day, and none stick with me. Yours did." He stepped closer. "Don't make me kiss you to prove it."

Somewhere deep inside, I caved, my feminine core wilting at the words, the need in me overpowering any rational sense. I didn't say anything, didn't move forward, didn't react ... but he saw something on my face and reached for me. His hand closed around my waist and pulled me forward, until I was flush against him, my heels not high enough to bring our eyes level.

It was a smooth move, too quick for me to react, too natural for me to fight. He held me against him and looked into my eyes in a moment, not of hesitation, but of anticipation. He lowered his head and pressed his lips to mine.

God. It was a soft kiss that asked permission. My hands weakened against his suit, and I gave up with the second kiss, one that brushed more firmly across my lips, opening my mouth. In the third kiss, he owned me, the contact deepening, a delicate play between two mouths born for each other, one where arousal flared, breaths quickened, and our hands tightened and traveled, first needy, then frantic. It was a kiss that seduced, then branded. A kiss where he gave as much as he took, and I lost as much as I gained.

He broke free, and my world spun back into place. I tried to find my thoughts, my sanity, my control. How had he decimated everything with just a kiss?

TEN

"I should go back to my friends." I stepped back, one heel skidding across the floor, and I grabbed the railing to keep upright. He watched me closely, in complete control of himself, and I hated how calm he looked at a time when my heart was galloping around my chest.

"Don't leave." He stepped forward and I shrank a little against the railing. He stopped, considered me, and then withdrew, his hands raised. "Okay. Maybe I misread you. I'm sorry about that."

He didn't misread me. In fact, if he could read anything, he'd know I was a half-second away from barreling into his arms and getting another kiss. My weight stuttered on my stilettos, torn between sprinting toward the exit and flinging myself at him.

I'd kissed a lot of men in my life, but never had an experience like that. I didn't know how to handle it. I didn't want that level of chemistry infused in a situation I was already struggling with. Why had I come up here? Why had I let the girls bring me to this club? Why had I answered his text?

I edged toward the stairs, each step a struggle in self-control. *I don't like to waste my time, Bell. If you don't want me to chase you, I won't.* I could leave. Walk down those steps, find my friends, and go. Never see Dario Capece again.

The thought wounded me, and the fact that I cared? That absolutely terrified me. The confident girl who had tossed back barbs with this man just minutes ago was gone, rattled to the core by the impact of that kiss.

A kiss. Two lips touching. Colliding. Deepening. It happened a thousand times a day, yet I didn't seem to be able to handle this one.

"Don't worry." His words stopped my retreat and I looked at him, finding a moment of grounding in the solidness of his eye contact. "I won't kiss you again unless you ask me for it."

The sentence had enough mocking ego in it for my backbone to peek her head out of hiding. I straightened a little, forced my vocal cords to work, and attempted a dismissive sniff.

It didn't do much, but I still saw the softening of his eyes, the hint of a smile on those deliciously addictive lips. God, I wanted to kiss him again. I wanted to shove him down in one of those club chairs, hike my dress around my waist, and grind my panties across the seam of his zipper. I wanted his hands in my hair, my skin against his skin, and to see in his eyes some of the discomposure I felt rippling through me.

For me, sex had always been about control. Now, just from a kiss, I felt powerless and afraid. Needy for more.

It made no sense.

"How many women do you sleep with?" My palm was sweaty, and I clutched the railing tighter, my need for information winning the battle against flight.

He tilted his head at me. "I have a mistress of sorts. And a waitress I occasionally fuck."

"It seems like you've got enough women already. Why go after more?"

"They don't mean anything to me. Maybe I'm ready for someone who does."

It was a reference to more than just passion and pleasure, and the sort of statement that normally had me breaking out in hives. I didn't flinch, and it was official. I'd gone completely mad.

"Tell me about this boy toy of yours from the university."

His tone was so innocent, the comment so loaded. It caused my attention to flee relationship talks, ricochet off the man who had followed me, and plunge into a pool of fear. *He knew about Ian.* I had forgotten, for a moment, who he was.

"Stay away from Ian." Fear crystallized deep in my ribcage. I'd heard the stories. There were some casinos you could fuck with. Count cards. Get sloppy. There were others you avoided. Dario Capece's, you avoided. Did he rule his relationship prospects with the same iron fist?

He chuckled. "I'm not going to touch the man, Bell. I just want to know the extent of your relationship."

I shook my head, his easy tone only half-extinguishing the alarm bells ringing through my head. "We're not *in* a relationship. It's just…" I didn't know how to describe my sexual fling with Ian, not in words that didn't make me sound like a carefree slut. I raised my chin and forced my voice to remain strong. "It's just a physical thing."

"I can't imagine any man being happy with a strictly physical relationship with you."

"Yet, that's what you're proposing. Right?" I released my hold on the railing, the kiss' effect fading, our focus on Ian giving me the distraction my sanity needed.

He didn't answer the question. Instead, he pulled at the end of a bright blue shirt sleeve, adjusting it under his suit jacket. "I have to be careful who I allow close to me. It doesn't make sense for me to get involved with a woman in a relationship. It's too risky for me."

He was giving me an out. If I wanted Dario Capece to walk away from me, all I had to do was say the words and tell him that Ian and I were dating. It wasn't that far from the truth. I could take Ian up on his dinner invite. But it wasn't what I wanted. Not with Ian...

"We're not dating." I don't know why I said it, but I did. I don't know why I stepped closer, but I did. Maybe it was because my lips were still tingling from his kiss and the chemistry between us was crackling like a live wire.

I wondered how much he knew about me. He'd had me followed. Knew about Ian. Found my phone number. Probably done a complete background check and history. Did he know about my poor upbringing? Dad's drinking? The night I was raped? Had the last forty-eight hours been a dissection of my life?

The last forty-eight hours... I stopped as something mentally clicked into place. "That guy at work ... the one who offered me money to sleep with him. Did he work for you?"

To his credit, he didn't deny it. "He did. In this town, with your looks..." He lifted one shoulder. "A lot of the girls earn a secondary income. I needed to know if you were one of them."

"I didn't *apply* to be your girlfriend." I spit out the words, my irritation turning to anger. "How fucking egotistic are you? You think that once you check off all of my boxes, that I'll just jump into your arms, grateful to be a side piece of ass?" I closed the distance and shoved him as hard as I could with the palm of my hand, his chest like a stone column. "Next time, just ask a girl and find out for yourself."

He caught my hand. "I'm not proud of the methods I've used, but I'm not some bartender on the Strip. I can't afford strangers in my life, and I expected..." He swallowed and held the thought for a beat. "I expected to be disappointed, to find an excuse to leave you alone." He released my hand. "I didn't."

I dropped my hand from his chest and watched as he stepped away, his gaze holding mine.

"I know it's a lot to think about." He slid his hands into his pockets.

I swallowed. "I don't even know what *it* is."

"Yeah." He chuckled. "I'm trying to figure that out myself. With other women, it's been simple. With you..." He broke eye contact, turning slightly toward the exit, then glanced back. "I have a feeling it won't be. Let's start with something simple. I'd like to see you again. Dinner, the next night you have off."

The closest thing I've ever had to a date was with Elliot, a dinner at TGI Fridays on prom night. We split a cheese fries appetizer and I spilled a drop of honey mustard on the skirt of my dress. It had been the most basic of events, one I'd never had the urge to repeat.

He took another step toward the door and nodded at me. "Goodnight, Bell."

I turned back to the club floor, unable to watch him leave and unsure of what to say. I waited for half of a hip-hop song, then glanced back.

He was gone, and somehow, void of any sense, I wanted him back.

I felt the poke of a long fingernail in my side and turned my head, meeting Meredith's quizzical look.

"What's wrong?"

I shook my head. "Nothing." I rested my head against the glass, comforted by the cool surface of Lydia's window.

I'd bet the title of this club that you want me to fuck you. Yeah. He'd been right about that.

I don't fuck strange women that I know nothing about. I'm not proud of the methods I've used, but I'm not some bartender on the Strip. I can't afford strangers in my life. I understood that he lived a different life than the rest of Vegas. I understood that he had to be careful who he went to bed with. But did that excuse his invasion into my life? It didn't, and it did. I could become offended and riled up about it, or I could accept the situation and look the other way.

If you're struggling with a moral line caused by my wedding ring, I can assure you that my wife doesn't care who I fuck, only that any indiscretions are kept secret. What woman could marry a man like Dario and not keep him to herself? I felt an unfamiliar flare of anger and wondered if it was what jealousy felt like. *I have a mistress of sorts. And a waitress I occasionally fuck.*

That's what he wanted. Another mistress. Or another "occasional" waitress. That was really the bulk of it. Sure, he was attracted to me. Sure, we had chemistry. Sure, he made me feel things that no other man had. But was that worth it? Or was that even *more* reason to run the other way?

I'd like to see you again. Dinner, the next night you have off.

I closed my eyes and tried to forget everything but couldn't block out the hurricane force of that kiss.

I shook, poured, and slid the martini to the side. Using the bottle opener, I popped open two Bud Lights and set them on my tray. Balancing it on my shoulder, I caught Britni's eye. "The skinny guy at four wants an ashtray."

"Got it."

She took my place behind the bar, and I moved through the floor, heading to the top table, and thinking about the remaining to-do items on my list. *Don Julio to the bald guy at three. Hot tea to the woman at two. Cigars to the tuxedo at craps.* I walked, smiled, delivered, and failed miserably at the biggest item on the list: *Don't Think About Dario Capece.*

It was an especially difficult task in a room full of men like this. All were power-hungry. Sharks. Egos bigger than their dicks. Dicks more active than their luck. All of them striving to be Dario and none of them succeeding. It was a powerful thing to think, in a room like this. But it was true. I didn't know why he was different, but he was. And all I could think about was his dinner invite. What would a dinner alone with him be like? Had I agreed to it with my silence?

I delivered the cigars, the tea, the tequila. I high-fived the CEO of the MGM when he won a hand. I downed shots with a group of Chinese investors and ate breadsticks and Alfredo sauce with the boys back in the control room. I watched the hours tick by and didn't check my texts or look for his call. I laughed, pocketed tips, and bet Lance and Rick a hundred bucks that someone would vomit before the end of the night.

I lost the bet, went double or nothing on a quick game of War, and talked celebrity gossip with Britni on the way to our cars.

At the red light three blocks over, away from the eyes of anyone, I checked my phone. I skimmed through a coupon from Best Buy, a voicemail from Meredith, and an obnoxious group thread from my roommates that stretched 41 texts long. Then, at the bottom, sent five hours ago, there was a text from Dario.

—When is your next night off?

A simple question, but one that assumed an outcome.

I typed out a response slowly, questioning the action even as I hit send.

Sunday

Sunday. As good a day as any to meet with my devil.

I closed the text, took a deep breath, and locked the phone.

ELEVEN

DARIO

Gwen moved like a cat. A Siamese, one born into a life of luxury, one that turned with fluid grace and could waltz up beside you without making a sound. Dario watched her pick through the Vuitton duffel, her brow creasing as she lifted a shirt out of the depths and held it up.

"There's a stain on this." She turned, tossing it to the side. "Tell Max tomorrow."

"Yes, ma'am." The assistant scurried to the blouse, tucking it under her arm, and returned to her spot by the window, hands clasped before her, face pinched. It was funny, in a sad sort of way, how afraid everyone was of Gwen. Dario often accused her of liking it, a claim she would laugh off, her eyes squinting, and he could see, even as she scoffed, that it secretly pleased her.

In some ways, the fear of her was ridiculous. She was kind, the sort of woman who remembered everyone's name, birthday, and problems. She was generous with her money, time, and favors. And she was calm and rational, a good yin to his yang, a voice of reason in an industry that often needed one.

In other ways, the fear of her was entirely accurate. Not because of the woman that she was, but because of the man she came from. Robert Hawk. A billionaire with as many demons as dollars and the recklessness to turn those demons loose without provocation. Dario hadn't so much *married* Gwen as rescued her.

And she hadn't so much married him as *promoted* him. One night, one ceremony, and he had moved from Biloxi mid-level scum to Vegas elite.

"That's it." Gwen zipped the bag shut and patted it. "Take it to the car, I'll be there shortly."

"Certainly." The woman's shoes squeaked across the floor. "I'll see you there."

She stretched, rolling her neck and glancing at him. "You've got everything this weekend?"

"Of course." He smiled at her. "Just be safe. Tell Nick I'll break his arm if you have so much as a mosquito bite."

She poked him as she walked by. "Not fair. I'm going to have a mosquito bite."

"Maybe I just want to break his arm." He followed her down the hall and into the kitchen. "When are you coming back?"

"Tuesday night, I think." She opened the fridge. "Any more information on that small casino you looked at?"

He settled in at the island and watched as she brought out a bottled water. "Nothing yet. They aren't interested in selling, so financials are an unknown. I'm keeping my eye on it but may have to move on to something else."

She stuck the water bottle into her purse and headed for the elevator. "Well, don't work too hard. And tell Meghan I said hi." He scowled, and her eyes widened in faux innocence. "What?"

"You aren't supposed to know about Meghan."

"Oh please." She waved a hand dismissively at the mention of the mistress. "My spies hear things. Just like yours do."

"You can tell your spies that Meghan isn't worth watching. That's old news." Old news as of yesterday, the blonde taking the news with a curse-filled rant that had stopped abruptly with her parting gift—diamond earrings that had made her shriek with pleasure and scamper off to pack.

"That's a shame." She scrunched up her nose in the way that always broke his composure, and he smiled despite himself. "Just don't have too much fun while I'm gone. I'm still the queen of this castle, you know."

"You'll always be queen." He stopped her in the elevator's entranceway and turned her to him. "Now be safe."

"You'll always be *my* queen." She amended his words quietly, and he watched her eyes, saw the way they flicked down to the floor before coming back to his. "That's what you usually say."

Fuck. He smiled, a gesture of reassurance and apology. "Of course. You know you're my queen."

She lifted a brow, and he could hear the words she didn't speak, words that hung in the air between them, suspended in time, even as they said their goodbyes, kissed, and she stepped into the elevator. *Am I?*

She was. They were bound by more than just ten years together, by more than friendship and love. They were bound by a thousand layers of contracts and holdings, of investments, debts, partnerships, and legalities. They were bound by the wrath of Robert Hawk and Dario's addiction to a heartbeat and power.

She was—*had* to be, his queen. Thinking about anything else, about the *possibility* of anything else, was insane.

BELL

"Talk to me about null and alternative hypotheses."

I rolled over, resting my head on Ian's stomach and groaned. "Oh my god. I'm sleeping with a nerd."

He laughed, and the abs against my cheek bounced a little. Okay, so he was a hot nerd.

"I hypothesize that further talk of hypotheses will nullify your chance of a second round," I mumbled.

"I hypothesize that you are going to flunk the final if you don't actually study with me."

I groaned louder and rolled over, scooting up his body until I was face to face with him. "I thought that's why I was sleeping with the instructor. So I didn't *have* to study."

"Oh no," he said gravely, his adorable forehead pinching. "Fuck buddies have to study. Girlfriends are the ones that get a free pass."

"What?!" I pouted. "That doesn't seem fair." I ran my finger along a ridge of his abs.

He choked out a laugh. "Is it *that* painful of an idea?"

"Being a girlfriend?" I grimaced. "It's not you," I hurried to say. "Any girl would love to date a…" I held up a finger and concentrated. "Let me remember how my roommate put this. A… 'hot, smart guy with a job and a delicious Irish accent'."

"You forgot to mention my incredible bedroom skills," he pointed out.

"Yeah. Thankfully she isn't aware of those." I rolled off of him and stood, stretching. "I've got to run."

"Wait." He sat up and caught hold of my hand, pulling me back onto the bed. "I'll drop the dating talk."

I smiled. "Thank you. Being a girlfriend…"

"I know. It's not what you want."

He kissed me and then changed the subject, dragging down my shorts, pulling up my shirt, and unhooking my bra. He slid his fingers into my panties, and I closed my eyes, a moan falling from my lips. I arched into his touch and tried, to the best of my ability, to push Dario Capece from my mind. *This* was what I wanted in my life. No complications. Fantastic sex. Work. School. My friends.

Not being a girlfriend. At least, not to Ian.

I was becoming less sure of how I felt about everything else.

"Who's hungry?" Lance kicked open the door to the control room, then maneuvered in, his hands full of bags from.... I leaned sideways on the couch in an attempt to read the ticket. Thai Garden.

I raised a hand. "Me. Feed me now, oh great leader."

"About time. I'm starving." Rick grabbed a bag from Lance and started pulling out mini boxes of takeout. I heaved myself off the couch and grabbed a handful of paper plates. My phone buzzed from the coffee table, and Lance snagged it, glancing at the display before he handed it over. His brows raised.

"What?" I snatched it from him.

"Nothing."

I glanced down, saw Dario's name on the text message notification, then swiped open the message.

—*the Irish boy isn't good enough for you*

I locked the phone and tossed it onto the couch. Sitting down, I used chopsticks to pull out a chunk of noodles.

"Dario Capece?" Lance asked.

So much for him not commenting on it. I ignored him, scooping up a mouthful of Pad Thai.

"What about Dario Capece?" Rick chomped on the bait like a rabid raccoon.

"He's texting B."

"What about?"

Rick's question hung in the air and, with only three of us in the room, was impossible to ignore.

"Stupid stuff." I shrugged. "You know guys like him. They think they can take what they want. It's not anything serious."

"It's not anything serious?" Lance repeated. "B, I'm pretty sure that every *fucking* thing Dario Capece does is serious."

Rick followed suit. "If Capece is interested in you, you've got to keep a lid on this. You know who his father-in-law is, right?"

I finished chewing and took a sip of my soda before answering him. "Super-rich guy. And ... let me guess—some mobster?"

Lance and Rick exchanged a look that had me setting down my paper plate. "What? Spit it out."

Lance leaned forward, pressing his palms together before speaking. "He's not connected, it's more that he's a fuckin' psychopath. He cut the fingers off his last GM when he suspected him of embezzling. Had the guy so scared, he didn't even press charges."

Rick nodded. "A decade ago, before Dario came around—the Majestic was losing cocktail waitresses. Not because they were quitting, but because they were *disappearing*. Rumor on the Strip was that he liked to keep them as pets."

"Pets?"

Lance jumped in. "Chained up in his basement. A few parents called the cops, reported their daughters missing, and LVPD sniffed around Hawk, but they could never find anything. Plus, you know those guys. They got half the department in their pockets."

"And you guys don't?" I smiled, but they didn't take the bait, the somber expressions on their faces causing me to change tactics. "Fine. You've scared me, okay? I'll stay away."

Rick wasn't done. "And don't talk to anyone about this. Not your roommates, or Britni, or *anyone*. You need to gush over Capece's gigantic cock? Tell us about it."

"A modified version, please." Lance grinned at me. "I can't have my ego damaged by some Italian asshole."

I rolled my eyes. "I'm not going to need to share any sordid details. Like I *just* said, I'll stay away."

"Sordid?" Lance laughed before popping a crunchy noodle into his mouth. "You can't use big words like that in here, B. Rick gets confused."

Rick flicked a soy sauce package toward Lance in response, and I stood up, reaching for it and dropping it into the takeout bag.

"You. Guys. Are. *Pigs*. Are those small enough words for you?" I dropped the bag on the table before him and smacked Lance on the back of the head.

He laughed in response. "But seriously, B. Watch your back."

"Forget watching your back. Just don't let Capece *put* you on your back," Rick added.

I thought of the fantasies that had plagued me ever since that kiss in the club. His eyes, burning across my skin, my legs open, his fingers and mouth strumming over me in sweet concert. *Don't let Capece put you on your back.* I winced and tried to redirect my thoughts, turning to their stories of Robert Hawk, chopped-off fingers, and missing cocktail waitresses. Waitresses like me, serving drinks, counting tips, and trying to get from one week to the next. Girls kept and probably killed by a psychotic billionaire whose daughter was married to Dario Capece.

Girls like me didn't have a great track record with luck, and a dinner on Sunday night would be hell on my odds.

"I don't like to waste my time, Bell. If you don't want me to chase you, I won't."

He had said the words with such solemnness. Maybe he *would* leave me alone. Maybe all I had to do was tell him to go away, and he would disappear. Problem over. Fates averted.

I sat down on the couch and reopened his text.

—*the Irish boy isn't good enough for you*

I ignored the barb and settled back against the cushion, thinking of my promise to the boys, to stay away from Dario. I typed out a response.

please don't contact me again

I reread the text before sending it. Moved my thumb over the Send button and paused. It was short and sweet, with no room for confusion or misinterpretation. Polite yet firm. I sent the text before I had a chance to change my mind.

TWELVE

For the entire shift, the text followed me, taunting me, and I was almost sick with nerves by the time I watched the last customer stumble out. I should have felt resolution. Peace. Instead, it felt like a mistake. A mistake I couldn't talk to anyone about. A mistake that had Dario's voice whispering in my ear, the phantom brush of his fingertips on my shoulder, his kiss on my neck. A kiss I'd never feel again.

I had lost control with him, my stability seeming to dissolve the longer I'd stayed in his presence. It was all just as confusing as the conflict I'd seen in his eyes.

I carried empty glasses and wiped down the bar, thinking of his hand closing around my waist, drawing me against his body, the soft give and dominance of his mouth against mine. The look of torture in his eyes when he'd stepped away from me.

"The women don't mean anything to me. Maybe I'm ready for someone who does."

Had it all been bullshit, lines of seduction that a dozen Vegas brunettes had heard? I stacked my tips, then handed them through the cage. Maurice spread the chips, then counted out my bills, passing them over with a smile.

"Thanks."

He nodded, then locked the drawers. On any given night, there was a few million in the cage. I've watched them count out the stacks, had seen the nights when the armored truck had to deliver extra, and nights when they carted away the profits. It was a good business to be in. I tucked my cash into my pocket and moved to the control room. Grabbing my phone, I held my breath as I unlocked it and opened my texts.

Nothing. No text and no missed call. I'd sent out a grenade, and he hadn't responded at all. I should be thankful.

I moved past everyone and out to the parking lot. I unlocked my car, got inside, and swore, hitting the steering wheel with enough force to hurt my palm.

I told him I didn't want him to contact me again. He hadn't, and the result was one that made me want to tear out my hair and scream.

I knew what I liked. What I wanted. Emotion-free, orgasm-filled sex.

While Dario Capece might be looking for the same thing in a side piece, I could already tell that—with him—my emotions wouldn't behave. A physical relationship between us might take my cold and lifeless heart and actually cause it to beat. To hum. To swell with blood and emotion. To *hurt*.

It was Sunday afternoon and I was in full pity-party mood. In bed at three o'clock. Class assignments finished, I was bingeing on reality TV with impressive dedication.

If I hadn't sent the Worst Text Ever, I'd be prepping for tonight's date with Dario. Instead, I was elbow-deep in some housewives show where everyone seemed to be broke and bitchy.

It was ridiculous. Ian asked me on a date, and I blew him off without a second thought. I did the same thing to Dario Capece, and I was chewing through my fingernails like a meth addict in rehab.

My phone buzzed and I catapulted over the covers, frantically tossing aside pillows until I pulled it out. *Ugh.* A text from Ian. I closed it without reading it and settled back against the headboard and pulled my bag of Doritos closer. I was being pathetic. I hardly knew the man. I shouldn't think twice about turning down his dinner invitation or never speaking to him again.

I shouldn't.

I shouldn't.

I shouldn't.

My mom hadn't raised a starry-eyed weakling. I reached for the remote and clicked on the next episode.

A few minutes before eleven, there was a soft knock, and I turned my head as the bedroom door creaked open. Meredith stuck her head in.

"Oh good, you're awake."

I paused the show and lifted my soda to my mouth, waiting to see what she wanted.

"There's some old guy here to see you."

She couldn't mean Dario. While he was in his mid-to-late thirties... "old guy" wouldn't be the terminology she'd use. Not for him, and not by her—a girl who'd recently dated a forty-two-year-old surgeon and didn't take any of our shit about it. I pulled back the covers and stood, her eyebrows raising at my messy hair, hot pink leggings, and Save the MF Whales shirt.

"Sexy."

"You know it." I stretched, mentally flipping through my visitor possibilities.

"Guy looks like a cop."

I passed Lydia in the kitchen, the smell of microwave popcorn thick in the air, and swung open the front door to—bonus points to Meredith—an old guy. Six feet tall, in a suit, with thinning hair and a military-precise stance. For a senior citizen, he was in shape, thick and muscular, with a glare that would get me to confess almost anything. "Can I help you?"

The man's eyes moved to Meredith, who peered over my right shoulder, then back to me. "Miss Hartley, if I could have a word in private."

I looked past him and saw what Meredith missed, the Rolls Royce idling behind her car, its headlights dimmed. I elbowed my roommate back, lowering my voice. "I got this."

I stepped out on the porch and pulled the door behind me, ignoring the man and heading toward the car, my socks moving silently down the concrete drive until I was beside the Rolls and knocking on the window, the glass moving beneath my knuckles. Dario Capece was unveiled, and my heart both cracked and soared at the sight of him.

I crossed my arms over my chest and attempted to appear aloof. "Too fancy to ring your own doorbells?"

The window stopped, and the glint of his watch caught the streetlight. I couldn't see him well, his features dim, but his voice was clear and firm, and tugged at every string of arousal I had. "I was trying to be discreet."

Behind me, there was the snap of a lighter, and I turned to watch the older man lean against our front porch column, his cigarette glowing to life. I looked over the glossy curves of the Rolls. "This car isn't exactly discreet."

It was small talk, useless words that danced around what I should be saying. *I told you not to contact me.*

He nodded to the passenger side. "Get in. I want to show you something."

I tucked a chunk of dirty hair behind my ear and cursed myself for being so slack. I should have showered. Brushed my hair. Should have been at least slightly optimistic that Dario Capece would put up a bit of a fight.

His eyes caught the movement, and I watched as his gaze moved down my body, taking in the outfit. "Nice socks."

My socks didn't match—one gray, one white, and I huffed in irritation. I'd bet someone laid out his socks each morning. I'd bet they were in perfect neat rolls in their own special drawer in his closet.

"Come on. You don't need shoes. Get in."

I frowned. "Your mom ever teach you how to say please?"

His mouth twitched, and the playful glint in his eyes almost melted my panties right off. "*Please* get in the car."

I opened the door to a car worth more than my life and entered an interior that reeked of wealth. I shut the door and locked myself in with the one man I should avoid, the one I had promised Lance and Rick to stay away from.

I should be afraid of him, of everything in his world and the risks that he carried. Instead, I got into his car, without my phone or purse or shoes, and trusted him to keep me safe. He waved at his driver, then rolled up the window and turned to me.

"I'm sorry for coming by so late."

I said nothing, tucking my palms underneath my thighs and watching as the driver got in. A divider rose with a quiet hum, blocking him from our view. I nodded in the general direction of the front seat. "Who's the guy?"

Dario stretched out his legs, crossing them at the ankle, and I peeked at his socks. Yep. Matchy-matchy. Dark with a pattern.

"That's Vince, my head of security. He's worked with me for a long time."

I thought back, to the first night I met him, and tried to remember if he'd been in the front room. Maybe he had. I'd been distracted by the two big guys, linemen who had practically snarled when Tim and Jim had approached them. I felt the car shift into gear and looked out the window, the night too dark to see anything. "Where are we going?"

"Not too far. Don't worry."

"Somewhere that doesn't need shoes?"

I ran my hands along a group of controls on the door, finding and activating the seat heater and a massage function. Underneath me, the leather minutely shifted, a soothing roll of action that felt heavenly. I sank into the seat and Dario chuckled.

"Having fun?"

"This massager is much nicer than the one at the pedicure place."

"I'd hope so."

He reached forward and pressed a button, a footrest appearing, my chair reclining slightly.

"Wow." I closed my eyes and let my arms hang limp. "I don't know why you scowl so much. This is all I'd need in life to be happy."

I heard the shift of him, felt the brush of his arm, but didn't open my eyes.

"Do I scowl?"

There was humor in his tone, and I risked a peek, turning my head to see a hint of a smile on his lips. "Oh yeah. Big time."

"I only scowl when I'm being tormented by a beautiful woman."

"Oh please." I reached forward and found the seat control, returning it to the upright position. The car rolled over a speed bump and barely rocked. I wanted to ask him why he showed up at my house in the middle of the night. I wanted to ask him where we were going. I wanted to ask him what he meant by "tormented."

I swallowed my questions, and looked out the window, watching neon signs pass, their colors muted by the tint. I suddenly felt like a kid. Next to Dario's powerful presence, I felt so young so…inexperienced.

It was unnerving, but in an entirely different way than I'd felt that night at the barn. While I felt powerless in his presence, I also felt protected, his strength giving me comfort instead of fear. As the Rolls hummed down the Strip, I felt another foreign emotion. *Excitement.*

This was his turf. His domain. The car slowed, and I straightened as it turned into the entrance of the last place I wanted to be.

THIRTEEN

"The Majestic?" I turned and looked at him, panic starting to thump through my chest. We shouldn't be here. I thought of Thursday, just three days ago, and how brazenly I'd followed him into that private alcove in the club. Then, I'd only been thinking of his wife. I hadn't thought about her father, and all of the danger that being Dario Capece's fling might put me in. "Why are we here?"

Dario cocked his head at me, a question in his eyes. "You're worried. Why?"

My hand tightened on the door handle, as much to hold the door closed as it was to shove it open and escape.

"I can't walk in there. People will see us together. They'll—"

The Rolls Royce continued through the valet area and down a hill, slowing before a gate, which slowly opened.

"We aren't going anywhere that anyone will be able to see us. Trust me."

I leaned against the door and watched as we drove down a parking garage tunnel, weaving around until we pulled into a small spot, one caged in by concrete walls. "This is a bad idea."

Dario reached forward, opening a compartment and pulling out a bottle from the ice. "If you don't want to go in, then we don't have to. But I want to show you something. Something I think you'll like."

He held out the bottle of water. I took it, unscrewing the lid and taking a sip. The car shuddered, and the walls beside us started to move. I froze.

"It's an elevator. It's taking us to the premier level. It's perfectly safe, I promise."

An elevator. For a car. I've lived in this town for two years and thought I'd seen everything. Still, tonight was the first night I'd ever been in a Rolls. And now, the first time I'd ever taken a car into an elevator. The movement stopped and the doors opened. The sedan rolled forward, down a row of garages, one opening halfway down. We pulled in, and I turned to see the garage door closing. I thought of his promise that no one would see me. I thought of Lance's story of cocktail waitresses disappearing and understood how—with a setup like this—it could occur. "Is this where you live?"

"No. We live a few levels up."

We. A subtle reminder that this man was not up for grabs. Where was Gwen now? Was she above us, wondering where her husband was? And why, of all places, had he brought me here?

His door opened, and I watched as he stepped out, his hands moving to the front of his suit and fastening the button there. It was the middle of the night, and he was in a suit, getting out of his Rolls Royce. I looked down at my baggy T-shirt, at the chocolate stain from a Crunch ice cream bar, and my mismatched socks.

He closed the car door, and it softly clicked into place. My stress level spiked.

His security left through a side door, and I took the hand that Dario offered, letting him lead me to the double doors at the end of the garage. There was a keypad and he released my hand, gesturing to it.

"The code is 04182996#."

He waited, and I realized he wanted me to enter it. I hesitated, my fingers on the white keypad, and he repeated the code. 0-4-1-8-2-9-9-6. I typed in the code, the digits familiar.

"My birthday..." I mused. "And the last four of my phone number. Creepy." I hit the pound key and the lock quietly buzzed, a green light illuminating.

"I wanted something you'd remember." Dario reached for the handle and swung open the door. "Go ahead."

I walked through and stopped, the short hall opening to a two-story living room, one with a million-dollar-view of the Strip. The room had low-slung white leather couches, a giant flat-screen on the wall, and deep blue walls dotted with colorful paintings. To the left was an all-white kitchen, with a six-top table and fireplace. I walked to the windows, which stretched from the floor all the way to the second-story ceiling. Moving closer, I watched the Bellagio fountains dance.

"Is this where you bring all your girls?" I turned away from the view, watching as he moved into the kitchen.

"I ended my relationships. With the waitress, as flimsy as that was and..." He tilted his head as if reluctant to say her name. "Meghan."

Meghan. She could be the nicest girl in the world, but I already hated her. I leaned against the window, curling my toes inside my socks, against the slick wood floors. "You broke up with them?" I lifted one shoulder. "Why?"

From this spot, I could see the ring on his finger. From this spot, everything I saw belonged to The Majestic and his *wife*.

"I'm making room for you in my life."

It'd been seven days since we met. Seven days, and he'd ended two relationships, had me followed, tried to trick me into being a prostitute, and brought me here. I crossed my arms over my chest and looked away. "You shouldn't have. And I'm not entirely sure you actually have." I huffed out a laugh and tightened my arms.

He pulled open a few drawers before finding a wine opener. "I have. You drink wine?"

I wandered away from the view and leaned on the counter, my gaze taking in the spacious and modern kitchen. It was all white granite and stainless steel and I watched Dario crouch before an open wine cooler. "Yeah. Something sweet, if you have it."

"We have it." He fished a golden bottle from the cooler and stood. The under-cabinet light was on, and it lit up his delicious features. His sleeves were rolled up to the elbow, the top button of his dress shirt open, and his forearm muscles flexed as he opened the wine. I watched his face, the strong features relaxed, half doused in shadow.

He was painfully attractive, in his movements as much as his genetic makeup. He was the manliest individual I'd ever met, from his dominant presence to the sheer strength of his build. He popped the cork and set the bottle down, tossing the opener aside.

"Trying to get me drunk?" I wandered around to his side of the counter and braced my palms on the granite, hoisting myself up and sitting on the edge. He only had one wine glass out, and I watched him fill it up halfway.

He ignored the question and handed it to me. "Here."

"You aren't drinking?"

He headed to the fridge, and as he passed, gently squeezed my knee. The gesture was sweet, an unnecessary touch of affection, and I lifted my glass to my mouth to hide the resulting smile.

"I'm fine with water." He opened the door, the fridge neatly filled with rows of soda, juices, and water.

I watched him reach in and grab a bottled water. I thought about my dad, the way his eyes lingered on alcohol as if it was liquid gold. I set down the wine glass. "I don't have to drink."

He straightened, leaning against the opposite counter and twisted off the water's cap, raising a brow at me in question.

"I mean, if it tempts you. I can just have water."

His mouth curved as he brought the bottle to his lips. "I'm not an alcoholic, Bell."

"Oh." I wrapped my fingers around the stem of the glass.

"Sometimes I drink. Typically, I don't." He finished off twenty ounces in a single swig. "And I'm definitely not going to drink around you."

I stopped, the rim of the glass at my lips, and watched him toss the empty plastic into the trash.

He moved forward, his hands pulling my knees apart, and leaned forward, caging me in. "I need all of my wits around you."

I puffed out a scoff, taking a deep sip of the cool and flavorful wine before placing the glass down. I wanted to kiss him. The urge was so strong that I had to focus on moving the glass away just to keep from grabbing at him. "Why is that, Mr. Capece?"

His eyes darkened, and for a moment, I saw our future. The growl of my name as he thrust into me. The grip of my arm when we fought, the hood of his eyes when he was about to come. He *liked* when I said his name. He'd like it more if I was on my knees before him, my mouth open, eyes begging.

"Every man needs his wits around a tempting woman."

I rolled my eyes. "And every man needs a line that isn't generic as hell."

"*Nothing* about me is generic." He stepped back, and my body missed the warmth and presence of him, the lost kiss crying out in the space between us. Snagging my wine glass from the counter, he downed it in one gulp. "Let's go out on the balcony."

Forty-two stories up seemed like a million. I stopped six feet from the railing and felt as if I was teetering on the edge of it.

"Not a fan of heights?" he asked.

"No." I settled into a padded chaise lounge and kicked my feet up onto it. Reaching down, I pulled off my dirty and mismatched socks before I had to endure another second of them.

He walked over to the railing and put his weight on it, looking down at a gridlock of traffic and movement. "I'm terrified of heights. I fell out of a window when I was fourteen." He turned to me, holding out his arm and pointing to a scar that ran halfway down his forearm. "Broke my arm and lost enough blood to drown a rat."

His story didn't match with the easy way he rested against the railing, his weight heavy, as if daring the iron barrier to give under the pressure.

"You don't look scared to me."

"I'm good at covering it."

He jerked his head in the direction of the fall. "This scares the shit out of me. The height, the fall and what that distance could do to a body. But this railing is safer than that chair, safer than being close to you."

"Then why am I here?"

He pushed away from the railing and stepped forward until his body blocked most of the view. The wind howled and I watched those gorgeous forearms as he brought his hands to his hips.

"Because I'm shitty at listening to reason. Because my wife is out of town and I have three uninterrupted days to figure out who Bell Hartley is and why I can't stop thinking about her." He met my eyes. "I think you need to figure out why *you* are here. You've got at least three good reasons to have slammed the door in Vince's face."

It was a fantastic point. I brought my knees to my chest and stole a glance of him out of the corner of my eye. He looked fearless. Strong. Damaged and repaired perfection. I met his eyes and felt my heart twist.

Why *was* I here?

Because he might be worth the risk to my heart.

"So… you brought me to a hotel suite." I gave him a playful smile in an attempt to avoid the question. "Hoping to get lucky?"

"I was hoping you'd like the suite."

"It's a suite." I shrugged. "It's fine."

He found that amusing, his mouth twitching. "A thousand-dollar-a-night suite, and it's *fine*. You're a tough woman to impress."

"I'd rather be impressed by you, rather than your real estate holdings."

"The suite was meant as a gesture of my commitment to a relationship with you. I've seen where you live. I've seen how hard you work. I want to provide for you, to give you a safe place to live."

"You want me to *live* here?" I twisted in the chair and looked back through the large windows, re-examining the suite with new eyes. Gold-print wallpaper. A thick fur rug on top of the walnut-colored floors. A far cry from my crowded room, in the house that never sleeps, with the affordable rent.

"You'd like it here. Daily maid service." He ticked off the pros on one hand. "All the room service you'd ever want. An expense account at the stores."

He wanted a mistress. Someone he could keep quiet and happy with credit cards and jewelry. A new Meghan. Maybe, at an earlier moment in my life, with another man I couldn't care less about, I might have been tempted. Now, I was only sad, feeling the ghost of Dario's girlfriend hanging out in the space between us. "Was this Meghan's?"

"No. I gave her until the end of the month to move out of hers."

I made a face. So generous of him. So handy that he had a stack of available places to house his prospective fucks. "How long did you date her?"

He moved forward and sat on the end of my chaise lounge. "About five months."

Five months. I thought of my pathetic night of moping, my descent into reality TV and ice cream. That had been after seven days. Five months would destroy me.

Our heights now equal, I studied him. "How long do most of them last?"

He reached for my hand, pulled it into his lap, and traced his fingers over the back of it. "I don't want to talk about other women. I want to talk about us." He looked at me and frustration tightened his features. "What don't you like about the suite?"

I curled my fingers around his. "The suite is fine. The offer isn't. I'm not interested in being taken care of by you."

He pulled on my hand and patted his lap. "Come here."

Here was a word with limited possibilities. I considered them, examined the ridiculousness of sitting on his lap, then obeyed. I crawled across the chaise and moved onto his lap, straddling him.

He tugged on my T-shirt. "I am a businessman, Bell. I'm open to negotiations."

He didn't understand. All his money, all his power, and he didn't understand the simplest thing about a woman's heart. It wasn't up for negotiation, and my biggest struggle wasn't in where I would live, but if I could protect that heart from him. I shook my head and tried to find my way back to a safe place of reason. "I told you not to contact me again."

He sighed, his eyes studying mine, and when his hands slid upward, underneath my baggy tee and up to the curve of my small breasts, he saw the change in my eyes, the weakness of my composure, the depth of my need. "I tried, Bell. I tried to leave you alone."

I hated him. I hated that with such simple words, with such a small touch, I was sucked into his orbit. Every rational thought said to back away. Every rational objection demanded I climb off his lap. Instead, I leaned into his touch.

His hands tightened and his mouth crushed against mine, soft velvet that took as much as it begged. My body reacted and I reached for him just to stop from falling.

I've kissed a lot of men in my life. Our first kiss in The Gold Room seduced my mind. This one broke the first chain around my heart.

DARIO

Their kiss escalated and her legs slid around him, wrapping tightly. When he stood, she didn't let go, her mouth hot and needy against his.

"Take me to the bedroom," she demanded, diving back onto his mouth, her hands fisting in his hair.

He stepped into the suite and her legs found their ground. She stepped away and through the bedroom door, a devilish gleam in her eye. He watched her disappear into the dark room and his cock twitched.

With her, everything was different. She hadn't asked him to get rid of Meghan or Laney, yet he had. He'd booked this suite out for a year, and she had turned her nose up at it. He was three steps behind, chasing her for attention, yet terrified of her at each step. Vulnerability was a luxury he couldn't afford, and each interaction with her brought it in spades.

He stepped into the room and shut the door, watching her turn, her eyes alive with desire.

He needed to get the upper hand, or he needed to let her go. It was that simple. But just as equally, it wasn't simple at all.

He toed off his dress shoes, then reached for his belt and undid the clasp.

FOURTEEN

BELL

There were few things hotter in this world than watching Dario Capece unzip his pants. He let them fall to the floor, and I watched him step out of them with the feral ease of a lion.

"Get on the bed."

I backed up until I bumped against the king-sized bed, my hands fumbling as I slid onto it. He undid his second and third button, then gripped the collar of the white dress shirt and pulled it over his head.

He was all muscle and black boxer briefs. The briefs were thin and silk, clinging to him enough that I could see the stiff outline of his cock. I wanted to turn on all the lights, to illuminate him further, but the dim light from the bathroom was enough to tell me everything I already knew. He was beautiful.

He stalked forward and the details came into view. The scars that dotted his landscape, short and long slashes of a history I didn't know. The thin dark hair, clipped short, on his chest. Thick abs. Strong shoulders. He reached forward and an impressive bicep flexed.

"Wow." The word fell out, and I covered the slip with an embarrassed grin.

He cocked a brow but said nothing. He tucked a tendril of my hair behind my ear and leaned forward, placing his hands on the bed beside me and lowering his mouth to mine. He paused, and I pushed forward, my lips against his, my tongue greedy when he finally opened his mouth.

"Dario…" His name was a plea uttered in between kisses, my hands moving up his chest, squeezing and testing the muscles, sliding over his shoulders and stealing into his hair, pulling on the dark strands. My bare feet reached forward, my sole bumping over those muscular thighs and found his cock, my soles coming together, and I used the thin gap between them to grip his length, his underwear lubricating the movement.

He groaned and straightened, pulling at my shirt. He was hidden from sight, and I yanked at the cotton, clearing it from my head and clawing for him. He stepped back and I followed, almost falling off the end of the bed and onto my knees, the fur rug cushioning the impact. I tucked my feet beneath me and my new position put his crotch front and center before me. Beneath the black fabric, his cock twitched.

I reached for it and he gently pushed my hands away. He looped his fingers underneath the waist of the underwear and pulled down, the material silently dropping to the floor.

I stared and forgot, for a single moment, how to breathe.

DARIO

His attempt to gain the upper hand was going haywire. She was on her knees, in the most subservient position he could envision, and still held all the power. The way she looked at his cock ... he groaned and stepped closer, his hand settling on the back of her head and pulling it forward till it met his shaft.

"Just kiss it."

She obeyed, her eyes meeting his as she planted a line of soft kisses along its length. She opened her mouth and he almost broke in the moment her tongue darted out and flicked against the underside of his shaft.

"How many men have you done this with?"

She only shook her head in response, refusing to answer the question. It didn't matter. From this point forward, her mouth was only his. That's what mattered. His to kiss, his to enjoy, his to experience. He couldn't bear the thought of her on her knees before another man, couldn't bear the thought of another man witnessing this sight, experiencing the tentative touch of her wet tongue sliding along his length. He threaded his hands through her hair and gripped it, tilting her head back, her mouth open as if waiting for more.

"God, you're beautiful."

She was. Too beautiful for a scarred-up thug like him. Too pure for his violence. Too naive for his deception.

She paused at the head of his cock, and he reached down, gripping the base of it and gently running the crown of it over her open lips. She flicked her tongue out, and he grinned. "Tease."

"You're the one who's too bossy to let me do a proper job."

It wasn't fair, the combination of assets that this woman possessed. The fearlessness. Sexuality. Wit. She was the most tempting woman he'd ever experienced, and that was dangerous. She closed her eyes and took him down her throat, a wet flex of sensation that had his balls clenching, the pleasure so great that he took a long moment of selfish enjoyment. She bobbed her head, taking him as far as she could, and it was one of the hottest feelings he'd ever had.

The sensation, paired with his long abstinence ... he stepped away from that mouth before he got distracted from his purpose—bringing her pleasure. He nodded at her to stand up. "Take off your pants."

Meeting her eyes, he prayed for forgiveness over the shit-storm he was about to start.

BELL

"Please..."

I clawed at the sheets and begged, for the third time, for him. I turned my head and bared my teeth, biting at his bicep muscle. He growled and pulled my hair, removing my teeth from his skin. He was above me, his forearm alongside my head and holding his weight, his body light atop mine. Too light. He pressed forward with his hips and his bare erection slid over my mound. I was so wet the motion was audible, the slick meeting of our bodies perfect, had his cock been just an inch lower.

"I need it." I panted the words, my hands gripping his hips, trying to pull him tighter to me. He shut me up with his mouth, his touch moving from my breast and sliding down to the place where our bodies met. I tightened, already aware, from earlier orgasms, of what his fingers could do. I clawed at his back and yelped when he pushed two digits inside of me.

"One more and I'll stop," he promised.

I didn't want him to stop. I wanted hours of this, assuming *this* included penetration of more than his fingers and his tongue. Not that I was complaining. God knew that foreplay was a lost art, one this man had mastered. But it wasn't fair to have such a beautiful dick and torture someone by withholding it.

"*Fuck* me." I gritted out the command, lifting my hips off the bed as his fingers hit my g-spot.

"I don't have a condom."

Ugh. A piece of sense in this torturous session. I tightened my grip on his back and gasped as another orgasm built—the third so far tonight.

"I—" I stopped as my legs tensed, my back arched, the orgasm swelled. Bold and glorious, it ripped a soundless scream from my throat as he furiously worked his fingers, his eyes tight on mine. Chords of intense pleasure rippled across me and I bucked against his hold, riding out the sensation, then curled in, everything fading into a mess of languid aftershocks. His hand softened and retreated as he lifted off me. I saw, in the haze of pleasure, his large frame settling back on his knees as he jacked off quickly, his fist a blur of rough motion. He held me down with his other hand, keeping me in place.

"Stay still."

"Just like that."

"God...."

He tensed, his face tightening, and came on my stomach, some shots hitting my breasts, and he held my gaze the entire time—an intense connection I couldn't look away from.

We hadn't even had sex. Just bodies, mouths, fingers. Friction, teases, touching. Whispers, pants, and begs. I'd gone further in the backseat of a car with my second boyfriend.

It should have felt minor. Instead, it felt like the biggest thing I'd ever done.

※

I cinched the belt of the thick and fluffy hotel robe and stepped into the bedroom, my feet leaving wet footprints on the floor. Through the open door, I spotted Dario in the kitchen and headed that way. He sat on a kitchen barstool, his phone in hand, head down. At my approach, he turned. "Enjoy the shower?"

I smiled. "It was heavenly."

He reached out, pulling me against his thigh and planting a soft kiss on my temple. I looked over the plates of food spread out on the counter. "You ordered food?"

"Just some snacks." He pulled a plate of chocolate-covered strawberries closer to me. "You want something to drink?"

"Water, please." I bit into a strawberry, cupping my other hand underneath it to catch the bits of chocolate as they fell off it. "Oh my God, this is good."

His hand tightened around my waist, a soft squeeze of affection, and then he reached around me for a water bottle. I went to stand, to move to the empty stool next to his, and he held me in place, twisting off the cap and passing the water bottle to me. He glanced down at my robe and I caught a whiff of fir trees from his freshly-shampooed head. "The shops are closed until the morning. I can have Vince bring me a change of clothes, but you're going to be stuck in that robe, or naked, until morning." The corner of his mouth lifted, and I loved the way it warmed his eyes.

"Hmmm...." I sucked a bit of strawberry juice off my fingertips. "Robe it is."

He scowled and I laughed. I stood, moving down the plates of food and eyeing their contents.

"So, tell me, Bell Hartley..." He rested his forearms on the counter and studied me. "What *would* it take to get you to move in here?"

I coughed a little at the abrupt change of subject. "What's your reason for wanting me to be *here,* specifically?"

He reached out and grabbed a piece of sushi with his fingers, dipping it into the soy sauce before bringing it to his mouth. As he chewed it, I followed suit, snagging a crab-topped piece, my own attempt a little messier than his had been. His vulnerability faded, and I watched as he shuttered back into dominance. "It's easier for me if you're here. I could meet you during the day or at night. Discreetly."

I made a face at that statement, my stomach still unsettled with the entire situation.

He watched the expression and patted the closest stool, spinning to face it. "You don't like me being married. So, let's talk about that."

I perched on the stool, taking a sip of water as he scratched the back of his head.

"I told you that Gwen and I ... we aren't monogamous. We also aren't physically involved with each other."

I held up a hand and stopped him. "At the Gold Room, you said that it wasn't my business why your marriage is the way it is. I'm not sure it's my business, now. But while your marriage freaks me out, it's not the only issue I have."

I took a breath, trying to decide how much of my soul I wanted to bare. "I've never been interested in being someone's girlfriend before. Emotional feelings ... my heart doesn't seem to work that way. Which is a good thing, I think. At least, I've always seen it as a good thing."

I looked at him, my confidence faltering. "But with you, I am worried that I will become emotionally attached. And I want, the first time I fall for someone, for it to be a winnable situation. You... your marriage..."

"It's a losing situation," he finished flatly. "Is that why you told me not to contact you?"

I nodded. "Plus, there's your father-in-law. I've heard that he ... well, he scares me. What I've heard of him scares me."

He smiled sadly. "I'm sure that what you'd heard of me scared you as well."

I said nothing, busying myself with a crunchy stick that tasted like apples and cinnamon.

Silence fell and when he finally spoke, the broken edges of his voice caused me to look up and into his eyes. "Gwen and I... we're both broken. We fit well together because of that. We've survived things together that have made us stronger. And we sometimes forget how difficult our world might seem to someone from the outside, looking in."

He closed the distance between us and tugged gently on my robe, pulling me toward him.

"Don't worry about Gwen's father. I've spent a decade insulating him from our lives." His hands tightened around me, his mouth found my neck, and he planted a soft kiss there. "In regards to your heart?"

He pulled away and looked down into my eyes. "I can't protect that. And I can't promise you anything. That's a risk you're going to have to decide whether to take." He tugged on the end of my wet hair. "Come on. Let's move to the dining room."

FIFTEEN

I flipped over puzzle pieces quickly, getting them face up and keeping an eye out for edges. Dario stood across the teak table, doing the same. The puzzle had been found on our hunt for a fireplace remote, and I'd given him a thumbs-up when he'd held it up.

I was in a bathrobe, a fresh bottle of Moscato open, a full wine glass beside me, doing a puzzle with one of Vegas's most elite. *Talk about weird*. Dario had answered the door a half hour ago, taken a duffel bag of items from Vince, and was now bare-chested, with workout pants hanging low on his hips. I thought the suit had been sexy. Half-dressed Dario was downright edible.

I found an edge piece and passed it to him. "Did you always work in casinos?"

"Pretty much." He tossed a piece into the pile. "I started in security, worked my way up, moved into hosting, then up from there. But that was back in Biloxi. I ran a casino down there, the Beau Rivage."

He glanced at me. "Ever been to Biloxi?"

I shook my head. "I haven't been much of anywhere. But you probably already know that."

"In fact…" I looked over at him. "What *do* you know about me?"

He shrugged and sat on the edge of the table. "I know you grew up about eighty miles south of here, in a town about the size of my cock."

I laughed. "I've seen your cock. Mohave is a wee bit bigger." I threw a puzzle piece toward his head, and he caught it mid-air. "But hey, I like the visual."

He smirked, a cocky smile that curled past the expensive bathrobe and found its way to my inner core.

"What else do you know?"

"Hmmm…" He tapped a piece against the table, then connected it to another. "Your mom is a waitress. So were you, before Cheech and Chong brought you to Vegas."

I nodded and thought of my mom. She always smells like the diner —fried food and cigarettes. When I was little, I would burrow into her body, and search for the scent of sugar. It was always there, hidden in the folds of her apron or the collar of her shirt.

"And your dad liked to drink." He didn't look at me when he said the words, yet I felt them sneak across the table and poke me.

"He did."

Dad had been a drunk. Dario could say it as nicely as he wanted to, but that was the truth of the matter, and everyone in town knew it, had told me it every day of my life. The cops had called him it, that night, when he had brought me in to file a report. When they'd sneered at the story of my rape, Dad had all but deflated. He'd stumbled to the side, the alcohol still strong in his system, then sank against a dingy wall in that Mohave police substation. He'd looked at me as if he wanted to die.

"He *did*," I repeated the words with more strength. "But he stopped." I moved to the head of the table, where a corner piece caught my eye. "He stopped drinking a few years ago."

"It's nothing to be ashamed of," Dario spoke quietly, as if I was a spooked horse he needed to soothe. "My dad was the same way. Only he didn't stop. Not when he killed my mom with his driving, and not when his liver gave out two years later. He drank right up until the day he died, damn whatever the doctors said."

He looked up, and there was a bitter sadness in his eyes. I put down the puzzle piece and moved around the corner of the table. Wrapping my arms around his waist, I pulled him to me, resting my head against his chest and squeezing him against me. "I'm sorry," I whispered.

He ran his hand softly over the top of my head, following my hair down my back and tugging softly on the ends. "Nothing to be sorry about. It was a long time ago. And my mom knew what she was risking, getting in the car with him." He pulled away from me enough to look down into my face. He ran his fingers over my cheekbones as if dusting them off, then leaned down and pressed his lips—for just the briefest of seconds—against mine. "But, thank you."

He pulled away from me, and I watched him circle the table, his eyes back down on the pieces, a long tumble of a sigh coming out of him.

I waited for a moment, then twisted my hair into a knot and tucked it under the neck of the robe, searching for a change of subject. "When'd you move to Vegas?"

"About thirteen years ago. Gwen and her father came to Biloxi to scope out our operations. I took them to dinner, turned on the charm." He winced, and I noticed the dark turn of his features, the quick change of his eyes, a tensing of his build. "The charm didn't work on Gwen's father."

"I heard he's crazy."

Dario didn't react, he only flipped a five-sided piece over on its back. "Most people in this town are. But yes, if you run into him on the street, you should turn the other way."

"I was a little more concerned about running into him in this hotel." I gestured to the suite. "Or in here."

He looked at me, and there was a real moment, one where he dropped any act, and I let him see my fear. "I'd never put you in danger. I wouldn't bring you here, *move* you here, if there was any danger."

They were words meant to reassure me. They didn't. "So you agree —an encounter with her father would put me in danger?"

"That's not what I said. But yes. I'm not going to bullshit you on that. Hawk won't ever know about or understand my relationship with Gwen. He doesn't know anything about what I do in my spare time, and he doesn't know that she's at our ranch right now because she likes the way our lead cowboy fucks her." He rested his hands on the table and held my gaze.

"Doesn't that ... bother you?" It seemed crazy, for him to sit here with me, messing with a pile of puzzle pieces, while his wife was with another man. It seemed crazy that *she* would be okay with some sort of arrangement that lets him have mistresses. If he was my husband, I'd have a chastity belt around that man's waist. I'd chop off one of his appendages in the middle of the night if he so much as kissed another woman. If he was my husband, it would break my heart for him to be here, right now, looking at a woman in this way.

"Does it bother you that Rick fucks Britni after work some nights?"

I threw up my hands and a piece of blue cardboard flew through the air, a laugh shaking out of me as I tried to hold the unexpected outburst in. "What the fu—What does *that* have to do with anything? How do you even *know* that?"

"Answer the question." The words were an order, an edge to their corners, and a part of me swooned at the dominating tone. "Does it bother you?"

My response was half of a strangled laugh, half a snort of derision. "No."

Not that I had even *known* about Rick and Britni. But ... thinking back, there had been plenty of signs, all which had gone right over my head.

"*Why* doesn't it bother you?" he asked.

"I don't know ... I—"

I scratched an itch on my arm and blew out an exasperated puff of air instead. I knew what he was getting at. "Because I don't like him like that. Besides, he's my friend. It isn't the same. She's your wife."

"In name." He slowly trailed his fingers through a pile of pieces, watching them tumble down the sides. "I imagine, if I had married a different woman, I wouldn't feel the same way."

"Meaning what? That you cheat on her, but wouldn't cheat on another woman?" I snorted in disbelief.

He studied me. "My marriage is a clusterfuck of situations that would take an hour to explain—and it's not my story to tell. It's Gwen's. We got married and both knew what we were getting into, and exclusivity wasn't part of it. But I can be loyal. I haven't needed to keep my dick to myself, so I haven't. But if I fell in love, if I—" He stopped himself, his face tightening from the effort.

What had he been about to say? Where was he going with that thought? *I can be loyal. If I fell in love, if I—*...

He picked out a piece and looked away. I reached for my wine glass and fought the urge to reach out and shake all of the unknowns out of him.

On the balcony, the wind pressed against me like a Black Friday crowd. I watched him light a cigar by the railing, his hands cupped around it in an almost tender fashion.

"You smoke?"

He flipped the lighter closed and drew on the end of the cigar. "Occasionally. When I need a distraction."

He stared out at the view, a canvas of neon lights and moving traffic. I expected him to look at me, to follow up the comment with what he needed a distraction from. He didn't, and I wrapped the blanket a little tighter. I looked out on the horizon and saw a faint glow.

"Look." I pointed. "The sunrise."

Had it been that long? I glanced back at the table, at the half-completed puzzle and the empty bottle of wine. My mind moved through the conversations and the pauses. He had told me stories of growing up in Louisana, of swamps and voodoo. He'd talked about Vegas, of places he wanted to take me and dishes he wanted me to try. I'd told him about the horses I grew up caring for and my first days at The House. I laughed at his ridiculous ego, and he'd told me that my smile made him happy.

He straddled the chaise lounge and sat down, patting the spot before him. "Come here. Sit."

He held the cigar to the side and moved back, reaching out when I sat down and pulling my back flush against his chest.

Together, we watched the sky change, a bright orange wave sweeping over the buildings, the streets almost empty. I followed a street sweeper as it moved down the Strip and saw a police car stop beside a woman.

The city, coming to life.

Our night together, ending.

His hand cupped my chest, holding me to him, a firm squeeze of reassurance.

I turned my head, resting it against his shirt. "Do you think you'll live in Vegas forever?"

"Probably. Why?"

I looked out on the city, one I felt swallowed by. Funny how, on the street, I never realized its enormity.

Up here, it seemed like a monster.

I sighed. "I don't know. Just wondering."

He pressed a kiss against the nape of my neck. "Come on. Let's go to bed."

In bed, we didn't talk. He shed my robe like it was tissue paper, then pulled my naked body against him, my back to his chest, his arm around me. I tried to stay awake, tried to memorize all of the pieces of this moment. The smooth sheets. His warm body. The muscles of his body. The brush of his lips against my back. The husk in his voice when he said my name.

"Bell."

The dawn light streamed through the room and highlighted everything in its path. Expensive fabrics. Stainless steel. Marble. Wood. I swallowed and could still taste the wine on my tongue. There was still the faint smell of cigar on his skin.

"Bell." He tightened his grip on me and I realized I'd fallen, or almost fallen, asleep.

"Yes?"

"Thank you for tonight."

I wasn't sure what he was thanking me for. I drank his wine. Butchered his puzzle. Went to third base and didn't give him much of an ending. Kept him up way past the hour when a businessman should sleep.

Still, I smiled. "You're welcome. Thank *you*."

He kissed my shoulder, and I closed my eyes, letting the pull of sleep drag me into its depths.

I woke to blood.

SIXTEEN

The blood was on the sheets, long dark streaks that had dried, flecks of black dotting the white surface. I held my breath, pulling back the sheets carefully, and lifted my hands, half-expecting to see them stained red. They weren't. They were pale and clean. I looked back at the bed, Dario's side empty.

"It's okay."

The sudden voice had me shrieking, my hands clutching the sheet to my naked chest, and I whipped my head around to see him in the doorway.

"What happened?"

He shut the door and strode toward me, his hands busy on the cuff of his left sleeve. "I didn't realize I was bleeding like a stuck pig until I bent down to check on you and saw the blood on the sheets."

His demeanor was calm, his voice wry, and I relaxed my grip on the sheet. I noticed the bright light from the window and glanced at the clock on the bedside. Almost noon.

"Let me see the cut." I reached out for him.

He sat on the edge of the bed and lifted his elbow, exposing the back of his forearm.

I hissed. "Jesus."

The cut looked deep and painful and already had a salve applied over it, a greasy substance that wasn't stopping the blood. I watched a line of it drip down and he pressed a pad of gauze to the spot.

"It's fine. I've got a doc in the living room, he'll give me a few stitches."

"What happened?"

He shrugged. "Just some business that turned sour."

"It's not even noon yet."

I thought of Vince, and the men he'd come to The House with. "Why isn't your security protecting you?"

"It's fine." He leaned forward and kissed the top of my head, a dismissive gesture that only added anger to my worry.

"It's *not* fine. When did you leave? Why didn't you wake me up?"

He stood up and the tenderness fell off of him. "I run a business. A lot of businesses. I can't sleep until noon on a Monday."

"I didn't ask you to sleep until noon. I asked why you didn't wake me up. Did you even sleep?"

I could see the answer in his face, in the tired lines that pulled at the edge of his features.

I yanked back the sheet and got out of bed. Stepping into the bathroom, I threw the door closed, waiting for the satisfying slam of the wood. There was none, and I turned to see his body blocking the opening, stepping forward, closer. He came up behind me and pressed me hard against the counter, his hands sliding down my arms and he gripped my wrists, pulling them behind my bare back. I struggled, then stopped, the fight futile. He surged forward and I felt the hard length of him against my ass.

His eyes met mine in the bathroom mirror, then dragged down the length of my naked body. "You think I had sleep on my mind?"

He transferred both of my wrists to one hand and used his other to slide up my stomach, his touch dominant as he ran his palm over my breasts. My nipples pebbled under his touch and I fought the contact, pushing back on him with my ass, irritated for being aroused at the sight and feel of his touch. He groaned at the increased contact, his eyes meeting mine in the mirror, and my angry facade slipped for a moment when a grin broke through my scowl.

He caught the smile and shook his head. "You're gonna be the death of me."

The words were a growl against my neck, and he kissed the spot and pulled off of me, the heat between us fizzling out into nothing. I saw a fresh smear of blood across his white dress shirt and pointed to the spot. "I bet you keep your dry cleaner busy."

"At times."

A line of blood dripped off his hand. The soft splat caught my attention and I watched the bright red drop stain the grout line between two marble tiles.

"Who cut you?"

He shook his head slightly. "A nobody."

I'm a nobody. A naked nobody who caught Dario Capece's eye. One he found entertaining and decided to keep around. I swallowed, and the sour aftertaste of last night's wine hit my tongue. "What happened to him?"

Dario lifted a robe off the hook and passed it to me, watching as I shrugged into and tightened it around my waist. "Does it matter?"

I considered the question, staring at the dark spot of blood on the floor. I shook my head. "No."

"Miller Lite?"

The waitress held up the bottle, and I raised my hand. "That's me."

She held out the beer and I half-lifted out of my seat to grab it.

"Super classy, Bell," Meredith mused.

"We're at a strip club." I shot the response back to Meredith, who completely missed the comment, her hands moving to wave frantically at the disco-haired brunette who had just come on stage in roller-skates.

"Look! That's Tracy!"

"She's going to spin on the pole in those skates?" Lydia asked.

"Shut it. It's her first night," Meredith snapped.

As if we needed the reminder. That was the reason we had trekked across town to Saffire—to provide emotional support for Meredith's friend. The girl had finally succumbed to the hole which claimed half of hot Vegas women: stripping or prostitution. She had chosen stripping ... but we'd suspected she'd dive into hooking pretty soon. It was too tempting for most of them, especially with the cocktail of drugs they passed around backstage. I watched her slowly circle the pole, her hands reaching back to pull at the strings of her top and thought of the guy at The House. The one with the chip—Dario's chip—and the fifty-thousand-dollar offer.

Maybe I was just a few bad months away from this myself. I watched her turn, saw the tight pinch of her features, the nervous press of her hot pink lips, and tried to imagine myself on stage. I tried to picture the lights, the stares, the sweaty hands and offers, the backroom jerk-offs and sugar daddy setups.

I thought of Dario's sleek suite with the million-dollar-view. That morning, Vince had stocked the closet with designer pants and a silk top, the tags still attached. In that opulent bathroom, I'd pulled on a thousand dollars worth of new clothes. I'd bent down and fastened the strap of a Prada sandal. I'd walked out and kissed a man who may have beaten someone up just hours before.

My throat closed and I tightened my hand around the beer, lifting it to my mouth.

The strip club manager liked us, sending over champagne and food. We got drunk, cheered on Meredith's friend, and talked about celebrities and classes. I laughed when Lydia got on the table and danced. I flirted when the hockey players next to us got friendly. I let a big Ukrainian goalie pull me onto his lap and sing me some song about beautiful women.

Throughout it all, I thought of Dario.

I thought of the way he'd dropped me off, his Rolls pulling up to my driveway, his hand passing me the suite's access card. He'd told me to text him if I needed anything, and to use the place whenever I felt like it. I told him I wasn't ready for it, and he pushed the card on me anyway.

I'd hid it in my T-shirt drawer and vowed not to use it. I'd changed out of the new clothes, hung them in my closet, and decided I wouldn't wear them. I'd scrubbed the scent of him off in the shower and fought the smile that came as I thought of him.

I had to remember our differences. I was nobody and he was somebody. I was single and he was married. I was too young and naive, and he was too old and ...

There were too many words to complete that sentence. He was too *everything*—a black hole that could suck me in without even feeling the crush of my soul.

"They don't mean anything to me. Maybe I'm ready for someone who does."

I couldn't get him out of my mind. And worse, I didn't want to. I tipped back my third beer and looked away when the goalie smiled at me.

DARIO

The room was blindingly bright, the fluorescents reflecting off the white tile walls. Dario shut the door and flipped the lock, giving his eyes a moment to adjust. He stepped forward, undoing the buttons of his dress shirt and taking his time as he eyed the two men slumped against the far wall. One moved his foot and the chain scraped against the concrete floor. The bigger of the two lifted his head.

"Who's there?"

Dario didn't respond, shrugging out of his shirt and examining the bandage on his forearm. The bleeding had stopped, thanks to the neat line of stitches from the doc. Not the first stitches he'd received this year, and probably not the last. He hung his shirt carefully on the door's hook and stepped closer to the two men, his dress boots clicking against the concrete floors.

There was a special place in hell for men who hurt women. He'd learned that at an early age, when he'd watched his father beat the shit out of his mother when the Saints would lose, or when his beer was warm, or when his luck at the casino had turned to shit.

It was why Dario didn't drink. Or gamble. Or watch football. It was why he'd forced the Cajun drawl from his speech and abandoned work boots and jeans for suits and ties. It was why he'd avoided the fishing boats and had gotten his first job on the casino floor.

His entire life, he had strived to be the opposite of his father. Now, he looked down into the swollen face of a man so much like him it made his fists ache.

"If you're gonna kill us, just do it already." The man coughed, and a spittle of blood came out.

"I'm not going to kill you."

He'd decided that after seeing the look in Bell's eyes when she had asked him about the man who'd cut him. He'd seen the worry there, had noticed the way her mouth had tightened, her jaw set. If she ever brought it up again, he wanted her to be happy with his answer. And if making her happy meant keeping people alive, then fine.

He squatted before the man and examined his swollen face, the eyes now puffy slits, the top lip split and hanging in an unnatural way. This one had squealed when he'd tied him down, his fat body flopping against the restraints. It'd taken two of them to get him into place and into a position where he could use the bolt cutters and the cauterization tool.

The man's lips cracked open. "Why are you doing this?"

An excellent question. The man must have been surprised at the dark suits waiting outside the small-town bar. He must have been confused when they duct-taped his mouth and handcuffed his wrists, must have hated the back of the Hummer, especially once they closed the lid. Fifteen minutes later, when they'd tossed in the second man, he'd probably wondered who he'd been, had probably been annoyed by the stranger kicking and flailing inside of the tight compartment. He'd certainly seemed surprised when Dario had pulled off his blindfold, and he'd realized the man was his son, also prisoner inside this room.

All day, Dario had left them alone. Plenty of time to think about who he was and why he was torturing them. Dario grabbed the man's shirt and pulled him forward. "You tell me why I'm doing this."

It was the same command he'd given the men that morning. And all morning, the two men had confessed. Thefts. Deceit. Abuses. Rapes. They'd given names and dates, details and apologies.

But they hadn't given Dario what he wanted. And they still didn't realize what this was really about.

Dario thought of the file he had received on Bell, the court-protected seal worthless when the right cash hit the right hands. He'd opened it without the proper reverence, unprepared for the horrible details that had covered those pages. Details that had never had a resolution. That beautiful girl, damaged by these monsters. That beautiful girl, ignored and disrespected by the system put in place to protect her.

It'd taken a week, but they were here now. Sniffling. Weak. Afraid. He leaned forward and pressed his fist into the bloody crotch of the man, putting his weight into the action, and appreciated the painful wheeze that resulted.

"Tell me. Tell me what you've done."

Finally, the man's mouth moved and the right words came out.

SEVENTEEN

BELL

Lydia groaned. "I can't believe you screwed us out of front row seats, Bell. You know I've never been to a hockey game."

Meredith nodded. "Plus, he was *hot*. You should have at least taken his number."

I shifted my weight and pushed the seatbelt tongue into the buckle, thinking of the cute Ukrainian, his cautious smile and the gentle way his fingers had curled along my lower back. He'd offered us front row seats and a tour of their facilities. He'd also asked me to come home with him.

There'd been a moment where I'd thought about leaving with him. He'd leaned in close, whispering in my ear, and I'd thought about turning my head. Letting him kiss me. Seeing if there was a connection—the sort that might lead to a night of rumpled sheets and moans and orgasms.

But I hadn't. Instead, I'd pulled away from his lap and turned down the hockey invite, and absolutely none of it made sense because I shouldn't, *couldn't*, make decisions based on Dario, or on any man's weak comparison to him. And that had been half the problem—that the goalie, that Ian, that *every* man seemed suddenly unimpressive when compared to Dario's pull on me.

"In regards to your heart? I can't protect that. That's a risk you're going to have to decide whether to take."

I'd always been a gambler, with my money, my time, my safety ... but never my heart. Still, didn't it mean something that it was even *at* risk? Didn't the fact that I had the potential to fall for someone mean that I should take the jump?

For four days I'd been mulling over that question. Four days. Countries made peace treaties and war decisions in less time. I'd buried myself in studying and work and had made no headway with the decision.

I could take the jump. Be Dario Capece's girlfriend. Live in his million-dollar suite. Accept his decadent lifestyle and ignore the wedding band on his finger. I *could* do it.

But would I? *Should* I?

Meredith turned on the radio, and I rested my head against the window. When we got home, I changed into sweats, washed my face, and called a taxi.

The access card got me into the garage, and I rode the giant car elevator up on foot. When I got to the coded door, I paused, taking a moment to remember the sequence. Birthday. Last four of my phone number. 04182996#. The lights changed and the knob gave underneath my palm. I pushed the door open and stepped into quiet tranquility, everything smooth and perfect. A lamp on the entry table illuminated woods, leathers, and fabrics, a gorgeous place I didn't fit into.

I moved into the bedroom and stripped, leaving my clothes where they fell and crawling into the bed. I unlocked my phone and stared at the text from Dario, sent a half-hour ago.

—*Let me know when you're home safely.*

It was the same text I'd gotten the last three nights. Short and sweet, easy to ignore. But, I hadn't. Each night, I had texted him from bed, my phone now filled with short chatter about my shifts, classes, and life. I typed out a quick response.

I decided to come to the suite for the night. I hope that's okay...

—More than okay. It's yours, for as much or as little as you want to use it.

I settled into the pillows and curled onto one side, cupping the phone close to my face. The bed, which had seemed so cozy with him beside me, suddenly felt cold and empty.

The bed feels lonely without you :(

I repositioned the pillow under my head and watched as dots appeared, then his response quickly followed.

—Is that an invite?

yes

—On my way.

I grabbed one of the giant feather pillows and pushed it between my knees, settling into a cocoon of comfort. I laid the phone on the bed beside me and watched the clock, wondering how long it would take him to pull on clothes, make an excuse to his wife, and come down to this level.

Though, maybe he didn't need to make excuses to her. According to him, they slept in separate beds. Maybe he just came and went as he pleased, and she did the same.

I was half asleep when the bedroom door clicked open, my head lifting off the pillow enough to recognize his build. I threw back the covers, inviting him in, and smiled when I felt the warm length of him, curling up behind me.

He kissed my bare shoulder and I felt his arm tighten around my waist. Before I could tell him *goodnight*, I was asleep.

I dipped a strawberry slice in whipped cream and brought it to my mouth, the sweet taste mixing perfectly with the chilled mimosa. I stepped away from the tray and curled up at the end of the couch, picking up the note that had been on my bedside table and rereading it for the tenth time.

I could wake up to you every morning.

I smiled and wandered into the bedroom, picking up my phone to text him. He'd beaten me to the punch, and I opened a text from him, sent just a few minutes ago.

—**Want a massage? I can have a team at your suite in fifteen minutes.**

I tapped out a response.

I'm not claiming it as "my suite" just yet.

The phone rang, his name lighting up the screen. A hundred men couldn't have stopped me from answering. "Hey."

I could hear the chimes and cheers of the casino in the background. "Good morning, beautiful."

I yawned in response, stretching my legs forward and examining the polish on my right big toe.

"I hated leaving you this morning."

I smiled. "You should have woken me up."

"You looked too peaceful. Listen, I'm about to walk into a meeting. I've got to go but let me send up Paul. Every woman at the spa raves about his hands."

"You really want another man rubbing all over me?"

He lowered his voice, and I imagined him ducking his head and moving away from his staff. "You haven't met Paul. I'm not too worried about it. Plus, I like the idea of you being naked. It'll get me through the next hour of spreadsheets with Chinese investors."

I eyed the clock, a sleek piece that hung next to a blood-red painting. "I better not. I need to head home soon and study a few hours before work."

"This weekend, I'll have the staff outfit the suite. I don't want you trekking back and forth over things you could have there. At least until you move."

"I'm *not* moving."

He laughed, and maybe he'd heard the waver in my voice. "Okay. Whatever. It's there if you want it."

His voice became muffled, and I heard bits of a conversation, something about rooms and time. He came back on, and there was a new clip to his tone, a business-like edge that lost all of its playful warmth. "I've got to go."

I said goodbye and ended the call, feeling detached from him, wanting a moment of before, where his voice had curled around the edges, and there'd been a smile in his tone.

I swung my legs off the couch and stood, thinking of Vegas traffic, of the taxi line and crowds of tourists. I sighed and sucked the last bit of whipped cream off my finger.

Time to get back to real life.

DARIO

This late at night, the view was all lights, a hundred tiny specks of pulsing color. He rested his weight on the railing and looked at the smaller hotel beside them. The curtains were open in some of the rooms, bits of people seen, movements recorded, shadows on balconies. The door behind him slid open and Gwen stepped through, coming to stand beside him.

"It's good to be home." She rested her head on his shoulder.

"You don't mean that." He smiled to soften the words, and she laughed, pushing her thick dark hair over her shoulder. Her hair reminded him of Bell. They had the same dark coloring, the same long hair. Gwen's, he'd handled a hundred times, knew the scent of her shampoo, the texture of its strands. Bell's… he'd barely had a chance to grip, to pull, to appreciate.

"You're right. I miss it already. And the horses miss you. You should go there soon. Ride BB. He needs the work."

"How's Nick?"

Her back stiffened a little at the cowboy's name, but she hid it well, turning to lean back against the railing, her glass of wine brought up to her lips. "He's good. Said to tell you hi."

"I bet he did." It came out wrong, as if he cared about her cowboy fuck toy, though he knew the man was more than that. Honestly, if anyone had married Gwen to save her from her father, it probably should have been that strapping stretch of masculinity and good intentions. Lord knew the man was protective enough of her.

But Nick hadn't married Gwen. Dario had. Nick hadn't even known Gwen back then. Dario had wanted an empire, and Gwen had needed a savior.

It had worked out for both of them. It had been perfect, thirteen years of side fucks and friendship, of mutual respect and understanding. Only now, suddenly, it felt like shit. It felt like she was still trapped, and both of them were still dancing for Robert Hawk.

From contentment to misery. How could everything change in just weeks?

He knew, of course. It was Bell. Ten thousand cocktail waitresses in this town and he had to meet the one that might break him. The one that might ruin everything he and Gwen had built. The one that might be worth it all.

The one that might not be.

He thought of last night, how it had felt, having her in his arms, listening to the soft sighs as she slept. It'd been over a decade since he'd slept beside a woman other than Gwen. And his nights with

Gwen had been perfunctory, each staying on their own sides of hotel beds, their pillow talk filled with financials and business plans.

He had liked sleeping next to Bell. In the half hour it had taken him to fall asleep, he'd felt a level of calm and contentment he hadn't experienced in years. And that, in *itself*—fuck the addictive way she'd wormed into his mind—was a problem.

Gwen's arm slid around his back and she looked up at him. "I was going to watch some TV in the theater room. You want to join me?"

He shook his head. "No. We've got someone in the cage." It was a lie. The cage was now clean, disinfected with bleach, a fresh coat of paint covering the bloodstains. Bell's rapists had been set free, dropped back in their shithole lives with a very clear understanding of their mistakes.

Gwen's face curled in distaste, as he'd known it would. "Well. Go easy on him, will you?" It was funny. As bloodthirsty as her father was, Gwen was the exact opposite. Her gentle nature, despite her upbringing, was something he'd always loved about her.

He glanced back at the view, the city stretched before them, the city they owned. He followed the Strip down, let his gaze linger on the patch of buildings where The House was, and thought of Bell.

The way she'd panted beneath him, her hands gripping his hips, trying to pull him tighter to her. The way she'd looked curled inside a robe, a puzzle piece in hand, smiling at him.

He should probably watch some TV with Gwen. Talk about business, laugh at some stupid show, and enjoy some time with his best friend. *Like they'd always done.* Pushing her off and avoiding moments like those felt wrong. Wanting those moments with Bell … that didn't feel fair to Gwen. *Shit.*

Instead, he kissed the top of her head and stepped away, heading inside. He could go to his office for an hour. Push around some papers and pretend he's beating the shit out of someone.

He ran a hand over his mouth and swallowed a groan. Talk about properly fucking things up.

EIGHTEEN

BELL

Some nights, when The House was closed, we played poker at Lance's. Strip poker, if we got drunk enough.

Tonight, we were definitely drunk enough. I tipped back a cold bottle of Miller Light and eyed my cards, my jeans and tennis shoes already kicked into the pile of clothes beside the table. The rules were simple. If you won the hand, you got the pot, and your clothes stayed on. If you lost, a piece of clothing hit the floor. I had panties, a bra, T-shirt and sweatshirt standing between me and stark nudity.

"Come on, B," Lance urged. "You ain't got shit."

I glared at him and ran a thumb along the side of my first Ace. The second Ace, cozying right next to it, I ignored. "Raise, twenty."

I pushed the chip into the pile and studiously avoided Rick's eyes, who sat to my left. It was a ploy, one that he bought with a laugh and a push forward of chips.

"Re-raise. I'm putting Bell all in."

I made a face, then pretended to catch the action, pursing my lips together and raising my eyebrows at Lance. "Please call this asshole."

Lance shrugged. "You know I can't say no to a lady." He eyed Rick's chip stack. "I can cover your stack. I'm in."

Rick stood, flipping over two pair, kings and queens. "Go ahead. Give me your money and take off those clothes." He pointed at Lance. "Keep yours on. It'll be more of a win if I *don't* see your dick tonight."

Lance read the cards and winced, tossing his into the center of the table. "Come on, B. Tell me you've got three of a kind under there."

I flipped over my Aces, which paired nicely with the fourth-street Ace, and lifted both hands in the air with a whoop loud enough to raise the dog's head. "And *that's* how you do it."

I pointed to Rick, then Lance. "Both of you, keep your underwear on. I'm taking my money and running."

I pulled the pile of chips toward me and picked through them. Britni, who had perched herself at the bar, wandered over to help me. I caught the brief eye contact between her and Rick, then she looked at me and smiled.

"Good hand."

"Thanks. It was about time. I've had crap luck all night."

She stacked a tower of fives and slid them toward me. "That's why I bowed out once the strip poker began. I'd be butt-naked in five minutes."

Rick stood up, moving past the table and heading to the kitchen. He reached out to squeeze her shoulder. I wanted to smack myself in the head for not seeing the signs earlier.

I counted out my chip stack and pushed it toward Lance. "Four hundred and forty."

Not bad for a night off work. Maybe I'll quit The House and become a full-time player. Lance's eyes met mine over the table, and he smiled. "Nice play."

"Hard to lose with pocket aces."

He stood, reached for the baseball cap that held our buy-ins, and started to count out the cash.

I watched my bare legs as they shimmered under the water, my limbs distorted by the hot tub's churn. Beside me, Lance was quiet, his arms splayed out to either side, a cold beer in one hand. He pressed it against my neck, and I smiled. "That feels good."

"I know. I'm tempted to jump in the pool to cool off."

I tilted my head, considering it. "Nah. Too far away."

He laughed, bringing the beer to his lips and tilting it back.

I watched the inside of the house, the figures of Britni and Rick moving through the kitchen, then disappearing into the living room. "You think they hook up?"

He chuckled. "Absolutely."

I closed my eyes, enjoying the heat from the tub, the massage against my back. I contemplated loosening my bra, the underwire a bit uncomfortable, but left it alone.

"How's your boy?"

I cracked open one eye. "Which one?"

There was the flash of white teeth in the dark as he smiled. "Oh, so it's like that?"

I shrugged, closing my eyes again. "I don't know. It's a mess."

"But you've seen Capece again."

I wet my lips. "Yeah. He wants me to move to The Majestic, to a suite there."

He started coughing mid-sip and leaned forward, setting his beer on the ledge and wiping his mouth. "What the fuck, B? And you haven't said anything?"

I scissored my legs under the water. "I'm not moving in there. You know me and relationships. We hide from each other."

"Huh." The skepticism seeped through the word and I rolled my eyes, wondering exactly how transparent I was. He picked the beer back up and took a sip. "Must be nice, to have spare condos lying around."

I snorted and looked over at him. "Oh yeah, because you need that?" I waved my arm in the air, gesturing to the empty pool deck. "All these women, everywhere. God, where are they all going to sleep?"

The water was unexpected, a splash of heat, and I sputtered, using my hands to force a wave back in his direction.

"Shit. Stop. Truce. Watch the beer." He held it out of the way and waited for the hot tub to settle.

"Besides, you don't have a wife you have to hide women from." I sat up, moving away from the side of the tub and into the center of the space, skimming my fingers along the top of the water and watching the water spray. "Tell me I'm being an idiot by seeing him."

Lance tilted the beer bottle to one side and eyed it. He was quiet for a long moment before speaking. "You're being an idiot. But I can't say, if I was in your position, that I wouldn't do the same thing."

He lifted his shoulders, the muscles bunching under his handsome face. "He's a good-looking, rich, powerful guy. That's not an easy thing for a girl to walk away from." He set down the beer and lifted his hands, linking his fingers and resting them on top of his head. "But like I told you before, you need to be careful. I don't want you getting hurt."

"I know." *Be careful. Don't get hurt*. I didn't know if he meant my heart or my body, but I didn't know how to protect either, short of staying away from Dario altogether.

And the last week had proved that I wouldn't be able to do that. I was already, after just one sexual session, a hundred texts, and two sleepovers, in too deep. I could feel my fall, I just didn't seem to have a way to stop it.

DARIO

Dario leaned against the wall, crossing his arms over his chest and listening to the floor manager go through pre-shift. As the woman spoke, he let his eyes drift over the assistant managers, assessing each one as he moved. There was a position opening up at the north location, and he wanted to promote from within.

Against his thigh, his phone vibrated. Reaching into his pocket, he pulled out the cell, swallowing a smile as he saw the text notification from Bell.

—I can't stop thinking about your cock

Jesus. A groan slipped out of his mouth, and he coughed to cover the sound, making eye contact with the manager before stepping away, out the side door and down the hall.

He moved briskly, his head down, fingers on the screen.

Tell me.

This hall was too long, his office too far. He jogged up the back stairs, nodding to employees as he passed, and shoved open the door, moving down the gilded hallway of the executive level.

His receptionist rose at his approach, and Dario cut off his greeting with a terse shake of his head. "Not now. And no interruptions."

The receptionist nodded, lowering himself back into the chair, and Dario could die in his office of starvation before the man would open the door. That was the benefit of hiring the right people and training them properly. They stood, jumped, sat and stayed where you told them to. They kept their mouth shut and didn't see anything. They refused bribes and were paid handsomely as a result.

Dario shut his office door and placed the call.

"Hey." She sounded lazy, as if she hadn't yet gotten out of bed.

"You were thinking about my cock?"

She sighed, and there was the rustle of fabric against the phone. "Yep."

"I'm going to need more information." He sat down at his desk, his dick already half-hard from her text. Now, with her voice, the soft huff of her breath ... he imagined her in her bed, naked, her dark hair messy, eyes hooded, hands running over stiff nipples and in between her thighs.

"I don't think I've experienced its full potential."

He had to chuckle at that. "No. You haven't."

"I'd like to."

He glanced at the clock and tried to place her schedule. "Shouldn't you be in class pretty soon?"

"I'll leave in a few minutes. Right now, I really wish you were here." She huffed out a breath and he imagined the sensation along the ridges of his cock, her hands sliding along his thighs, her eyes on him, her lips wet, tongue darting out. He thought of how she had licked his length, the way she had grinned, the flick of her tongue, her capable grip.

Maybe it was the distraction, the idea of her mouth, her body, the possibilities, but he told her the truth. "I don't know what to do with you, Bell."

"What do you mean?"

He should change the subject. Evade. Redirect her attention to the organ between his legs that was screaming for release. Instead, he continued down the path of destruction. "Our relationship is a risk to my marriage."

The lazy drawl dropped from her voice and it sharpened into steel. "First off, we aren't yet *in* a relationship. Second, I thought you had some arrangement with her. Your waitress, your mistress—"

"I didn't care about them."

He interrupted her, his words hardening, his arousal fading. A shame, since that's what this was supposed to be. Fucking arousal. Bell was supposed to be a piece of ass. A piece of ass that showed up and sat and bent over where he told her to. A pretty face, nice ass, and entertaining mouth, like all of the others. She was *meant* to be like the others, yet hadn't been. From the very beginning, she had flipped that possibility on its head. How?

He was suddenly mad without reason, his earlier realizations coming back stronger and sharper, their negatives all he could think about in the wave of fear. *She might break him.* Ruin everything for Gwen. Lose everything they'd fought so hard to have.

"So, because you *care* about me ... that's why I'm a problem for you?"

"Yes. It's not that complicated of a fucking concept." He growled the words with a ferocity that few women had seen and pushed himself to his feet.

"Well, join the fucking club! You think I *want* to like you? You think I *want* to be sitting here, all swoony-eyed, unable to get you out of my fucking head?"

He took a deep breath at her words. This was, without a doubt, the most fucked-up argument on the planet.

He should have become a fucking choir boy when he married Gwen. He should have become abstinent and not dipped his cock into whatever woman caught his eye and risked falling into love.

Not that this was love. It couldn't be, not this soon. She was a liability, and he was the king of this town. Any spark between them would trigger a bomb, one with Robert Hawk's name on it. Any love between them would only end in tragedy, the sort that involved body bags and evidence lockers.

He'd been stupid. Egotistic. Cocky. He'd thought with his dick and his heart, and not his brain.

He ended the call before he did any more damage.

NINETEEN

DARIO

"You've got to do something about these sluts."

Dario pulled apart the roll, steam breaking free and curling into the air. He reached for the butter and ignored the comment from Robert Hawk.

"They're all over the bar at The Majestic. We're not running a brothel, Dario."

He looked up, meeting the older man's sharp eyes. "They aren't prostitutes, Robert. They're models. We're strict with them on that."

Which wasn't to say they didn't have a stable of escorts. Two percent of last year's bottom line had come from those girls. But that was run through a separate corporation, one that Robert Hawk didn't have his fingers in.

"I don't care if they're models. They don't belong in my casino. The men are here to play, not get distracted by skirts short enough to show their pussies." The man snorted and lifted his glass, glaring at their waiter.

"You aren't supposed to be at The Majestic." Dario kept his voice mild but pinned the man with a look capable of breaking glass. "We have an agreement, one that doesn't involve you harassing our employees or our guests."

"I wasn't harassing anyone." The man sat back, shoving his glass to the side and waiting as a fresh whiskey was set down. "And it's my damn casino. What's the point of having one if I can't check in on it?"

He lifted the whiskey and paused, pointing his finger in Dario's direction. "You think you can do whatever you want, without me checking on my investment? It doesn't work like that."

"Your investment has tripled in value since I stepped in." Dario cut a wedge of steak and stabbed it with his fork. "I'm not going to measure dicks with you, Robert. Just stay out of the casinos and count your millions at the end of each month." He lifted the piece of meat to his mouth. "How's the horse business?"

"Fuck the horses. I killed one last week. Damn thing came up limping. Worst business to be in."

Dario took a sip of ice water. "You seem to enjoy it."

"I enjoy winning. The rest is bullshit, a complete waste of time and money. Speaking of which, how's my little girl?"

It was interesting, the way that Hawk viewed his only daughter. A waste of time and money was one end of his emotional spectrum toward Gwen. The other end was a maniacal possessive pride, one that insisted his daughter succeed in everything, yet never move more than a step from his control. It had taken three years and delicate maneuvering to engineer the marriage between them and the manipulation of Robert Hawk. It had been the most difficult business deal Dario had ever entered into. A business deal still very much in play.

Dario finished chewing and swallowed. "She's good. Spent last weekend at the ranch."

"I keep waiting for a grandchild. I'm going to be hobbling around on a walker at the current pace of your dick."

Hawk would be dead in the ground before Gwen ever brought a child into the world. She had a hormone implant that guaranteed that.

Dario shrugged. "We're trying. I've told you before about her doctor's report."

Robert Hawk looked away, the mention of the doctor's report ending the conversation as quickly as it had started. There was no doctor's report, at least not one that verified Gwen's concerns. She hadn't checked to see her fertility feasibility but they both doubted her ability to carry a child. Those three weeks in Mexico, the things that had been done to her twelve-year-old body…

Dario's stomach clenched and, for the hundredth time, he considered killing the man. "Maybe you should have thought about your future grandchildren when she was in Mexico."

The words hung between them, and Hawk's eyes sparked with anger, a flash of rage that was quickly buttoned down and tucked away for later. Dario often wondered what happened after their meetings, if all of Dario's pokes exploded out of Robert Hawk and onto an innocent victim. He often wondered if he should think less and shut his mouth more.

But he couldn't keep silent about some things. Hawk's refusal to pay a million-dollar ransom had led to Mexican kidnappers savaging his daughter. Dario had been the one to avenge that crime. It'd taken three months in that sweat-filled country to track down the assholes, ones who'd barely remembered the event until he'd reminded them. By the end of the trip, they'd remembered everything and burned and bled their way into hell.

It had felt good. It had made Gwen happy, but hadn't brought back her innocence. Just like his recent activities hadn't brought back Bell's. Was it a coincidence that both of these women had such brutal pasts? Maybe that psychiatrist from Sacramento had been right, the one who had gotten drunk on mojitos and analyzed him over nachos and salsa in that airport lounge. Maybe he did have a white knight syndrome.

"You don't know anything about Mexico. And I'm not talking to you about it here. It's none of your goddamn business."

"She's my wife. It's always my goddamn business." Dario spoke calmly, lifting the napkin and wiping his mouth. Balling up the fabric, he tossed it on the table. It landed next to his phone, which buzzed to life, the display lighting with a number he instantly recognized. Bell's.

Hawk's eyes moved to the phone. "You need to take that?"

Dario ignored the question, sitting back in his seat and letting the phone buzz, his posture relaxed despite the clench of his jaw. "Don't change the subject, Robert. You were asking about Gwen."

Hawk's eyes stayed on the phone and he reached forward quickly, snagging the cell off the table and tapping the screen to answer the call. He lifted the phone to his ear and held Dario's gaze.

Underneath the table, Dario's hands clenched, every muscle in his body fighting to stay relaxed, to keep himself from leaping out of his seat and snatching the phone from the man's liver-spotted hands.

The psychopath smiled, then drawled into the receiver. "Hello?"

Dario could hear something, a delicate voice that spoke. Hawk asked who she was, glanced at the screen, then held the phone out, across the table.

Dario took the cell, releasing a contained breath when he saw that the call had ended. "Don't touch my fucking phone again."

The man raised his eyebrows in a mild manner. "She sounds like a beautiful woman."

It was bait, and Dario avoided the trap, schooling his features into a manner that didn't scream his thoughts. *What had Bell said? What, if anything, did Hawk know?*

"Do you know why I picked you to marry my daughter?"

Dario stayed silent and fought the urge to check his watch. This lunch had already gone on too long. A rehash of circumstances wasn't going to help that.

"I picked you because you told me that you would be loyal to her and to my business interests." Hawk took a long sip of his drink, then smacked his lips together. Dario examined the lines that formed around his mouth, the dry spots on his cheeks, the watery blink of his eyes, the scab on the top of one ear. Robert Hawk was getting old. "I picked you because I liked how you carried yourself, and I liked how you handled situations."

"Is there a point to this?" Dario caught the waiter's eye and lifted one finger for the check.

"You've gotten too big for your redneck Cajun britches."

Dario smiled. "That's a matter of opinion."

"You don't pay *me* the proper respect." The older man slapped his hand on the tablecloth with enough force that the silverware rattled.

Dario said nothing. He'd learned, after a decade with this man, that he'd burn himself out. The waiter eased by and he passed him the credit card.

"Who was that on the phone?" The man's eyes bulged, the table rocking slightly as he leaned forward and spit out the question. Dario said nothing and Hawk's finger jabbed the air between them. "If you've got some slut on the side, I swear to God—"

Dario interrupted him before the threat could be completed. "I'm loyal to Gwen. I always have been. And I'm loyal to your business interests and investments. Just as I've always been."

He took the check folio from the waiter and added a generous tip, then scrawled his name across the bottom and stood. "And Robert?" Tucking his credit card back in his wallet, he leaned forward and rested a palm on the table, leaning forward until he was eye level with the older man. "Don't *ever* fucking threaten me."

Walking away, Dario's heart pounded against his chest.

BELL

I watched Ian walk across his room, his build thin and lanky, the muscles popping from his frame as he changed from his button-up and khakis into workout clothes. *This* is who I should be with. Safe. Secure. Sweet.

Boring.

He hadn't seemed so, three weeks ago. He'd seemed sexy, then. The bad-boy professor who bent the rules by bending me over his desk. The bad-boy professor, taming his wild ways and legitimately interested in taking me on a date.

I couldn't do it. I couldn't give him false hope for a relationship that would never happen. While Dario and I seemed to be barreling down the road toward some version of a relationship, I hadn't returned any of Ian's calls or texts. I'd ghosted him out, and he'd called me on it after class, pressuring me into this meeting at his house.

Now, he turned to grin at me, and I thought of Dario. I'd called him just before class, needing to hear his voice. I hadn't liked the way our last call had ended—a fight with a gaping cliffhanger. A fight where he said he cared about me. A fight where I'd shouted out more confessions than I'd planned or expected to.

But Dario hadn't answered my call. A stranger had. I'd hung up without giving the man my name and had waited for Dario to call me back, to explain.

No call had come. And now I was in Ian's apartment, which was a mistake. I had realized that the minute I stepped into it. He'd moved forward to kiss me, and I'd side-stepped the action. Now, I settled into the sofa and looked up at his ceiling.

"I'm sorry," I apologized for the third time. I'd made a mess out of my attempt to end our fling. Lots of stammering and over explanations, none of which had mentioned Dario and all of which had put the blame solely on my fear of commitment.

"It's okay. I get it." He walked over and rested his hands on the back of the sofa, looking down on me. "It isn't like you misled me. I'm the one who tried to change the rules on us."

He was so freaking nice. Nice, and so completely different than Dario. When Ian looked at me, my chest didn't ache. And Dario had the ability to decimate my self-control with just a look, to scatter my intentions with the crook of his mouth. If Dario had reached for me ... side-stepping would have been useless in the face of our connection.

I waited until Ian straightened, then I sat up on the couch. I glanced over at my book bag, the canvas tote silent for the last hour. I hadn't checked it during class, had forced myself to leave it in my bag during my drive to Ian's. Now, I walked over and unzipped the front pocket, reaching in and pulling out my phone.

I unlocked it and frowned at the unfamiliar No Service alert on the display. I clicked on my texts. My email. My messenger.

"What's wrong?" Ian asked.

My cellular network was completely gone, the words Verizon missing from the screen. How long ago had this happened? I thought about its silence during the last three hours. I had assumed that Dario hadn't felt the need to call me back, but maybe he couldn't. Or maybe ... he was the cause of this.

I grabbed my book bag and pulled it over my shoulder. Glancing at the clock on Ian's wall, I quickened my movements.

"Heading to work?"

"Yeah. Look…" I slid my palms into the back pockets of my jeans and wondered if a fourth apology was needed.

"Don't worry about it." He leaned forward and kissed my cheek. "Just… know that I'm here if you change your mind."

I won't. I muted the words and gave him a half smile instead. He tossed my keys toward me and I caught them mid-air.

"Study for the final. You've got five days."

I groaned. "Yes, sir." I swung open the door and waved to him, grateful the end of the semester was so close.

I took the stairs down to my car. Checking my heart for damage, I could practically feel it beam back at me, lifting one artery in an enthusiastic high-five. Why couldn't it be so resilient with Dario?

TWENTY

I got to work early, but the back lot of The House was already full. Lance's H1, Rick's Mercedes, the house cars ... and a Rolls that stuck out like a virgin in a strip club. I parked my car, stepped out, and eyed it.

The driver's door opened and a three-hundred-pound navy suit nodded at me and opened the rear door, waiting expectantly for me to come over and get in. I glanced at Lloyd, who stood by the back door and lifted his chin to let me know that he had me covered.

Three weeks ago, I'd have balked. Asked questions, or just ignored the man and gone inside. But in my new life where I slept in strange penthouses and ate room service and was courted by powerful men ... I obeyed. I ducked into the backseat, unsurprised to see Dario sitting there, his phone to his ear, his legs stretched out and crossed at the ankle. He patted the seat next to him and held a finger up to his mouth for me to stay quiet. The driver shut the door and I inhaled Dario's seductive scent. Today, it was an expensive cocktail of something heady and sexual. Just a whiff of it, and I wanted to crawl over that seat and put his cock in my hand.

The thought gave me a shot of arousal, one so strong that I actually moved, crawling forward and kneeling before him, grateful for the roomy backseat. I ran my palms over his knees and up his thighs, the expensive fabric smooth under my hands. I squeezed, the muscles tensing under the touch, a hard iron of corded tendons and thick quads. He watched me, his eyes darkening, and just the look on his face—I grinned up at him and he didn't respond, his eyes following my movements, his feet adjusting, legs spreading to give me more room.

"It's not worth that. I've seen the financials. You can't lowball me on one end and talk it up on the other. Either it's gold or it's shit. Pick a position."

I slid my hands higher and ran my palm along the seam of his zipper, isolating him through the fabric. It twitched, stiffened, grew. He shifted lower in the seat and pulled at the strap of my top, getting it off of my shoulder, then moved the cell phone to his left hand and did the same with the other. His fingers trailed across the neckline and slid under the cotton, dragging it down and exposing my bra.

His eyes locked on the skin, savoring the dip of my cleavage, and the worship, the need in his eyes … sixty seconds in his presence and I was already wet.

He laid the phone on his shoulder and I could hear a man speaking, figures and occupancy rates, the shuffle of papers and a second voice chiming in. It sounded like a meeting, a group sitting on the other end of the phone. A group who might hear whatever I was about to do. I reached forward and quietly pulled down his zipper.

DARIO

This woman was fucking nuts. He'd come here to have a serious conversation with her, to talk through everything, and she was mixing his common sense with tequila and downing it for sport. He should be pushing her off. Giving her the sort of look that put a thousand casino employees in their place. He should finish this call—a call that could make or break this negotiation—and then deal with her.

She worked her hands through the thin opening of his zipper and the pocket of his underwear and wrapped her hand around him, the throb of his cock pounding at the delicate yet firm touch of her hand. *Jesus.* He stared at her, his eyes struggling between the playful curve of that mouth and what lay underneath her top. She pulled him free and his thoughts scattered at the sight of him in her hand. He pulled her shirt lower, his dick twitching at the sight of her breasts, pale and firm, covered with a black lace bra.

She let go of his cock and pressed on his thighs, pushing herself up his body. He shifted against the seat, and she straddled him, her knees tight to his hips, his cock still at attention between them. She leaned forward, the fabric of her shirt tickling him, and put her mouth to his ear.

"My phone isn't working."

Yes. Hence his need to waste thirty minutes of a back-to-back day by sitting in this parking lot and waiting for her. He slid his hand through her dark hair, exposing her ear, and put his mouth against the spot. "Vince has a new one for you."

Changing her cell had been necessary after her brief exposure to Robert Hawk. That brief flash of her number across the screen had been enough for that psycho to memorize the number and sic his dogs on it. The moment Dario stepped outside the restaurant, he'd had Vince on the phone, and initiated contact with their men at the cell phone carriers. Eight minutes after he'd called Vince, her phone had been shut off, the service suspended, and all ownership information on her account cleared. If Robert got curious about the female voice on the other end of the call, the cell phone number would get him nowhere.

Ten minutes after he'd called Vince, there'd been men on campus, she'd been located in class and discretely protected. Seeing her now, safe and untouched, gave his heart a well-needed rest. Thinking about the fact that she'd been at that professor's house for the last hour, doing who knew what, made him jealous as *fuck*.

Her hand found his cock and squeezed it, and he let out a rough breath. He tilted his head down, pressing his lips against the hollows of her neck and kissed her there.

He interrupted his acquisitions head in the midst of his monologue. "I need to look at these figures and wrap my head around the changes. Let's talk tomorrow—same time." He ended the call without waiting for a response, then tossed the cell on the other seat, his hands moving to her waist. She leaned back, working her grip up and down his shaft and looked at him.

"What happened to my phone?"

"I had it turned off." He slid his hands up her torso and moved the right one, pulling the top of her bra down and sitting up, his mouth finding her nipple.

Her hand tightened around him. "Why?"

He swiped his tongue across the nipple's tip, then looked up at her. "The man who answered my phone—I didn't want him to be able to contact you."

"I didn't say anything. When he asked who I was, I just hung up."

He squeezed her waist, then gently pushed her off of his lap. "Good." He nodded to the other seat. "Sit down. I need to talk to you."

She looked down, her hand still gripping him, his dick at full mast and not listening to the itinerary. She let out an awkward laugh, then released him. "Oh...kay." Adjusting her skirt, she moved to the seat, her arms crossing over her chest in the petulant move of a child. "This feels like I'm in trouble."

Dario tucked himself back into his pants, wincing at the action, and zipped himself up. "You went to the professor's apartment."

"Yep." She snapped out the word in an insolent fashion, and his anger mounted at her nonchalance. He forced his features to stay calm, his voice mild. "Why?"

She looked at him. "I needed to end things with him."

Half the tension leaked from his body. "And did you?"

"I did." She glanced at her watch, a cheap ceramic number that was beneath her. She deserved everything. A Rolex on that wrist. Diamond studs in those ears. La Perla supporting those breasts. Her own Rolls and driver. "I have to go to work." She glanced out the window, toward the building.

"You're fine. You didn't seem concerned about the time when you had my dick in your hand."

Her eyes flashed, and maybe he'd gone too far. But this … this was nothing compared to what he'd felt, watching his security's footage of her strolling out of that prick's place, a smile on her face. He'd lost it. He hadn't moved a muscle, hadn't broken a sweat. But mentally, he went six rounds with that pencil thin fucker. Mentally, he'd broken his nose, pummeled his face, and pissed on his body.

Mentally, he'd professed his feelings for her and warned the man to stay the fuck away.

"I don't want you to see him again. Or see anyone else."

Another woman might have swooned at the words. She didn't. She stiffened. "That's a little hypocritical." She grabbed her purse and pulled it over one shoulder. "Bringing up Ian when you had two women on the side and are still *married*."

She sneered the words as if he was a selfish pig who just wanted a side piece of ass. And maybe that was what he *had* been. That was certainly how he'd treated every other woman he'd fucked in this town. But needing a fresh mistress wasn't what kept pulling him to Bell. And that realization proved why he should be fighting harder to stay away from her.

"You're a hypocrite." The second time she said it, it was softer, sadder, almost hopeless.

"Gwen and I are friends, and only married on paper. You and he were, best I understood it, *fuck* buddies. I ended any physical relationships when I met you." He swore and looked away. "I hate asking you for this. But I'm not asking. I'm *telling* you. You're not seeing him again, outside of class. Period."

Her lips tightened and she turned her head, looking toward The House. "I don't care about Ian. *I* ended that, so stop barking orders at me. And what's next, Dario? You going to tell me I can't work?

That you'll cover my bills, because you don't want strangers flirting and groping me in *there*?"

She tilted her head toward the building. "I'm not your employee. I'm not your girlfriend. I'm nothing." Her voice shook slightly. "I'm *nobody*. And I don't want your fucking phone."

She opened the door and stuck a leg out, the night air coming in and doing nothing to calm his fever.

He struggled against reaching out, grabbing her hand and pulling her back into the car and against his chest. He fought against calling her name, just so she'd look back. If she looked at him, she'd see. She'd see that he wasn't a selfish pig, that he did care for her, that his heart was struggling to find the right words without cutting his throat in the process.

If she just *looked* at him, she'd see how lost he was to her.

She stood up, shut the door, and walked away.

TWENTY-ONE

BELL

The kid on Table 4 was newly twenty-one, with a watch on his wrist that cost as much as my car. I took the empty glass he offered and smiled when his unfocused gaze found mine.

"It's my birthday," he slurred.

"I heard. Happy Birthday, Conner."

We'd gotten the story on him an hour ago, around the time that he'd taken out a second marker. Conner Brentwood. His Daddy owned fifty-six McDonalds in Texas. His Daddy sat to his left and had stared at my cleavage through his last three hands. They were down two hundred grand and neither seemed the slightest bit concerned about it. To Conner's right, a stripper from Saffire moved a diamond-encrusted wrist and pushed one of Conner's black chips toward the dealer.

"Come sit with us and play." He nodded to the seat next to the stripper.

I patted his shoulder and lifted his glass. "I'm good with drinks, bad with luck. Trust me, you don't want me around your cards."

He scoffed, and when I turned away, I felt his eyes drop to my ass. I gave the stripper a small smile and collected two more empties on my way to the bar.

Fifteen minutes later, when I stepped into the control room, I reached for my phone without thinking, then stopped.

"It's a bad habit to break," Lance smirked, watching me drop my hand with a frustrated groan.

Rick turned in his seat. "What? Tempting rich birthday boys?"

"No. Checking her phone."

I pushed my bag away. "I swear, you guys need a new hobby—something other than watching me."

Lance kicked his foot up and rested it on the desk, using it to swing his chair from left to right. "You can't exactly blame us. Your current situation is much more exciting than anything we are up to."

Rick tossed a handful of cashews into his mouth and nodded in agreement.

"So ... why isn't your phone working?" Lance looked at me as if he was about to analyze my response, and I pulled the fridge door open, grabbing a bottled water.

I twisted the cap off and took my time with a sip, thinking through how much I wanted to share. "I'm changing my number. Trying to ditch a credit card company."

They exchanged a look at my fib, and I scowled at them as I headed for the door. Joining Britni behind the bar, I pulled glasses out of the dry rack and stacked them on the counter. "Thanks again for this weekend."

She was covering my shift this Sunday so I could head home for my dad's birthday. I hadn't seen my parents in almost a month, and needed, for more reasons than one, a mini-trip away from this town.

"No sweat." She loaded up a tray and I watched her turn, noted her effortless carry of a dozen drinks. Like me, she'd practically grown up in restaurants, had waited tables since she was a teen.

Like me, she took classes during the day, partied as much as she studied, and didn't have a life plan that extended past next semester.

If she had been the one to greet Dario, would he have gone for her and never known my name?

No. I knew that deep inside. The pull between us…

I hadn't lived much. Done much. I didn't *know* much, but I knew that our connection wasn't normal. It was two planets colliding. Explosions. A black hole that pulled you in, regardless of the danger.

It felt like a once-in-a-lifetime connection, but everything around us was once-in-a-lifetime levels of fucked up.

I shouldn't have gotten mad at him and stormed off. I should have acted like an adult and had an intelligent conversation. I regretted it but didn't have a phone or his number to call him and fix things.

DARIO

He finished his work and stood, stretching. The condo was quiet, Gwen heading to bed a few hours ago. He was exhausted, but couldn't leave things with Bell as they had. He couldn't have that giant cliffhanger hanging over their relationship. He should have kept her in the car and forced her to talk, forced *them* to work it out.

But what was there to work out? He couldn't accept her being with anyone but him. And he couldn't leave Gwen—not right now. So, there wasn't anything for them to really work out. There was only her, needing to accept his demands, even if they weren't fair, even if he was a hypocrite.

He opened his closet and walked into the room, glancing at his watch. In two hours, Bell would be off work. Thirty minutes after that, he could have her naked and underneath him.

As soon as the thought came, he tried to kill it, to get the image of her, her back arching, eyes closing, skin flushing—out of his head.

Moving to the racks, he began to change.

BELL

Conner Brentwood had had too much to drink. Which, given his birthday and location, was pretty much a rite of passage. I switched his drink for ice water and yielded when he pulled me onto his lap, his clumsy hand trying to slide a green chip into my pocket.

"You take such good care of me." He sang the final words, and I smiled at him, the thousand-dollar chip warm in my pocket.

"I'm *trying* to take care of you. You keep drinking and you'll be hating me in the morning."

He scowled and scraped his cards against the table, asking for another hit. Another hit … on two nines. A five came up and he tossed the hand away, another five grand lost.

A guy at the end tapped on his empty glass and I untangled myself from Conner's grip. "Good luck."

He caught my hand and pulled it, not letting go.

I leaned over and put my mouth against his ear. "That big guy in the corner is just itching to throw you out. Let go of my hand or he's going to."

Conner's bleary eyes moved to Lloyd, who glowered in the sort of way that intimidated anyone with enough sense to breathe. Conner's grip loosened and I squeezed his shoulder and straightened.

I turned toward the bar, my eyes automatically skimming my other tables, looking for needs, for eye contact, for empty glasses. I was moving and thinking, a to-do list of orders building in my mind, and almost ran into Britni, who uncharacteristically stopped, right in front of me, in the middle of the aisle.

I moved to her left, and she blocked me. My eyes met hers and I raised one brow.

"Can you switch tables with me? Cover the top table?"

The top table was where the elite of our high rollers sat—the sort of men who made Conner and his daddy look like used car salesmen. It was the coveted table and one that Britni typically latched onto with the intensity of a honey badger.

Her offering it up could only mean that a major asshole was sitting there. I turned to glance over my shoulder, to see who the culprit was, but she stopped me.

"Lance told me to tell you that your guy is there."

My guy. At that table, it could only be Dario. I made the decision in less time than it took Conner to let go of my hand. "Let me get this round to my tables, then I'll turn them over to you."

She nodded, stepped to the side, and I walked toward the bar. With each step along the way, as I bent over the ice and grabbed bottles and mixed liquor, I felt his eyes. How long had he been here? I thought of Conner, the way he'd pulled me onto his lap—something that, given the timing, Dario had to have seen. I thought of leaving Dario's car, how I'd felt walking away. I had expected, with every step I'd taken, for him to call out, to stop me. And yet, he hadn't. We both had too much pride for our own good, yet he was here.

I delivered drinks, gave myself a stern warning to be strong, then climbed the short bank of steps to the top table. I stepped onto the level and locked eyes with him.

DARIO

It'd been seven hours since she'd knelt before him in the car, her hands on his thighs, her hands on his cock. She'd looked at him in a playful way that tugged at his heart and had eyed his cock in a devious way that lit fire to his arousal. Seven hours since she'd looked into his eyes with finality, then turned and left him stunned and alone in his car. Now, she met his gaze in the frustrated manner of a woman pushed too far.

But she couldn't give up. Not when, even as her mouth tightened, and her eyes moved away, the energy between them sizzled. Not when, as she rounded the table, and he followed her with his eyes, her cheeks flushed. Whatever it was between them, it wasn't a spark. It was a crackle of lightning, one that lit new wildfires whenever they came in contact. She might hate him right now, but she wouldn't stay away. Bell smiled at a man on the end, patted the shoulder of his companion, and finally, rounding the table's final curve, came to his seat.

Her eyes dropped to his glass, the bottle of water still half-full beside the tumbler. She reached for it, unscrewed the lid, and topped off his glass. She glanced down at his cards, then met his eyes. "I thought you didn't play."

Her knowledge of his reputation warmed him. He reached over, wrapping his hand around her slender wrist, and pulled her toward him. She stumbled forward and stopped. He released her. "It's a night for vices."

She moved closer, and God, he wanted to clear this room. To stand up and tell all of these assholes to go home. He wanted to grab her, to kiss her, to brand her as his own and lift her onto this felt table. He wanted to...

He forced himself to stop before his thoughts went carnal, before he had her shorts ripped open and loose around her ankles, before he was in between those thighs, first with his mouth, then with his cock.

It was too late. He shifted in his seat in an attempt to give his dick more room, to ease the throb of it between his legs.

She leaned forward slightly, lowering her voice, and he watched the pale pink of her lips and tried not to think about how they felt. "What are you doing here?"

TWENTY-TWO

BELL

It was unsettling, having him at The House. He was out of his usual suit, in a V-neck and jeans, his hair rough, jaw unshaven. He looked dangerous, as if he was short on sleep and on the prowl. He reached for his glass, and his muscular arms were a reminder of how he looked naked. I swallowed and waited for him to answer my question of why he was here.

He took a while, lifting his glass to his lips and studying me, tiny movements of pupils that said more than his words finally did. "You made it clear earlier tonight that working here was important to you. I came to check on my future investment."

His gaze flicked behind me, to the casino floor, and I understood. He wasn't talking about me, though there could definitely be a double meaning behind the words. "I thought you weren't looking at The House anymore." Rick and Lance weren't selling. *I'd heard them say they weren't selling.*

Still, the possibility existed. With Dario Capece, there was no such thing as denial. If he wanted something, he'd find a way to get it. I was proof positive of that.

He lifted his chin at me, studying my face. "You're here. That keeps my interest in it. Plus..." he glanced around the room. "There's no disputing that business is strong."

I ignored the observation, my chest seizing in a manner I'd never felt with him before. The possibility made me feel like a dog backed into a corner, my hackles rising, teeth baring in an effort to protect myself and everything that this place meant to me. Security. Friendship. Home. This *was* my home. My haven. He couldn't have it. He couldn't have my heart *and* this.

I shook my head and his brow creased, concern deepening his eyes to the color of espresso. "What's wrong?"

"No." My tongue wouldn't work, it stalled in my attempt to communicate my thoughts. I forced myself to focus and leaned forward, fighting to keep my voice at a level that wouldn't carry. "I don't want you buying this place."

"Why not?" His gaze sharpened, some of the compassion already waning in the face of a business decision. "I thought you'd like having me above you." His mouth twitched at the joke and his ability to see humor in this situation only fueled my anger.

"No, I don't want you above me." I straightened so quickly I almost knocked over his drink. His hand shot out to grab the glass and I ignored it.

"I could help you, if I owned this place." He nodded to my outfit, at the tray clenched in my hand. "Get you a promotion."

"And bend me over my desk during shifts?" I took a step back. "No thank you. If you buy this place, I'll quit." And I would. I would leave this place that I love—leave the money, my friends, and two years of history—before I would *ever* be his employee. It would change our entire dynamic if he were my boss. I would lose my ability to call him on his shit, would wonder if my sexual activities with him were continuing due to attraction or because of the pressure to keep my job.

I had enough trouble trying to sort out my feelings for this man. Adding this additional factor would drag my psyche through the shredder.

"Bell." He reached out and pulled me toward him, removing the tray from my hands and setting it on the table. I glanced at the dealer, who casually pulled the deck from the shoe and spread the cards on the table, taking his time in the reshuffle. Dario tugged at the edge of my shorts, refocusing my energy on him. "I get it. You don't want me to buy it." He shrugged. "So I won't."

So easy for him. Destinies changed, millions diverted, just like that. And all *because of me*. My irritation at the situation mellowed a little in the realization of my power.

"You won't buy it," I tested.

"No." He met my eyes. "You don't want to work for me?" He lifted his hands. "Then you won't."

"Fine." I straightened and lifted up the tray, snagging the empty water bottle off the table.

"Wait." He captured my hand, tugged on it. "I don't like how we left things earlier."

I turned away, pulling my hand free. I couldn't do this here and couldn't ignore a table full of Vegas's most important men to talk about my relationship—or lack of one—with him. Whatever and whoever *he* was to me.

I stepped away and when he called my name, there was an order in the tone. I stopped, looking back over my shoulder.

"Can I get a cigar?"

I nodded, and his gaze flickered, a break in the dominance where he pleaded with me for something and I resisted. When I turned away, I felt as if part of my heart ripped, left behind in the grip of his gaze.

I avoided the back room and Lance and Rick's questions. I busied myself with refilling the ice, taking water bottles to the security, and making sure that every person in my section was taken care of. I tried my best to avoid Dario, delivering his cigar in the most perfunctory way possible. Still, he haunted me. I was hyperaware of his presence, of his scent, of his eyes. The knowledge and feel of his attention was a heady mix of endorphins and arousal.

He bet recklessly. I watched his action out of the corner of my eye, every deal a new clue to the man. He participated in every hand, used side bets with no regularity whatsoever and never bought insurance. He split nines, doubled down on fifteens, and seemed to will the dealer to bust, over and over again.

An hour after he sat down, he was up four hundred thousand. Ten minutes later, I braved the back room. I walked in, and Rick and Lance looked up from the monitors.

"Holy shit, B. Can't you go distract this guy?"

I shrugged, grabbing a soda from the mini-fridge. "Trust me, I'm giving him all the 'go away' vibes I can."

I walked behind them and looked at the monitors, watching as his table busted. He tossed in his cards and leaned back, his eyes moving over the room.

"He's looking for you," Lance said.

I didn't move, watching as he scanned the floor. From this black and white image, his magnetism wasn't palpable, I couldn't smell his scent or feel his dominating presence. I felt safer in this room, locked away where my weak subconscious couldn't make stupid decisions. Next to him, three of the men stood, handshakes and goodbyes offered. I watched the dealer reshuffle and wondered if Dario would also leave, take this opportunity to stand and count his chips. He didn't. If anything, he settled deeper into the chair.

Rick nodded at the monitor. "Go out there. Try to get him drunk. Maybe that'll fix things."

I took a sip of the soda and glanced at the clock. "We're closing in twenty minutes. That'll limit the damage."

"And I've never been so happy to close. I'll call the cage, let them know he's cashing out large."

I moved back onto the floor, the room quieter now, most of the crowd thinned out. I glanced toward table four and noticed Conner and his father had taken their stripper and left. Their absence was a relief, one less thing to worry about. I looked up to the top table and Dario tilted back his glass, holding my eye contact. I climbed the steps to his level and stopped before him, speaking at a volume only he could hear. "Did you need something, Mr. Capece?"

"I think we both know what I need."

He swiveled away from the table and patted his thigh. "Come here."

I ignored the invitation and picked up his water, eyeing the low level in his glass. "Want a real drink?"

"No."

He watched me clear the trash from his cigar. I glanced at the end of the cigar, the expensive Cuban only half smoked. I grabbed the matchbook and flipped it open, dragging the match across the surface and holding it to the end of the cigar, letting the flame lick up the thin paper ends. I put the end in my mouth and sucked on it, my eyes on Dario. The corner of his mouth lifted. He reached out for me and I let him pull me onto his lap, his arm curving around my waist. The dealer paused, a card in hand, and Dario nodded.

I watched her distribute cards to him and the old man at the end, the only other player left at the table. I took a drag off the end, the dry taste reminding me of Sunday afternoons at home, my father sprawled over the end of the couch, football on the television. Once he stopped drinking, cigars had been his vice. Cigars and the Steelers.

Dario tilted his hand up. Queens. Two pale faces, both with crowns, sitting ducks in his hand. I looked at the cards and saw myself in one of them, Gwen in another.

"Should I split?"

I shrugged, looking away from the queens before I ripped them in half. "You don't want my advice. I'm terrible at cards."

It was half true. Poker was my game. Blackjack was my curse.

He flipped over the second queen and divided the cards, sliding five purple chips to match his original bet. And just like that, the stakes were doubled. Fifty grand. I drew on the end of his cigar and felt a little dizzy. He took it from me and brought it to his lips, his eyes on mine, his face close enough to kiss. It was erotic, the way he closed his mouth around it, the way his eyes glowed when he inhaled.

The dealer flipped a card over, setting it next to the first queen. An ace. Lucky girl. Dancing with the best card in the deck.

The second queen got her card, and I let out a disappointed breath at the result. A six. Paired with the queen, it was the worst hand in Blackjack. A terrible omen—one queen with the ace, one with the six. It wasn't hard to figure out who I was in this screwed-up analogy.

The dealer flipped over her cards. Nineteen. She slid Dario's chips together and knocked on the table, indicating the wash.

He leaned into my body and spoke quietly, his words warm against my neck. "Come to the suite tonight. Please."

Please. I don't know that any one word had ever had such power over me. I tried to push off his lap and to my feet, but he held me in place.

"I'm going fucking nuts without you. Please. Just for tonight."

This time, when I pushed off his thighs, he let me. I stubbed his cigar out on the table and grabbed his water, taking a sip of it before nodding to his chips. "You're cut off. We're closing up for tonight."

"Is that a yes?" He waited for a response and I wavered, my head a little loopy from the cigar.

"Maybe."

It was enough for him and he sat forward, pulling a chip from the stack and tossing it toward the dealer.

"Need a chip rack?" I asked. He nodded, and I turned to the older man, one who now stacked his chips with unsteady hands. "You too, Mr. Rodriguez?"

The man nodded and I grabbed the ashtray.

"I'll wait for you outside." Dario stood.

"I can drive myself." *If I go.* I wanted to add those three words, fought to speak them aloud, but couldn't.

"I'll wait."

I didn't respond, but on the way to the cage, I caught myself smiling and forced the gesture into a frown.

⊛

We left my car in the parking lot of The House. I figured, with the birthday boy's tip in my purse, I could more than afford a taxi home if Dario pissed me off.

"I'm sorry for being a hypocrite."

I turned to him, watching as he easily shifted the gears, easily manipulating the Aston Martin. It was the first time I'd seen him behind the wheel, the muscles in his forearms lit by the neon lights we passed.

"You know, I thought, for a little bit, that I might be okay with your marriage arrangement." I watched a drunk stumble almost into the street, then catch himself. It made me think of my dad, and how many nights we had picked him up from some back alley in Mohave. He had caused so much destruction in our lives, so much financial instability. But my mother had stuck by him, telling me that the vows they'd made were too important to discard. I couldn't easily accept that Gwen should be discarded either. He'd told me how our relationship could ruin his marriage, and I didn't want that burden on my shoulders. I thought I could bear it . . . "But it's too hard for me."

"I haven't had a physical relationship with Gwen for over a decade." He said the words quietly.

"You aren't with Gwen and you've ended things with everyone else. So…" I did my best mental calculation of the time. "You've been celibate for… three weeks now?" I coughed out a laugh, my throat still raw from the cigar smoke. "I don't know if I believe you."

He shifted into a lower gear and gave a sound that closely resembled a growl. "I don't care if you believe me. I'm not keeping my dick dry if you plan on seeing other people."

"I'd rather you sleep with half of the city than be married. I can stop dating people. You can't stop being married."

"Sure I can. It's called divorce. People do it all the time."

I looked away, my hand tightening on the strap of the seatbelt. "Don't be stupid. You're not going to get a divorce."

He fell silent, and the tension in the car thickened. I cracked the window, needing some fresh air.

His hand settled on my knee and his grip tightened a little as if afraid to let go of me. "Sometimes, I think I'm falling in love with you."

If I was a different one, the sort who had fallen in and out of love a half-dozen times, I might have laughed, scoffing at the unsure declaration.

But in that car, and with his man ... the words felt heavy and worthwhile, like a giant blow to the foundation of his life.

Sometimes, I think I'm falling in love with you.

I dropped my hand to his, and threaded my fingers through his, pulling it away from my knee and lifting it to my mouth. I pressed my lips to the back of his hand and inhaled the scent of his skin.

Sometimes, I feel the same way. I swallowed the words but still, my heart soared.

TWENTY-THREE

He pulled his shirt over his head, revealing the delicious stretch of his torso. It was knotted with muscles, the thick cords pulling, then relaxing, as he tossed the navy blue shirt aside. He reached over to turn on the shower and glanced over at me. I stayed in place, one hip against the bathroom counter. He dropped his hand from the shower knob and came closer. His presence had a heat, an energy, one that lit my skin on fire before his hands even reached for me. I straightened and he skimmed his palms under my shirt and pulled it over my head.

"You have no idea of just how much I wanted to lay you back on that poker table." He popped the top button of my shorts and carefully pulled down the zipper, leaning forward and kissing my shoulder, his teeth tugging playfully at my bra strap. He released it and worked the shorts over my hips, crouching down to slide them down my legs.

"One night, I'm taking you downstairs. I'm closing off VIP and I'm going to spread you wide open on the felt. I want to make you scream to the sound of slot machines and watch the footage later when I need to jack off." He growled the words, and they poured kerosene on my need. I shivered in the bathroom's cool air, and he quickened his movements, hooking his fingers under the edges of my panties and yanking them down. He turned me around, running his hands up the backs of my legs and over my ass, a groan coming from him as he gently slapped me. I arched my back, pulling the bra loose when he undid the clasp. I turned, reaching for his belt.

"No." He pushed my hands away and nodded to the shower, the glass already fogging up. "Get in and warm up."

I dipped my fingers under the hem of his pants and pulled, stealing a peek inside before I spun away from him and stepped into the shower.

God, this shower. Big enough for four people, it had body jets, an overhead rain head, and two handheld massagers. I felt the water hit me from all directions and closed my eyes, stepping under the overhead, my body temperature instantly rising.

I need this shower. This alone was almost worth swallowing my pride and moving in. He opened the door, stepped into the fog, and I remembered the other reason. More access to him. Huge shoulders, the rigid cut of muscles, deep notches of abs, his thick cock hanging, beckoning. I reached for it as he moved closer, wrapped my hand around it and felt it stiffen in response.

"Easy there." He pushed me away, turning me to the bank of

nozzles, and hot spray peppered my stomach as his big hands rubbed in soap, massaging my shoulders and back and sliding between the crack of my ass.

"I went fucking nuts inside when I saw you sit on that boy's lap." He nipped at my neck, scraping his teeth against the skin as his touch swept over my hip and moved in between my legs, opening up my thighs, his fingers teasing across my clit, a swirl of delicious pleasure. My mouth dropped open, my head fell back against his and I opened my legs wider, wanting more.

"It made me want to take you while he watched." He pushed his fingers inside of me, the thick insertion making me moan, my body clenching in response. "I'd make him sit there, his dick limp and useless, and see what you really need."

"Fat chance," I gasped, reaching out and bracing a hand against the stone tile, my hips thrusting against the movements of his fingers. "You'd have to fuck me in order to do that."

He growled, and I suddenly felt the press of a wet finger, hard against the hole of my ass. He kept his other hand working, his fingers dipping in and out of me with slick and fluid precision, each mini-thrust hitting my g-spot and turning my world fuzzy, my orgasm close, the new pressure on my ass turning up the dial in a way my body might not be able to handle.

He pressed harder, and the entry was so thick, it could only be his thumb. My world went black, my ass constricting, and the additional stimulation broke my orgasm free with blinding intensity.

Waves of hot pleasure expanded and flexed my body as his fingers moved, working me over. I screamed, my hand clawing at the wall, my body fighting against him, and he held me in place, his grip biting into my flesh, his thumb diving deeper into my ass, the filthy feeling only taking my arousal to a higher place.

The orgasm broke, the pleasure fading, and *fuck*. Fuck, I loved what he could do to me, the way he could play with my pleasure. He moved behind me, and I felt the bump of his cock against my thighs.

I needed to be closer, and turned to face him, grabbing his shoulder for support. He pulled my hand from it and wrapped it around his dick. I looked up at him, the spray dancing off his muscles, his eyes darkening when they collided with mine.

God, the way his cock stuck straight out, the way he hissed out a breath when I wrapped my hand tighter around his shaft. I ran my second hand over his balls, squeezing their heavy weight, and he groaned out my name as if in pain.

I moved my hand, working it to the head and back down. He stumbled back against the stone of the shower, resting his weight against it and pulled me closer. "Faster," he mumbled, and his mouth found mine as the hot water hit my back. I felt the stiff flex of him in my hand and worked it furiously between our bodies.

He was so big. So thick. Such an impressive cock that perfectly matched his large size and ridiculous ego. Maybe that's where that ego had come from—the confidence that, at any point in time, you had the biggest dick in the room and knew exactly how to use it.

Or so I assumed. As deftly as he brought me to orgasm with his mouth and fingers, I couldn't imagine how sex would be.

"I need to fuck you. God, you have no idea how much I need to fuck you." He pulled his mouth from mine and whispered against my lips. I kept going, my breath panting with his, my limbs still weak from my orgasm. His cock grew even stiffer, and he pinched his eyes closed, his body tensing, and I knew, in the moment before his cock flexed, it was happening. It was a moment of strength and weakness, all at once. I felt powerful, my hand stroking him through it, my fingers tight around his shaft, eyes dropping to watch the action, the water taking it away as quickly as it appeared.

His gaze found mine, and he pulled me forward for a kiss that seemed desperate in its connection.

He curled against me in bed, his skin hot, an arm wrapping around my chest. I clutched his forearm, pulling it against my chest and threaded my fingers through his grip. He kissed my back and pulled me even tighter against him.

"What time do you have to be up?" As I asked the question, I thought of the first night I stayed here and waking up to the bloody sheets.

"Not until eight." His voice was heavy, dragging on the edges, and it was the first time I'd ever seen him let down his guard.

"Don't leave without waking me up."

"I won't."

I wanted to tell him to promise me, but that seemed young and insecure. Instead, I tightened my hold on his arm and felt him clench around me, a blanket of warmth and security.

Sometimes, I think I'm falling in love with you.

It was the last thought on my mind before I fell asleep, a line that had me smiling, wrapped in his touch, the rasp of those words still audible in my mind.

THE TRUSTED ONE

"So, Bell Hartley is there now?" Robert Hawk peered at Claudia with an intensity that had once scared her. Now, it gave her a surreal sense of peace. That shift had come when she realized he would do anything to strengthen those he saw as his. And there were only two people in the world with that ownership. Herself and Gwen.

Claudia nodded at his question. "Yes, with Dario. Gwen's alone in the condo." She looked past him, at the monitors that showed the warehouse, individual squares displaying each woman in their cells. Only a year ago, she'd been one of them. Weak. Insolent. Unappreciative. The rumor mill had called them pets, but they didn't understand the beauty of what Robert Hawk was doing. It was a psychology project to him. Give women opportunities. Reward those who behave. Punish those who fail. Measure loyalty.

Of course, she had been different than the others. There was a reason Claudia was standing in his mansion, with the keys to an exotic car in her pocket. She was special. He'd told her that, after all the pain and the tests. He'd whispered it in her ear after she'd passed the final challenge and was given her freedom.

Now, Robert Hawk stared at the photo of Bell Hartley, one Claudia had taken as they'd left The House and gotten into Dario's car.

It was a shame, really. Claudia had been prepared, at the onset, to protect the girl. She'd been willing to overlook the fling that would surely fizzle out. But this girl and Dario had taken things too far. The looks that passed between them. The way that Dario was chasing her around like a lovesick idiot. Overnights together, leaving Gwen alone. And the final nail in both of their coffins—the phone call that had gotten Bell on Robert Hawk's radar. Now, there wasn't any hope for her and Dario. She'd been forced to tell Robert everything and had watched his quiet fury ignite.

"We need to end this problem now, before Gwen is aware of it." Hawk eyed her as if assessing her potential, and she straightened under his scrutiny.

"Do you want her brought to the warehouse?" She'd helped with that before. Drugged women with friendly shots at the bar, then helped them stumble to her car. This would be different. It'd be interesting to see how Robert Hawk treated a woman like Bell, who had done more than pick the wrong casino as her ticket into chains.

"No." He shook his head. "There's no point in training her. I need to send Dario a message, and her dead body will be more effective than her disappearance."

She nodded at the decision.

"Do you think you can handle it?"

The question surprised her. He was a man who liked his own dirty work, especially when blood was involved. To put this trust in her... she nodded quickly.

He leaned back in his chair and eyed her. "I can't do it. Not without Dario catching wind and ratting to the cops. But you..." he smiled. "You can be my secret weapon. He doesn't know you at all."

It was a reminder that stung. Gwen, whether she appreciated it or not, had been given the golden ticket of Hawk's attention and pedigree upon birth. Claudia, she'd had to sweat, beg, and earn each and every step into Robert Hawk's world.

"After this," Robert continued, "you can meet Gwen. Pass this test, and I'll set up a dinner, just the two of my girls. How would you like that?"

She nodded, emotion welling in her throat at the thought of sitting at a table with the two of them, as an equal. Finally, Gwen would know about her. Finally, Gwen would treasure her in the same way that Robert now did. "I can do it."

He smiled at her. "I know you can. And what's more, I think you'll enjoy it."

TWENTY-FOUR

BELL

My car ate up the miles between Vegas and my parents' house, the drive passing quickly in a mix of Beastie Boys and Sublime. I pulled up to the house around two and met my dad at the mailbox.

"Anything good?" I put my car into park and stepped out, watching as he slowly walked toward me, his hands thumbing through the thin stack of mail.

He finally looked up with a wry smile. "No Publishers Clearing House check yet."

I shrugged. "Yeah. Me neither."

He reached out an arm and pulled me into a hug, his shirt smelling of cigarettes and Old Spice. I lifted my chin and he kissed my cheek. "You look good, Bell. The big city agrees with you."

"Thanks, Dad. You're not looking too shabby yourself. Mom inside?"

He nodded, and we moved toward the house. I paused at the steps, letting him go ahead, and bent down, whistling to Rascal, who heaved himself out of the dirt and slowly made his way over, his back swaying, tail slowly wagging.

"Hey buddy." I patted his side, running my hands over his skinny ribs and up to his ears, scratching them in a way he liked, his back foot lifting and pawing at the air.

"You coming?" Dad paused in the doorway, holding the screen door open, and I could hear the sound of water and dishes inside, the smell of fried chicken faint on the breeze. Rascal lifted his head and sniffed, and I bent down to kiss his muzzle.

"I'll sneak you a piece later." I straightened, patting his head and nodded. "I'm coming."

Jogging up the stairs, I reached out and tugged at his T-shirt. "Happy Birthday, Dad."

He grunted in response. "Nothing happy about getting old, Bell."

I rolled my eyes, ducked under his arm, and entered the house. Across the living room, my mom turned from the stove, her face splitting into a smile, and she held out her arms for a hug.

I didn't have an excuse, running off to Vegas to live a life of sin. I grew up right. We attended church, ignored Dad's drinking, and prayed over every meal.

I didn't have *fancy* things, but I had things. My clothes were second-hand or Walmart specials, but they were always relatively fashionable. We didn't go on vacations, but we went to the movies on occasion, and to dinner enough times that I understood how to carry myself and didn't look like a hick when presented with a salad fork or restaurant bill.

We were good. As good as a family could be when the father passed out by eight, missed work as often as he attended, and couldn't get through dinner without a six-pack of Coors.

Then, *that* day happened.

The stable.

The police.

The statements.

The scorn.

The disbelief.

The shame.

And then we *weren't* good. We were bad, for months. Dad drank more, they started fighting, and Mom and I stayed at my grandparents' house as often as our own. There was a year where I didn't know what was happening, a year where I met with a social worker and failed tenth grade.

And then we were better, almost better than before. Mom and Dad got back together, he quit drinking, and I started counseling. Met Elliot. Came out of my shell with the tentative steps of a newborn fawn.

And then, two years after I graduated, Rick and Lance walked into my diner. They were full of swagger and money and fun. When they dangled Vegas in front of me, I snatched it from their grasp.

"Pass the gravy, Bell."

I passed the dish and watched Mom tuck a bit of silver hair behind her ear, her eyes on the dark liquid as she spooned it out.

"The chicken's good."

She nodded. "I made plenty. Enough for you to take some home to your boys."

I smiled, thinking of Mom's first meeting with Lance and Rick. She'd immediately labeled them as too thin, not properly taken care of, and in sore need of good women. Ever since then, she'd been trying to fatten them up, tame their wild ways, and get them married off.

She'd been unsuccessful.

Halfway through dinner, I realized something was wrong. They were uncharacteristically quiet, their questions less invasive, their conversations more on food and weather and less on nosing around my personal life. I glanced at Mom, who carefully scooped up some corn. I moved to Dad, who eyed his tea as if he wished it were stronger. "What's going on?"

They looked at me with the wide-eyed innocence of the guilty.

"What do you mean?" Mom took an unusually large bite of cornbread.

"You guys are being weird. No one's asked me who I'm dating, or if I'm on birth control, or how my exams are going."

"Well, why—how *are* your exams going?" She asked the question through the mouthful of cornbread, and little specks flew out and peppered the table.

I waved her off and latched onto my father, a man who hid secrets as well as Rascal hid a bone. Which was to say that all you had to do was mention the item, and Rascal all but led you to it in an attempt to keep you away. "Dad. What's going on?"

He lifted his eyes from his drink to me, then they ricocheted off to the right. "John Wright and his son got into some trouble."

It was so unexpected that I sat back, a little of my breath lost with the impact of his name. "Another girl?"

He shook his head. "No, no. Not that kind of trouble. Someone roughed him up. Roughed both of them up."

That wasn't exactly a shock. The pair were assholes. They couldn't walk into a place without offending someone, and they walked into a lot of places. I gave my best attempt at a casual shrug. "How'd you hear about it?"

Mom cleared her throat and leaned forward, gripping my hand. "Let's not talk about this at dinner. Especially, not the details."

Not the details? I pulled my hand from hers and stared at my father, willing the information out of him. "Can you just spit it out? What happened?"

He sighed, sitting back in his seat. "They were castrated. Got their balls cut off. And were beaten almost to death, according to Jimmy."

Castrated? I unexpectedly laughed, the sound bursting out of me in a horrific bark of sound, something that startled both of my parents, as well as myself. I clapped a hand over my mouth, swallowing the cruel sound before it repeated itself.

It wasn't funny. It *couldn't* be funny. But that's how my mind handled it. I didn't think about the look in John's eyes as he had held me down. I didn't think about the way they'd encouraged each other, the feel of their sweaty skin against mine, the smell of their breath, the painful invasion and my choked begs that only seemed to encourage them more.

Someone had cut their balls off.

My hysteria faded a little and I swallowed, trying to respect my mother and calm my emotions. "Who did it?"

Dad shrugged. "They don't know. No one had heard from them for a while, and John's wife finally called the police. They found them on a dirt road, ten miles outside of town, covered in blood and dust. They were trying to walk home and didn't make it."

"But they're alive."

I'm surprised that mattered to me. After so many nights of wishing them dead, I was shocked to discover that it did matter to me. I liked the idea of a ball-less Johnny better than the idea of a dead one.

He nodded. "Yep."

I examined his expression, then my mother's. In prior mentions of my rape, they'd always carried the same looks—a mix of regret and guilt and pain. But now, they looked almost relieved that something—perhaps karma—had handed my monsters their punishment. I wondered what my own expression gave away. Did it show the relief I finally felt, knowing that they would never be able to rape another girl?

After dinner, I curled up in one of Mom's afghans and studied. I worked through two classes, then set aside the books and watched Andy Griffith with them, lasting through three episodes before I nodded off. I woke up to the smell of Dad's brownies and struggled to sit upright. My father could cook three things, and brownies led the short list. I inhaled two and a half and a giant glass of milk, debated politics with Dad, then bagged some brownies to go and kissed them both goodbye.

I was in my car, heading home and thinking over it all, when I first thought of Dario and the chance that he was behind John and Johnny's incident. I hadn't told him about it, and Google didn't show any history of it when you searched my name. Dario shouldn't even *know* about it, but by the time I pulled into my driveway, I'd convinced myself it was his handiwork. I picked up my new phone, scrolled to his number, and sent him a text.

we need to talk

Maybe I was wrong. But maybe, probably, I wasn't.

TWENTY-FIVE

I pulled into The Majestic with a sharp squeak of tires and didn't pay attention to the woman in yoga pants who stretched against the entrance gate, her eyes recording everything about me by the time I inserted my gate card and pulled onto the car elevator.

When I blew into the suite, Dario was waiting by the window, his cell in hand. He turned slowly, his head lifting, eyebrows raising, and I watched as he pushed the phone into his pocket.

His gaze moved over my knee-high boots and thin sweater dress and his mouth curved upward in appreciation. "You needed me?" Three simple words he managed to make into a sexual invitation.

I dropped my keys on the entry table and crossed my arms over my chest. "I went home today."

He nodded slowly, his head tilting to the side as if remembering something. "Right. For your dad's ... birthday?"

"Yes." I snapped out the response and moved into the kitchen, wrapping a hand around the fridge handle and yanking open the stainless-steel door. The shelves were fully stocked, tiny clear cases holding a variety of fruit, salads and sandwiches. My hackles rose at the convenience of it all.

"Want to guess what I found out?" I bent over and pulled out the drink drawer, grabbing a bottle of beer and using the edge of the counter to pop off the top.

He gave me a slow grin, the sort that burned cities and broke hearts, the sort that almost crumbled my resolve. "No idea."

"Really?" I tilted back the beer and finished half of it. Swallowing, I scrunched up my face and tilted my head to the side. "Absolutely no idea?"

I walked over to him and walked my fingers up his chest.

He trapped my hand with his and looked down at me. "If you have a question, just ask it."

"Cut the balls off anyone lately?" I almost said their names and what they'd done to me. But if I was wrong, this wasn't a story I wanted to tell. And if I was right...

"Yeah." His face hardened, but those eyes softened, a push-pull of emotion that ran my emotions through a grinder. "And I'd do it again."

"Why?"

He shrugged and gently pulled my beer from my hand, finishing it off. He was so big, so strong. I was close enough I could feel the warmth of his body, near enough that we brushed against each other when we moved. With him, I felt untouchable. Protected. Loved.

I should have been afraid, but I only felt comfort.

"They hurt you." He set down the empty bottle and leaned back against the counter, pulling me to him, his hands running over my hair and then curling against my back. He spread his stance and gathered me close. "I'll never let anyone hurt you again."

"You can't promise me that."

He dipped his head, his lips pressing against mine. He moved closer and his kiss grew stronger, greedier.

"Dario." I gasped his name in between two kisses, my hands tightening on his bright blue button-up. He ignored it, his hands sliding around to grip my ass before pulling up my dress.

"Dario." I pushed hard on his chest and he stopped, pulling away. "We have to *talk* about this. I didn't tell you about what they did, you shouldn't have..." The sentence trembled, then stopped, my emotions too clogged to finish.

"You really want to talk about it?" He stepped back and lifted his hands from my body. "Fine. I have connections in Mohave. I read the police reports. Your statement and theirs. I saw the photos."

I closed my eyes, thinking of the photos. I'd had to strip naked. There was the flash of bulbs and the blank face of the police officer, her methodical examination done with latex gloves and quick movements that had contained little care. She hadn't believed my story. I'd seen it in her eyes, their disinterested movements over my scrapes.

Dario's voice deepened. "They got off back then. You got fucked over and they went free."

He was right. I had gotten fucked over. That was life in a small town, for a white-trash girl raped by one of the richest families in town. Johnny told them that it had just been me and him, behind the barn—and that I'd been after him for weeks. I hadn't helped matters by showering, scrubbing my skin so hard I'd practically bruised myself. That loss of evidence had been compounded by my drunk father, who'd taken two hours to sober up before he'd driven me to the police station. Our trip had been delayed further when he'd run off the road and into a ditch.

John and Johnny Wright had gone free. I had lost everything.

He carefully brushed a tear off my cheek. "I should have gutted them and left them in the desert for the vultures. I let them off easy."

I stepped away before I let out everything I held inside. I could feel the swell of emotions, the hot flare of tears, and swallowed it all. I made it to the fridge, found a second bottle of beer, and popped it open. "It wasn't your fight to take up. It wasn't your business to get into." I turned and met his eyes. "It was invasive for you to read that report, see those photos, track them down and speak to them."

"Trust me when I say that little speaking went on." He smiled, and it lit a fuse in me.

"You think this is *funny*?" I threw the bottle of beer without thinking, my arm rearing back, liquid flinging, and when I let go off the glass, it was intended for his head. He ducked to one side, and there was the loud sound of glass breaking. I flinched and didn't look to see the damage.

"I told you before. I needed to know what I was getting into with you."

"And?" I gestured to the situation in general and heard the thick clog of tears in my voice. "I'm a mess. Is that what you wanted? Someone with *that* in their past?"

"I didn't expect to find that when I looked into the police records of your town. *Fuck*, I don't know what I expected. But when I saw that, read that..." He looked down, considered his words, and then back at me. "I can't love you and not protect you. I can't love you and not *fight* for you."

The words rocked me. I didn't move, I stayed strong in my stance, kept my eyes on him, but inside ... the words swam through my bloodstream and fortified it. I swallowed as his words filled in the gaps, strengthened my core, and offered me something I'd never known before. I felt renewed yet betrayed at the same time. *He fought for me because I'd been hurt. He saw the photos, the girl who had been brutalized. The girl who'd lost every ounce of dignity.* His last words echoing through my mind. *I can't love you and not fight for you.*

I broke away from his gaze and tried to find my bearings. "This fight was already over."

"It was already over, and you lost." He pushed off the counter and approached me, my body stiffening as he grew closer, as he pulled at my wrists and dragged me away from the fridge and against his chest. "You're never going to lose again. You're going to be fucking Queen of this town and anyone who so much as sneezes in your direction will pay hell for it."

"That's a nice speech Dario, but it's all bullshit." I pulled, and he kept me in place, pinned against him. "Mistresses are never Queens."

"Don't call yourself that." He moved his hands to my waist, gripped and lifted me onto the counter, my hands finding his shoulders for support. I looked down at him from my new position and he slid his palms up my legs, sliding the bottom of my sweater dress up and exposing my thighs. "You're more than that."

His fingers reached my hips and his eyes dropped. Maybe it was cruel of me to have pulled off my underwear in the car, to have left them in my center console and waltzed into the suite bare and ready for him. Maybe. Or maybe, with everything else, he deserved it.

"Fuck." He hissed out the curse.

I'd waxed, the area smooth, only a thin line of hair just above my clit. He slid his hands inward, until he could reach out one thumb and run it over the sensitive flesh. I spread my thighs wider and he groaned deep in his throat.

"You're torturing me."

"Just fuck me. Right here." I sat back on the counter, my elbows supporting my weight, and challenged him with my eyes.

"I want to take things slow with you."

"Please." My voice broke a little with the word, my weakness showing, but I needed him. Right now, I felt too confused, too lost, too conflicted. I was grateful to him, but also mad. I swooned at his protection, but struggled with the realities of it. I needed to be grounded, I needed to feel loved, and I wanted, more than anything on this earth, to feel a physical *connection* with him. "I need it. You want it. Please."

"I'm worried..." His thumb, which had been gently swiping over my wet slit, pushed its way inside.

I almost came off the counter and saw the way his eyes darkened, his need as greedy as mine. How was he controlling himself? It'd been a month since he walked into The House. A month, a dozen orgasms, and I needed more. *I can't love you and not protect you.* That's what he'd said. "Worried about what?" I gasped, my nails digging into his shoulder, and this needed to happen right now. I needed to have this moment to right my sails, calm my emotions, and comfort my body.

When our eyes met, I saw his pull of emotion, saw the depth of his feelings. He destroyed their lives. For me. It didn't make sense, it was too early, we didn't know each other well enough, but fuck his *I think I'm falling in love with you*. He loved me. I loved him. Whether he put his dick in me or not—those facts weren't changing.

He dropped his gaze, concentrating on my pussy, and he crouched and lowered his mouth to the spot, his eyes closing as he ran his tongue along the folds, circled my clit, then gently sucked it as if he was a man desperate of thirst. He dipped his tongue inside of me, his hands biting into my thighs, and I let out a quiet moan as he straightened, his gaze still stuck to my open legs.

I spread them wider. "*Please.*"

Had I ever begged for it before? I didn't think so. I didn't think I had ever *needed* it like this before. It was a craving that hummed through my entire body, one that had my ass gently grinding against the counter the minute his hand settled in between my legs. He pushed a finger inside of me and I almost bucked off the surface. He pushed a second in, and I grabbed at the air, found his tie, and yanked the silk-blend fabric toward me.

His lips came down on mine, he curved his fingers inside of me, and I saw stars—the sort that brought orgasms in their wake, the kind that exploded pleasure centers and made me pant against his kiss, a low moan coming from my throat.

"If I have you, I'll never be able to let you go."

I babbled his name and clawed at his hair, his fingers gently massaging my g-spot, a smooth in and out and *ohmygod* motion that had me losing everything but the taste of his kiss, the feel of his touch, a need that was spiraling out of control and into something more.

If he didn't give me something, if he didn't pull out his cock and push this giant ache of want, I'd go crazy. I yanked at his belt, cursed against his kiss, and lost all reason when he quickened the motion of his fingers. "Oh my god, don't stop. Please. Please. Fuck. I. I. I...."

He yanked me to the counter's edge and worked a third wet finger inside. It took just the pressure, the wide stretch of entry, and I broke.

My hips furiously bucked against his hand.

His name rained from my lips, a mad chant of love and need and desire.

My vision blurred, fingers dug into his skin, clawed at his clothes, and found nothing but rigid muscle and heat.

I came in an avalanche of blinding, gripping glory, and I swore allegiance to him in the final moments of the blast.

I broke. I fell. I surrendered it all.

TWENTY-SIX

DARIO

Gwen was curled into a ball on the chaise lounge, a cup of coffee in hand. He stopped before her, holding out his hand. "Help me with these links?"

She carefully set down the cup of steaming coffee and reached forward, fastening the buttons and cufflinks with quick efficiency.

He nodded at the clock. "Shouldn't you be heading out to lunch?"

She made a face before settling back against the padded upholstery. "I'm just putting it off as long as I can."

He moved to the sofa, picking up the open laptop. "Did we get the projections from Tim?"

"Yeah. I left them open. Twelve percent higher than the Britney show."

He said nothing, scrolling down the document, his eyes moving over the numbers.

"One of us should meet with them."

He grimaced. "In San Diego?"

She reached for her coffee, studying the caramel depths of it. "You didn't come home last night."

He lifted his eyes off of the screen and looked at her. "Work ran late. I caught a few hours of sleep in one of the suites."

"With who?"

He closed the lid of the computer and stood, coming to stand before her. "What's wrong? You don't ever ask me about that."

She shrugged, lifting the ceramic mug to her lips. He reached forward, carefully pulling it out of her hands.

"Is it the waitress?"

He shook his head. "I ended that. This is a new girl."

She bit the edge of her bottom lip, a crack in her composure before she shot him a wry glare, one that fit their normal roles. "My husband, breaking hearts all over Vegas."

He didn't smile, didn't respond to the playful tones of her barb. Something was wrong, a chink in their seamless arrangement. He knew what the issue was on his end—he was falling in love with Bell. But he didn't know what was going on with her. And both of them having issues ... that was a situation that needed to be resolved. He set down her cup. "Talk to me."

Her eyes met his. "I could say the same to you. Is something wrong?"

He ran a hand over his face, smoothing the skin, and giving himself a moment to collect his thoughts. "I like her." *Nothing for you to worry about.* He couldn't voice that lie. Already, he could see the pool of trouble that Bell was going to cause.

"You. Like. Her." Gwen said the words slowly, as if her mind was trying to translate them. "Like. That's it?"

"Yes."

Her gaze found his and he felt exposed in the heat of her stare, the way she examined every tic of his face and looked for more. But she didn't know what deceit from him looked like. Not when he had never lied to her before, had never needed to, had never risked their marriage in this manner before.

"Don't worry." His words came out strong and powerful, protection wrapped in every syllable. He interrupted her examination with a kiss, leaning forward and pressing his lips against her forehead in a solid and firm movement.

It felt wrong and, for one of the first times in their marriage, he felt dirty.

GWEN

Her father sat across from her, his head down, focused on the rack of lamb falling victim to his knife. He cut it with quick and short precision, the blade flashing in the afternoon sun, each crunch of gristle and bone giving her a fresh shot of panic.

Every lunch with him was the same. A sixty-minute session of nerves and anxiety, lies and promises, threats and fulfillments. How had she ever survived twenty years under his roof? How had she emerged in one piece? What would she have done without Dario?

Three questions Gwen asked herself constantly. Three questions that never produced answers.

"Everything okay with you and Dario?"

She looked up from her wine to find him watching her, his lamb spared, his eyes pinned on her. She forced a smile. "Of course."

But it wasn't. For reasons unknown to her, their ground was shaky, the foundation cracked. Dario was failing to fix the issues, to right their heading. She thought of their conversation this morning, the way his voice had changed when he had brushed off his newest fuck. He had told her not to worry, had promised her that everything was fine. But it wasn't. Something was off. And chances were, this girl was the reason.

"I can keep an eye on him, if you'd like."

Her father's offer was a red flag, the sort she'd heard all of her life, a casual suggestion that had always ended in disaster.

I'll talk to him about your grade. Professor Vance, showing up in class with a cast on one arm, his eyes down, hands trembling when she approached his desk. The shiny and perfect A that had appeared on her report card, paired with a glowing recommendation letter for colleges, unrequested and filled with descriptions that sounded nothing like her.

She shouldn't disrespect you like that. Her friend Charlotte, who made a mistake and kissed Gwen's boyfriend. He'd broken their relationship off, Gwen had cried, and Charlotte had disappeared, her remains found nine months later, her bones picked clean by coyotes and vultures.

No date for prom? How can that be? The singer from the Backstreet Boys, who had shown up on their doorstep, a rose in hand, fear in his eyes. She had hoped for a kiss, but he'd practically sprinted away at the end of the night.

Her father was a man with unlimited means, yet *violence* was always the answer.

"I *don't* want you to keep an eye on him." She spoke emphatically, trying to get through his psychotic head, but her father's lips tightened, some idea behind the gesture. She reached out and touched his hand in an attempt to catch his attention. "Dad. My marriage is fine. Dario is great. I don't want you doing anything to mess that up."

He didn't respond, and her touch tightened. "*Dad.* Promise me that you'll leave Dario alone."

His gaze finally moved to her face and he gave a slow grin that only alarmed her further. "Of course. I'm not going to touch a hair on Dario's head. Why would I?" He spread his hands and raised them in the air. "Why would I? I love that kid."

And he always *had* loved Dario. It was one the reasons their marriage had worked. Her father had embraced Dario like the son he'd never had. He'd blessed their marriage and left them alone, never seemed to snoop around, or ask questions, or have any idea about their extracurricular activities.

So why the questions about her marriage? Maybe he had a plant out at the ranch, someone who had seen her and Nick. They hadn't exactly been discreet, hadn't felt the need to be on the three-thousand-acre ranch. And they hadn't wasted a single hour of last weekend. She swallowed a smile at the thought of Nick, naked in the sunlight, the muscles in his arms when he'd moved above her, the taste of his kiss in the morning before breakfast.

It hadn't been fair for her to press Dario about his feelings for this new girl. Not when Gwen had fallen for Nick years ago, their passion rekindled with every trip she made, her visits more frequent in the last year.

"Dario's the only one who's ever made you smile like that." Her father spoke softly, almost tenderly, and she looked up from her plate, unaware that her face had given away her thoughts about Nick.

She nodded tightly, letting him believe the lie.

"You know I would never jeopardize your relationship with him. I'd do anything to protect it."

She swallowed, reaching for her wine and lifting it to her lips, grateful for the distraction. She caught a glance at her watch and breathed a sigh of relief at the time. Lunch, almost over. Another grenade, almost avoided.

I would never jeopardize your relationship with him. I'd do anything to protect it. His words pounded through her head and she gulped at the wine, finishing the remainder of the glass.

BELL

I was running, feet smacking against the pavement, vintage Dr. Dre thumping through my earbuds when my phone rang. I wove around a brochure-passing stripper and pressed the button on my headphone cord, answering the call.

"Hello?"

"You sound busy." Dario's voice crackled through the earbuds.

I slowed to a walk, and glanced down the street where I could see the towers of The Majestic sparkling in the sun. "I got a minute."

"I'm heading to San Diego tomorrow, just for a night. Want to come?"

A seven-foot-tall transvestite tottered by on uneven platforms. I moved aside to give her some room. "Flying or driving?"

"Driving. The plane..." His voice fell off and I wondered, for a moment, if I'd lost him. "The plane would cause too many issues for us, right now."

"So we're talking about a road trip. You and me."

"Yes. I'll try my best to keep both hands on the wheel." There was a smirk in his voice and I grinned in response, the decision already made.

"I've got my last exam—I should be done around eleven. After that, I'm in." I turned back, picking up my pace and jogging toward my car. A night away from my issues and his marriage, on a trip all our own... it would be nice.

TWENTY-SEVEN

"I've got to step up my game." Dario stood in the middle of my room, his hands on his hips, and surveyed the area, every spare surface piled with clothes, books, and crap. He looked out of place, too big for this room, and too sexy for words in faded jeans, a T-shirt clinging to his build and a Breitling watch heavy on his wrist.

"What do you mean?" I pushed aside hangers and squeezed to the back of my closet, running my hand over items until I felt the scratchy fabric of my yellow dress. I wiggled it loose and emerged, running a hand through my hair and taming it back into place.

"Your room." He stepped over and peered down at my desk, my textbooks half covered by my recent Sephora haul. "It's ... crowded."

"Yep." I took a giant step over a pile of folded towels and tossed a lone shoe in the general direction of the bed.

"And this is your closet." He took in the cram of hangers, the pile of shoes in the floor, every inch packed to overflowing.

I squeezed past him and folded the dress into fourths, pushing it into the bag and working the zipper closed. "Your powers of observation are impressive."

"I don't understand." He glanced up at the fan, the blades sagging on the ends and covered in a fine sheen of dust. "You have a gorgeous suite at The Majestic. One with a closet five times bigger than this. And your own bathroom. And a second bedroom, with *its* own bathroom."

He folded his arms over his chest, blocked the exit to my room and pinned me with a stare. "Why stay here?"

I spied my phone charger and went for it. He waited as I wrapped the cord into a coil and added it to my purse. I glanced at him and realized this conversation wasn't going away. "This is my place. I have full control of it. I pay for it. You should understand why that's important to me."

"You like the independence."

"Yes."

He grimaced, but dropped his arms, moving to my bag and lifting it off the bed. "You deserve better."

"You're right." I wasn't talking about the room. I was talking about a covert night in San Diego since we couldn't go out in public here. I was talking about losing my cell phone because the wrong person answered his. I was talking about *us*, and he headed down the hall with my bag, either missing the inference entirely or ignoring it.

I flipped off the light and, like a good little mistress, followed him.

⬥

"Wow." I watched as the headlights flashed, the vehicle unlocking. "You shouldn't have."

He laughed, opening the back and swinging my bag inside.

"No, *really*. You shouldn't have."

In the middle of my driveway, cozying up next to my car, sat a minivan. A Honda minivan. I walked up to it and glanced in the backseat, half-expecting to see a car seat strapped in. There wasn't one, and I took a full tour around the van before glancing up at Dario.

"What? I don't seem like a minivan guy?" He reached forward, pressing a button on the key fob, both side doors engaging and sliding open. I laughed and raised my eyebrows as if impressed.

"I can also close them. Watch." He pushed another button. A loud beep sounded, the sort typically associated with a delivery truck backing up, and the side doors slid closed. He opened mine with a flourish, and I took a final look around, still expecting to see a limo tucked nearby, or a Range Rover, or his Rolls.

Nothing. This was it. Dario Capece was driving me to San Diego in a... I glanced at the brand emblem before tossing my purse into the floorboard and stepping inside. A Honda Odyssey. I waited until he got in, then pulled my seatbelt across my chest.

"No, you *don't* seem like a minivan guy."

In fact, had odds been put on that fact, I would have bet every dollar in my bank account that Dario Capece would have shown up at my house in something overly extravagant, something designed to impress, something that matched the wealth that dripped off of him. Even now, his jeans shifting against the cloth seat, his hand pulling designer sunglasses into place, he looked expensive.

He tossed the keys into a cupholder, and I noticed the rental tags on the ring.

"You rented this?"

"Yep." He reached over, grabbing my hand and pressing a kiss on it.

The man had a half dozen cars, easily. No need to rent anything, much less a mommy van with eight cupholders and a stain-proof interior. I took note of my suspicions and fastened my seatbelt as he pulled out of the driveway.

Finding an aux cable, I plugged in my phone, scrolling through Spotify and starting a Clint Black song. He nodded in approval and I pulled off my sandals and propped my feet on the dash.

We turned out of my neighborhood, and the minivan's engine roared, moving into a higher gear as Dario sped up. I settled deeper into the seat and reached for his hand.

DARIO

She was driving him crazy. Bare feet up on the dash, soles arched as if they were in the air with him between her thighs.

She didn't even realize it. She was teasing the fuck out of him and clueless about it. The song changed, a drumbeat starting, and she began to bob her toes to the beat. He forced his eyes to the road and willed his dick to calm down.

It was stupid of him to not fuck her. He was thinking of this as a woman would, thinking that sex would unlock some fountain of emotions between them. The problem was, there were already feelings between them. She was already his first thought when he woke up and his last before sleep. She had already eroded his self-control, his rules, and his boundaries.

And she was already in danger. He'd seen the look that had crossed Robert Hawk's face when he'd answered that call and heard her voice. Dario had felt the prickle of unease when he'd stepped out of the casino and into his car. He'd noticed, in subtle shifts and quickened speech patterns, the discomfort of his staff. Something was going on, and if anything happened to her, he'd burn the entire city to the ground.

As a result, he'd gone rogue.

Spending cash.

Giving Bell a new, untraceable number to reach him at.

He'd used a fucking taxi this morning, taken it to the airport, gone through the motions of getting a flight, then gotten a rental car and driven to Bell's.

Maybe he was being paranoid. It wasn't the first time Robert had answered his phone and heard a female voice. And it wasn't the first time, or even the tenth, that Dario had had a woman on the side. It wasn't like Hawk could sense his love for Bell, and there was no reason for him to suspect anything. Still, every sensor in Dario's body was blaring alarms at full volume. It was good that they were getting out of town. For at least a night, away from the city and Robert Hawk's goons ... she'd be safe. But at some point during this trip, he would have to tell her the truth—everything he'd bit his tongue on so far. And it wasn't fair to sleep with her before that, not when those truths would likely end things between them.

She turned in the seat, pulling her feet off the dash, and he let out a sigh, grateful for one less distraction.

"I'm hungry. Mind if we stop somewhere?"

He nodded and changed lanes, an exit approaching.

THE TAIL

The minivan changed lanes, and Claudia did the same, hiding behind a large semi. She watched until she saw the vehicle on the exit ramp, then followed suit as it turned right. When the van pulled into a gas station, she continued forward, turning into an adjacent fast food restaurant and parking. Watching the vehicle stop beside a pump, she picked up the phone and placed the call.

"Yes?" Robert Hawk spoke quickly, the phone answered on the second ring.

"They're stopping for gas."

"Watch, but stay hidden. Call me if anything changes."

Easy enough. She nodded, ending the call and putting the car into park. Taking a moment, she stretched out her legs, the muscles sore from tailing Bell's run, and glanced in the rearview mirror, the fast food sign bright and appealing. As if on cue, her stomach grumbled.

She hadn't had fast food in years. Her time in the warehouse had conditioned her stomach to the basic meals that servitude provided—cold subs delivered rarely enough to keep her hunger guessing. The subs were always leftovers from Hawk catering functions, some half-eaten, all delicious to their starved stomachs. Now, she eyed the Tex-Mex sign and remembered the last taco she'd had, over two years ago. It had been grabbed after work and choked down while driving home, a frosty soda gripped in one hand while she steered with her knees. She'd been so weak, back then. So focused on unimportant things like social media updates and fashion trends, TV shows and class schedules. She'd drowned her weekends in alcohol and distracted her boredom with sex. She'd had no idea of *life* until it had all been taken away from her.

And that was what Robert tried to give them.

The meaning of life.

The value of living.

The importance of submission and boundaries and respect.

Too bad none of the others had understood that, or listened to the whispered lessons she tried to pass on. They had all looked at her as if she was crazy, as if *she* was the one chained to a wall and *they* had all the answers.

The minivan's door opened, and Bell Hartley's head popped up. The infamous Dario Capece glanced over his shoulder at her, the gas pump in hand. She shut the door and came around the car, still speaking to Dario as she walked away ... and toward the taco joint, alone. Claudia reached into the passenger seat, found her phone and got three or four good pictures of Bell on her way toward the restaurant.

Claudia's stomach growled again, and she turned in her seat to watch Bell pull open the taco chain's door and disappear inside.

She tossed the phone down and turned off the car. Opening the center console, she paused, glancing from the switchblade to the handgun. Could she do this? She thought of Robert's promise, a dinner with him and Gwen, just the three of them.

She reached into the console and grabbed them, slipping the gun into the back of her jeans and the switchblade in her pocket. She was efficient in both weapons, thanks to hours spent with Robert. She'd learned the weak areas of the human body, knew how to stab, twist and slice the life out of someone. She'd practiced with the handgun at five yards, then fifteen, then twenty-five. She could hit the center ring of a bull's eyes seven times out of ten at all three distances. Bell Hartley wouldn't have a chance.

She stepped out of the car and toward the restaurant, one hand slipping into her pocket and palming the knife.

Poor Bell. So similar to Claudia, two years ago. A sitting duck. A dumb, hungry, sitting duck.

TWENTY-EIGHT

BELL

I read the back of the guy's shirt ahead of me and tried to decipher the Greek letters. Lambda...Phi? Lambda Omega? I gave up. Greek letters, like sorority houses, had never been my thing. I tried to imagine Dario as a frat guy and smiled at the thought. On the drive, he'd told me about his start in the casino business—a start that had skipped right over college and landed him in a security polo. In some ways, our upbringings had been similar: jobs at fifteen, lower-class families, drunks for fathers. But in other ways, I felt like my life was so much more fun than his had ever been. I had spent the last two years driven by parties and school. He had graduated high school and dove into double-shifts and management training, with a laser focus on success and little else.

The door to the Taco Bell opened, and I glanced over. A woman came in, and I looked back to the board, tapping my credit card against my leg, torn between a burrito or a taco. Probably a burrito. Less messy. Then again, we were in a minivan. It probably had baby wipes and a mini trash can. The frat guy ahead of me took his receipt, and I stepped up to the counter.

"Two beef burritos, please."

The cashier rang up the items, and I glanced over my shoulder at the restaurant. The girl behind me looked away. A guy walked out, pulling a toddler by the hand. Two guys sat by the window with trucker hats on. I shifted, suddenly uneasy.

After that night at the barn, this used to happen all the time. When I was alone and strangers were near, I would get panicky. My chest would tighten, and my mind would run through all the different scenarios that I was certain were about to occur. Most involved death and dismemberment, my mind a pretty dark and gory place.

It'd been a long time since I had felt this way. Now, in the brightly lit Taco Bell, it was stupid to be afraid. I turned back to the cashier. "And ... nachos with cheese. And a crunchy beef taco. And a Pepsi."

"Make that two Pepsis."

I jumped at the sound of Dario's voice, my head snapping toward him.

He frowned, his hand sliding down the small of my back. "Jumpy?"

I smiled thinly. "A little." I leaned against his chest, and he wrapped his arms around me, giving me a firm squeeze that melted away my tension.

The cashier snapped her gum and fixed us with a bored expression. "That it?"

"Add on a chicken quesadilla." Dario pressed a kiss on the top of my head and took the cups from the cashier, passing them to me. "I'll pay. Can you get our drinks?"

I took the cups and turned, heading for the soda station and dismissing my nerves.

THE EX-VICTIM

The minivan pulled into San Diego at dusk, the city lights a rainbow of colors. Claudia followed them over the bridge and onto Coronado Island. The road was crammed with traffic, and it was twenty minutes before they turned into the Del Hotel.

She forced her hands to relax on the wheel. She'd been so close. Thirty seconds from stepping forward and jamming the knife into her kidney. One quick stab and twist. She'd stayed behind her and out of sight of the cashier, debating over whether to do it there, or wait and see if Bell Hartley went to the bathroom. It was a good thing she'd hesitated. Otherwise, Dario Capece would have seen it all.

It didn't matter. She'd find another opportunity to get the girl.

The valet pulled the minivan forward, and Claudia followed the car into an exterior lot, finding a spot and settling in to wait.

Patience. That was all she needed. Patience, and the right opportunity to get her alone.

She had done this three times before. Watching a girl. Waiting for an opportunity. Taking her off guard. With each of those instances, the goal had been to take the girl, not kill her. But the process was the same, even though the stakes were higher. She closed her eyes and took a deep breath, remembering the moment she had been caught off guard. She'd been leaving work, walking through the casino parking garage and digging through her purse for her keys. She'd heard her name and turned, surprised by the man who'd collided with her. It had been her first contact with Robert Hawk, their introduction marred by the sharp prick from the needle, the drug hazing everything over in a cloud of delirium. She'd been afraid for only a moment, then sank into his arms. One moment, and Claudia's life had changed.

Now, all she needed was one unguarded moment with Bell Hartley, and it would all be over for the pretty brunette. One moment and Bell Hartley's life would end.

BELL

"Wow." Dario came to a stop and raised his eyebrows, his gaze taking an appreciative sweep over my body.

I held out my arms and did a full turn, my yellow dress spinning out with the movement. "You like?"

"Breathtaking."

He was pretty heart-stopping himself, dressed in a charcoal grey button-up and pin-striped dress pants, the sexy ensemble paired with a few days' worth of silver and black stubble. He stepped closer and I ran my nails through his thick hair. We kissed and I pressed against him, emboldened by the heels, which put me almost level with him.

"You're going to torture me in this dress." He pulled up the hem of it, one palm sliding over my bare ass and squeezing the flesh, his fingers tracing along the edges of my thong.

"That's the plan."

His eyes darkened as he explored the tiny scrap of satin that made up my panties. I smiled. I did want to torture him. I wanted him to crave me, wanted him hard and ready by the time we returned to this room. I'd been a patient girl for long enough.

I pushed off his chest and pulled my dress up, exposing the white thong he'd had his hands all over. Looping my fingers underneath the sides of it, I slid it over my hips and down to the floor. Stepping out of the thong, I walked to the dresser and grabbed my clutch, looking over my shoulder at him. "Ready?"

He bit his lip, his eyes dragging from the white lace to me. Letting out a low swear, he shook his head and gestured to the door. "Please. After you."

We ate oceanfront, in a little restaurant walking distance from the hotel. I dipped bread in olive oil and looked up to find his eyes on me, his expression guarded.

"What?" I put the bread down.

"I need to talk to you about something." He leaned forward and rested his forearms on the table. "Leaving Gwen is complicated. There are ... *issues* with her father, the man you spoke to on the phone."

"We didn't speak. I just said—"

He brushed off the words, holding up his hand.

I spoke before he had a chance to. "And I'm not asking you to leave Gwen. Not right now." The defense came out quickly, before I had a chance to think it through.

"I know you aren't asking for that. But I can't continue on like we are. It's not fair to you." He sighed. "And it's not fair to her. I haven't lied to Gwen in…" He stared upward for a moment, then gave a low, frustrated laugh. "I don't know if I've *ever* lied to Gwen. And what you and I are doing… it feels a lot like lying." His jaw tightened, and when his gaze caught mine, the weight in it was almost palpable. "How I feel about you … it feels like cheating. It *is* cheating."

"But…" I struggled to find my way through his words. "I thought you weren't cheating. I thought you had an understanding with her. I thought she had some guy she's messing around with—"

"I'm not talking about cheating on Gwen. I'm talking about cheating on *you*."

I inhaled sharply at the words.

"You're right, it's not fair to you, for me to have a life with her, one you aren't a part of. And the sad thing is…" He reached for my hand, gripping it between his palms. I held my breath and waited for the next line. When he finally spoke, it felt more like a dark confession than truth. "I'm in love with you. And I'm terrified at what I'm bringing you into."

I'm in love with you. The confession competed with the follow-up. *Terrified?* I curled my fingers around his hands. "Tell me what you are bringing me into."

Maybe, right then, I should have told him that I was in love with him too. But I'd never felt that, or said that to anyone before. And I needed to know, before I jumped off that cliff, what lay at its bottom.

DARIO

It wasn't his story to tell, and he'd never shared Gwen's story with anyone. But now, looking into Bell's eyes, he couldn't keep it from her. If he went forward with Bell, Gwen's story would soon include her, and she had to understand what she was getting into.

He paused, aware that this could destroy them. If Bell was smart, she'd run. Fake her way through the rest of their night, finish her giant box of Nerds on the drive home, and never answer his calls again.

His chest clenched at the possibility. He had told her he loved her and she hadn't responded—hadn't really given him much of an indicator, short of her rapid-fire orgasms, that she was ready for more. Yet, she was here, after dealing with all of his possessive and invasive bullshit. He released her hands, knotted his fingers together to keep from touching her, and shared everything.

The hell that Gwen grew up in. The abuse. The neglect.

Gwen's kidnapping, and Robert Hawk's refusal to pay the ransom.

The control that her father held over her life, the staggering accountability he held them both to.

"When I met Gwen, she was close to breaking. The night we met, she tried to commit suicide, was steps away from jumping off the roof of my Biloxi hotel. Security footage caught her in the stairwell and alerted me. I got there just in time."

He remembered the cool Mississippi night, the way the wind had whipped the dress against her body, the way Gwen had clung to the railing, her eyes darting between him and the edge. She'd been terrified of him, and that fear had broken his heart. He'd warred between stepping back and rushing forward. He'd ended up using the talent that had got him out of the swamp and into the casinos—his words.

He'd told her about his upbringing, his own mistakes. He'd promised her that whatever had brought her to this rooftop, he would handle. He'd sworn on his dead mother that he would protect her, rescue her, and fix everything.

And she'd believed him. She'd trusted him. When she'd stepped away from the edge and fallen into his arms, he'd had no idea of the enormous responsibility of what he'd just taken on.

But he'd never regretted it. Not as he'd grown to love the woman he was rescuing, and not as they'd built an empire together, one independent from her father. For a decade, they'd paid a heavy interest rate to Robert Hawk, both in money and morals, half of their activities as illegal as they were profitable. But finally, ten years after he'd married Gwen, they were legitimate. Their loan from Robert Hawk was a month from payoff, and they were thirty days from owning The Majestic outright, along with the other six casinos under its flag.

In a month, he and Gwen would be—at least on paper—free.

But never, as long as his blood was in Gwen's veins, would Robert Hawk let them go.

"What do you mean, let you go?" Bell leaned forward and touched his hand, pulling him back to the present.

Dario shook his head at the waiter, sending him away, and tried to find the best way to describe Robert Hawk's God complex. "He sees Gwen and me as assets and wants proper credit for our success. He doesn't think the way a normal person does. He's like a child who doesn't share, one that throws temper tantrums and pouts, and doesn't let others play with his toys. Only, his temper tantrums ruin lives. His pouts bankrupt companies. Gwen and I are his toys—Gwen, more than me. Hawk has zero accountability for his actions and half the police force is in his pocket."

Bell's face paled, and he could see in the quick way she reached for and sipped her wine, that she understood. He thought of his last statement and knew that she—more than anyone—understood what it was like to be at the mercy of a police force that turned a blind eye.

If she was smart, she'd leave him behind and never answer his calls again. Break his heart and save her skin.

He watched her swallow the wine, and her eyes met his.

TWENTY-NINE

BELL

I already knew about Robert Hawk, but I hadn't understood the depth of his reach until that moment, until Dario laid it all out across that candlelit table. He sat back, and my hair blew across my lips. I tucked it behind my ear and thought through everything he had said.

My thoughts didn't work logically. I wanted to break them down, to address each problem one by one. Gwen. Her father. His marriage. What he saw for our future. But all I could hear, in the thoughts that crowded my head, were Dario's words. *I love you.* He loved me. A man who controlled so much, a man pulled in so many directions by so many, a man so fiercely attractive I could barely breathe in his presence, who had broken through all of my walls ... he loved me.

He was waiting, and I reached for my drink, taking a sip of the sweet wine and giving myself another moment to think, to remember everything that he said. *Leaving Gwen is complicated.*

"I think you should talk to Gwen. Get her opinion on this."

He looked out on the water. "I didn't want to talk to her without working through it with you first. If you want to walk away, then there's no need to involve her."

I choked out a laugh.

"What?"

"Nothing. It's just…" I tried to find a way to explain the cowardice in that, if that was even the right word. "It sounds like you're hedging your bets. If I walk away, you'll just go back to her. Life goes on, everyone is happy." I raised one eyebrow at him. "Right?"

"No."

I leaned forward, putting my elbows on the table and resting my chin on my fists. "Sounds like it to me."

"If you walk away, I'll spend the next few decades fighting to forget you."

I snorted. "Oh, please."

DARIO

She didn't get it. She didn't realize her hold on him, the way that she had disrupted everything. Maybe … maybe that was his fault.

He forced his jaw to unclench, for his words to come out calm. "I'm not a man used to fighting for attention, Bell. I haven't been in a position to do a proper job of showing you how I feel about you. Part of that's due to my respect for Gwen. Part of it is because I've worried, if I showed you all of my cards, that you'll be careless with me."

But he already had shown her his cards, even if she hadn't recognized it. Protecting her from Hawk. Ripping apart that filth from her hometown. Giving her a new home, chasing her around like a love-struck teenager. Had any other woman walked away from him, he would have laughed. When *she'd* walked away, over and over, he'd followed. Waited for. Chased. His cards had been on the table from the moment he'd walked into The House and saw her. She just hadn't known where to look, and what they meant.

He pulled her hand toward him, cupping the small palm between his. "I love you. And I'm risking everything for you. Telling Gwen is a side effect that has no impact on the destruction you are capable of doing to me."

Her eyes softened, and maybe there was a chance, maybe she *did* love him, maybe he wasn't a crazy old man chasing a flighty college girl. She glanced down, and he steeled himself for whatever was coming next. "I'm worried you're playing me."

Insanity, coming from her perfect little mouth. How did she not know?

"It's just that, we haven't even..."

He tried to follow the sentence, tried not to get distracted by the way her teeth gently pulled across her pale pink bottom lip.

"We haven't even had *sex*." She leaned forward, whispering the words, and he laughed. So young, this one. So brave, so beautiful, but so young. Did she think *that* mattered?

"I told you why we haven't done that."

She cast her eyes to the side, glancing at the other tables to see if anyone was listening. Everything they'd talked about, and this... this is what she was worried about. This from the woman who was naked underneath that dress, her bare pussy in easy reach of his fingers and at risk of exposure from a strong breeze. He felt his cock stiffen and mentally forced the image from his mind.

"Yeah." Her lips pursed together in a beautiful pinch.

"Because I cared about you as more than a fuck. Because I was trying to keep..." He had *tried* to keep an emotional distance between them. Tried and failed. He had tried not to get in too deep. Tried and failed. Why was he still trying? What was he still fighting?

He leaned forward. "Is that what you want? It's important to you?"

She shifted in her seat, a blush spreading over those gorgeous cheeks. "I just want all of you. Not some censored version of you."

Censored. That was an adjective that had never been used to describe him. Then again, with other women, he'd had them naked and wrapped around his cock within hours. With other women, he hadn't been interested in anything *but* that.

He stood so suddenly that the table jerked a little. "Let's go."

"What?"

He pulled out his wallet and peeled two large bills off its clip, tossing them down on the table.

"Now. Come on."

He held out his hand for hers, and she grinned, grabbing her purse and standing. Her soft palm slipped into his, and they moved through the planters and toward the entrance.

"Want to walk back along the beach?" he asked.

She glanced toward the hotel, then out on the sand. Reaching down, she pulled off her left heel, then her right. From her new, diminished height, she jogged forward onto the beach, turning and giving him a playful look. She looked free and in love. It was a look he wanted to see every day, for the rest of his life. He caught up with her, grabbing her hand and pulling her against him.

She was a freaking minx. A sexy, adorable, beautiful minx. And she wanted him, *all* of him.

It was a blessing that scared the hell out of him.

BELL

He flipped the lock, pulling me into the room and onto the bed. He opened the sliding door, and the sound of the ocean came in, the scent of seawater, the cool warmth of the breeze. I lay back, my weight propped on my elbows, and pulled my feet up, my dress falling to my hips, everything exposed to him.

He stripped, his eyes on me, the moonlight reflecting off his build as it was unveiled. Those shoulders, the bulge of his biceps, the lines of his abs, the sharp cut of his hips. He was a fucking machine, and when he pulled down his underwear, he was already ready.

He ripped open a foil package and tossed it beside me. "I want you just like this, every night of my life."

His knees settled on the bed, the mattress shifting, and he parted my knees and ran his hands down my thighs. Between us, his stiff cock bobbed, and it was so thick I wondered if it would hurt. I reached between us and wrapped my hand around it. Squeezing the thick cord of muscle, I felt it respond against my palm.

"Lay back."

His hand brushed over my pussy, and my smile turned into a sigh of surrender, my grip falling off his cock, my back hitting the mattress. His talented fingers made soft contact with my clit, feather-light and circling, moving over the sensitive area in a leisurely fashion. He shifted, and I felt the thick intrusion of fingers, pushing inside of me. My body was slick and ready, and I lifted my hips off the bed in an attempt for more.

"God, you are perfect." He leaned forward, and my eyes pinched shut when his tongue replaced the movement on my clit, his fingers moving from thrusting to g-spot manipulation, everything in my world turning dark as pleasure overtook brain function, and my body surrendered to his mouth.

The man ate pussy as if it was ice cream. He feasted on it, moaned against my clit, and slid his tongue across every inch of it. A woman couldn't be self-conscious, not with the talented play of his mouth, his hands pinning my thighs open, the enthusiasm—no, worship—of his touch. My body tightened and he knew, his lips tensing, tongue flicking, and everything spiraled into a hot spin of pleasure, all of my senses building, twisting, exploding underneath that mouth.

"Oh… God… I…"

I surrendered to him, trusted him with its intensity, and didn't hold back, letting the orgasm bind and break me, the explosion ripping through me with exquisite clarity. I screamed, knotting my fingers in his hair, my thighs clamping around his head, my feet flexing against his back. I whimpered, the orgasm spreading, fading, my body jerking. My legs slid off his shoulders, and my hips bucked, an involuntary reflex, my pussy tightening, an aftershock of pleasure still sparking.

I moaned with unintelligible pleasure and he didn't look up from his cock, rolling the condom on with brisk efficiency. He sat back on his knees and pulled me forward, flush to him, my thighs against his, my legs falling open, void of any energy or control. My senses came back to life when he thrust forward, a slow, controlled movement that opened my body in an entirely new way.

Holy shit. I could feel him everywhere. Rigid. Thick. He filled me in an almost painful way, and if I wasn't still drugged and languid from my orgasm, I'd make him stop. I cried out, my hand pushing on his chest, and he leaned forward, the pain lessening, the angle better, his gaze holding mine.

"Give it a minute."

I'd give it all night. He pulled at my dress, dragging it over my stomach and exposing my breasts. He tilted his hips, went even deeper, and I couldn't believe this was happening. Him, naked against me. His muscular thighs, tensing. His cock inside of me. His eyes ran over my bare body, and he whispered my name. He slid his hands over my breasts, owning and caressing them with his touch. My body relaxed, adjusted, and when he moved his hands to my hips, his weight settling back, it didn't hurt anymore. His eyes met mine, and I smiled.

"Ready?"

I didn't know what I was supposed to be ready for, but I nodded. I nodded, and the man atop me exploded into action.

Had I ever been truly and properly fucked before? I thought I had. I thought I was experienced, thought that all of the men before Dario had exposed me to every pleasure center and position that existed. But in that room, I had a virgin's knowledge of what could occur.

He fucked ... and there was no other word for it. Hard, piston-like thrusts that didn't change in their repetitions. I didn't understand the beauty of it until the consistency of his actions led to the build. The build that grew and strengthened and twisted and bloomed, my orgasm the kind that shattered through me, a pleasure center exploding, and stretching. He barely stopped, but suddenly I was on my hands and knees, at his disposal. Animalistic and raw. He growled when he thrust into me. He gripped my ass, pulled me on and off of his cock, and set us into motion.

On my side, his movements slowed, his hands sweeping over me. Teasing. Cherishing.

My dress, fully off. His fingers, tightening in and tugging on my hair. His mouth on my nipples, the gentle scrape of teeth, suction of his tongue.

I crawled on top of him, my knees tight to his sides, his wet fingers dragging over my breasts, then gripping my hips. He pulled me down to his chest, wrapped his arms around me, and his hips took over our movements. That orgasm was the best, the longest, the highest. He rolled on top of me, growled out my name, and let himself come.

He was gorgeous when he came. That heat, that light in his eyes, flared. There was a moment of vulnerability, of raw and unprotected emotion. He grunted, his legs trembled, his hands tightened. It was long, and I could feel his cock flex, felt the warmth of his release through the condom, and I squeezed my body around him in response.

"I love you." I whispered the confession, and he rolled to his side, pulling me to his chest, his cock still inside me, and I felt his heart, the strong thump and hammer of it. His body was such an engine, a force of sexual nature, built to please and—in this moment—all mine. I relaxed my cheek against his chest, my legs sliding down, his intertwining around them.

"I love you, too." His fingers trailed over my bare back, and he lifted his head, pressing his lips to my hair. "I don't ever want another man to have you."

I think he meant physically, but emotionally, he was the only man who had ever truly *had* me. Would he be the only one who ever would?

I closed my eyes and couldn't, in that moment, find anything to say.

THIRTY

DARIO

He drove, his hand resting on the back of her seat, and glanced at her. She was curled up, her sweatshirt stuffed under her head, asleep. She looked so innocent. Innocent and brave. Giving that vulnerable and delicate heart and love to him. He had to protect her, take the trust she gave him and fulfill it.

An easier thing to want than deliver. Fuck, he was in one hell of a situation—pulled in different directions by two incredible women. One held his heart and his cock in her delicate grasp. The other held his head and his past in her fist. Gwen wouldn't let go easily. She would fight for him, for them. She would remind him of every promise he'd ever made and hold him to them.

Fuck. He rubbed his hand over his face and picked up his phone, then set it back down. Changed his mind again and sent Gwen a quick text message, letting her know he was on his way back. She replied quickly, asking about dinner, and he confirmed. *There.* A date set. Him and Gwen. It was time to tell her everything and hear her thoughts on the matter.

He'd been married to the woman for a decade but suddenly, with the dinner looming, he was lost at what to expect.

THE FAILURE

Claudia chewed at the edge of one nail, watching the back of the minivan as it changed lanes. This had been a complete waste of a trip, and Robert had been less than enthusiastic on their last call. The disappointment had been hard in his voice, each question another stab in her gut.

Why had they left mid-dinner? She didn't know.

Why hadn't Bell stayed at the hotel when Dario had met with the show runners? She didn't know.

Had she been in the meeting with him? She couldn't say. The talent office hadn't let her follow them up the elevator, wanting her driver's license and authorization from someone inside.

She had done her best, and it hadn't been enough. There hadn't been an opening, the couple glued together like lovesick idiots.

She turned up the air conditioning. She hadn't told Robert about their behavior together, afraid the details would anger him further. The way that Dario looked at her, the way he constantly touched her, pulling her into his side and kissing the top of her head ... it had made Claudia sick. Dario was married to *Gwen*. Devoted to Gwen. He was supposed to be in *love* with Gwen.

It was a wrong that needed to be righted. First, by Bell Hartley's death. And then? She tore off a piece of her cuticle and wondered what further punishment Robert would bring down on Dario Capece.

She glanced down at the notebook where she'd written down the code that Robert had given her. 04182996#. He'd gone into the Majestic's reservation system and pulled the access for suite 908.

It was probably better, killing Bell there. The Majestic was a controlled environment, one Robert could get her full access to. He would be able to kill security cameras and see housekeeping schedules. She would have privacy and less witnesses than at Taco Bell.

She released the gas, letting the minivan grow further away. Putting on her turn signal, she moved into the right lane and onto the next exit. Glancing down the road, she caught a final glimpse of the van before it disappeared from sight.

Soon. Soon, this task would be done. Bell Hartley would be dead. Dario Capece would be punished. Robert would be pleased, and Gwen's marriage would be saved. All thanks to her.

It would be the biggest test Robert Hawk had ever given her.

So far, she had failed. But soon. Soon, she would succeed.

BELL

"I'd like you to stay in the suite tonight."

I looked over, halfway through a Sudoku puzzle I had already screwed up. "Tonight?" I made a face. "I've got laundry to do." With my last two weeks filled with work, Dario, and exams, my dirty clothes pile had accumulated into a mountain. Now that the semester had ended, I had no excuse.

"Do it there." He rested one hand on the steering wheel, his other on my thigh.

"You want me to go home, pack up all my dirty laundry, and take it to The Majestic?" I laughed. "No."

"You know, we have services for that."

"I don't want some stranger going through my dirty clothes." Though... maybe I could get over that. The thought of never doing laundry again was definitely tempting. I turned the page and started a fresh puzzle.

"You can do laundry tomorrow. Just stay there tonight."

I looked up, curious at his insistence. "Is it a sex thing? You had one taste at what I've got, and now you need it every night?"

He chuckled. "It's not a sex thing."

"Is it my sparkling personality? You need more of it?"

He grinned and released my thigh, stealing my hand and pulling it into his lap. "Guilty. I am addicted to your sparkling personality."

"That's a common issue, you know." I straightened in my seat. "I have to send certified letters and hire professionals to handle the personality stalkers. It's exhausting."

He lifted my hand and ran his lips over my thumb, then gently nipped it. "I will try not to be exhausting. And I refuse to accept certified letters."

I giggled when he flicked his tongue over my knuckle, the flutter reminding me of his talent against my clit. I shifted in the seat, and his gaze darkened.

"You're lucky you're wearing jeans. If you were in a skirt right now..." He shook his head, his eyes on the road.

"If I were in a skirt, I'd have my panties pulled to the side and your fingers inside me."

He made a sound low in his throat, one that sounded suspiciously like a growl. "Dirty girl."

I laughed. "Not ... yet."

I unbuckled my seatbelt and flipped up the armrest. He watched the action, his mouth curving into a smile. Then, I took full advantage of the minivan's lack of center console and got on my knees, unzipping his pants and taking him into my hand. As we grew closer to Vegas, I showed him exactly how dirty my mouth could be.

GWEN

Her husband was nervous. She could see it in the stern jerk of his head at the waiter, the way his fingers drummed on the table, the adjustment of his tie.

She waited until their drinks were served, then leaned forward. "What's wrong? Is it something that happened in San Diego? Or..." She looked down at her place setting, moving the silverware into a neat row. "Has my father done something?"

Ever since that lunch with her father, she'd been filled with a sense of dread, the weight of an impending event. She'd tried to follow its thread, tried to figure out its source. Nick at the ranch? Something with Dario?

"Your father hasn't done anything." He smiled at her, a gesture meant to reassure her. It didn't work. She'd seen enough of his smiles to know which ones meant what. There was the smile he gave when he was amused. The one that spoke of fondness. The one that was forced. The one that hid something.

This smile was that last sort.

She sighed. "Just tell me. Whatever it is. You're driving me mad."

His jaw tightened, and he finally, after a long period of silence, nodded. "I'm in love with someone. The new waitress I met."

In some ways, it was as unexpected as a bomb. While she had fallen in love with Nick, Dario had always been the casual one. All the women he'd been with ... none of them had kept his interest or posed a threat to her. Sure, the women had developed attachments to him. It was hard to be around Dario and *not* fall in love with him. He was so big, so *impressive* in everything he did. She remembered the night she met him—before he ruled over Vegas, back when he was just a casino general manager. Even then, he'd taken her breath away. So sexy. So brooding. So intense and charismatic. When he'd looked at her, it had been as if he really *saw* her. When he listened to her, it was as if he took each word in and *valued* them.

And now, this beautiful, powerful man—her man—was in love with another woman. A cocktail waitress. She laughed despite herself. Talk about a step down.

"Don't laugh."

"I'm sorry." She lifted a hand to her forehead and rubbed it. "Fuck."

This sucked, and mostly because he wouldn't bring this up unless it was serious. And if it was serious, then it was an issue. "What does she know about me?"

"Enough to understand the situation. She doesn't need me to do anything."

"You mean, leave me? She doesn't need you to leave me?" The words came out harsher than she had intended, and his face hardened in response.

"I'll never *leave* you. You know that."

He emphasized the word "leave" and that was a tell in itself. He wanted a divorce. He would support her, protect her, but wanted a divorce. What did a world look like without him as her husband?

She shook her head. "No. I can't. He'll..." She looked up at him. "He'll kill me."

She whispered the statement and believed every word of it. Her father would *kill* her. Not physically, but the mental strain, the exhaustive chess games of manipulation he played, the stress and the torture he would put her through... she'd be back on a rooftop, wanting to end it. Only this time, there wouldn't be a Dario to save her. This time, she'd jump.

"Gwen."

Her father *could* fix this. One call and he'd take care of the girl. She'd be gone, and Gwen would be safe for another decade, maybe longer. Dario wasn't a man who fell in love easily. Even their marriage, their ten years together ... it had never been *true* love— not the sort of reckless heady emotion between two souls. Their love had grown slowly, a friendship, fed with mutual respect and adoration for each other.

Her breath stalled at the path she'd just considered. That was the danger in being Robert Hawk's daughter. Spend enough time around evil, and you start accepting the options it provided.

She looked at her husband. "How long has this been going on?"

"Not long. A month or so. Less than two."

The signs were all there. Gwen had known about him ending things with Meghan, had noticed the new suite that he'd pulled out of the rental pool. Suite 908. A new home for a new girl. Typical behavior, yet when combined with his late nights and distraction, it was alarming. Her anxiety worsened.

He reached out and grabbed her hand. "I'm not doing anything right now except talking to you about this."

"No." She shook her head, a short and jerky movement that caused a twinge of pain in her neck. "No. You can't." She pulled her hand away. "You *promised* me."

He had promised her safety, to be a conduit between her and her father. He promised to be her right-hand, to help her rebuild The Majestic's reputation. He had promised to marry her, to take her out of that house, to give her a new life. He had delivered on all of those promises, for all of this time. He *couldn't* stop now. He couldn't throw her away just because he had fallen in love.

Love. God. How terrible was she to not want him to be in love? He deserved that. He'd done so much for her. Was it fair for her to hold him hostage?

"Don't make me be this way." She held his eyes and begged him with her gaze. "I just ... I'm not ready. You can date her, you can love her, just don't... don't leave me."

She was pathetic. Where was the strong woman that was supposed to reign over this town? Where was the woman who had done so many great things in the last decade?

But Dario had been beside her with all of those things. Encouraging her. Comforting her when she was exhausted. Giving her a kick in the ass when she was afraid. Handling the dirty details while her hands remained clean.

She stared at him and saw a pain that matched her own. He was one of two of the best men she knew, and her confidence in his loyalty had been unquestioned. He'd never ask anything if it would cause her pain, yet as she searched his face for an answer, she only saw disaster.

THIRTY-ONE

BELL

"So....?" Meredith raised an eyebrow at me and turned away from the stove, a prepackaged bag of chicken stir-fry beginning to crackle in the skillet. "How was San Diego?"

I popped a baby carrot into my mouth and leaned against the kitchen counter, buying some time as I crunched through it. While I'd confessed to her my continued relationship with Dario, I hadn't shared any details about Gwen's father. "It was good."

"Good?" She put down the spatula and crossed her arms over her chest. "Come on now. We're alone in the house, for the first time in forever. Spill. Is his bratwurst as talented as it is delicious? Or is he all sizzle and no substance?"

I laughed. "Oh my god. Leave your Top Chef obsession out of my sex life."

"Ah-HA!" She pointed at me. "So there *was* sex. Come on. Spill it. I'm growing cobwebs down there. Let me fuck vicariously through you."

I elbowed her out of the way and picked up the spatula, pushing around the vegetables and flipping over a few chunks of chicken. "Fine. There was..." I closed my eyes and exhaled deeply. "Good sex. Insane sex."

"Better-than-Ian Sex?" she challenged.

"Can't-Even-Remember-Who-Ian-Is Sex." I fixed her with a look and she bounced a little in place.

"Damn, girl. That's not even fair." She opened the cabinet and pulled out two paper plates, setting them out on the counter. "Especially since this glow seems more than just post-orgasm." She leaned forward and peered at my face as if examining it for evidence. "Dare I say..." Her eyes widened. "Holy shit."

I shoved her away. "You're so dramatic."

"You're in *love* with him?" She glanced over her shoulder as if Lydia and Jackie might suddenly pop out of spin class and into the hall.

"Correct me if I'm wrong, but I thought you were just ... I mean, he's married, right?"

"Right. And we were casual, or I was trying to be casual but ..." I turned down the burner and set the spatula down. "I don't know. I couldn't stay away from him. I tried. And you know me. I fought against feeling for him with every ounce in my being, but it still happened."

That was sort of a lie. My love hadn't just *happened*. It had perched on my shoulder in the casino, and followed me through every subsequent interaction, taking its time to slip into my heart and suction-cup itself to every artery until I couldn't help but breathe it in. I had been done for the minute our eyes had met.

"Can't say I'm surprised." She opened up the fridge and reached in, grabbing a two-liter of Diet Coke and twisting off the cap. "Something's been different with you, ever since you met him. Not to be all Debbie Downer on you, but what's the plan from here? Is he gonna leave his wife?"

"I don't know." I pushed my glass toward her and watched as she refilled it. "He's talking to her about it now." I glanced at the clock and imagined the two of them at an intimate candlelit table, discussing their marriage. A stab of jealousy and fear hit.

What *was* the plan? Did we even have one?

—*I spoke to Gwen.*

how'd it go?

—*Not great. Come to the suite tonight.*

your manners suck

—*PLEASE come to the suite tonight. My cock misses you. So does my heart.*

it's been four hours. Your cock is high maintenance.

—*text me when you are on your way*

omg. stop.

—*I love you*

FINE. I'll be there. give me a few hours

—*I love you*

I love u too. I'm sorry about Gwen.

—I'll figure it out. Be safe.

I read his last text with a smile and tossed the phone onto the bed. Turning back to my suitcase, I pulled items out and returned them to their proper place. I thought of Dario's comments, his critical appraisal of my room, his urge to stay in the suite.

Just a few weeks in his world, and I could feel the pull, the easy intoxication of it all. I could say yes and have daily maid service. Say yes and never do laundry again. Say yes and kiss goodbye to frozen pizzas and fast food, credit card debt and car payments. I could quit my job and spend my days poolside, my afternoons shopping, my nights drinking expensive wine and bouncing up and down on the most powerful cock in Vegas.

It would be easy.

I stopped before the tall mirror in my room, twisting my hair up and turning my head, imagining a string of diamonds around my neck, chandelier earrings hanging from my ears, a glittery evening gown hugging my curves. I dropped my hair with a shaky inhale. In the last month, I had searched the Internet for photos of Gwen and Dario, had seen countless images of the statuesque brunette at charity events, ribbon cutting ceremonies, and social events. She didn't look like a girl who grew up on welfare. She didn't look like someone who once stood, bruised and shivering, in a police station and told a story that no one believed.

Guilt stabbed at me, because she also didn't look like someone who grew up with a psychopathic father. I wouldn't trade childhoods with her. I don't know anyone who would.

I turned away from the mirror and hated every bit of this situation. Yet, I couldn't walk away, not from the man who now owned my heart.

DARIO

A few hours. Enough time for him to get Gwen home, spend some more time with her, and then leave. A few hours would give them enough time to talk through this and find a solution, or a few possibilities. He sent Bell a final text and switched his phone to silent, pushing it into his pocket. Looking into the bathroom's mirror, he straightened the line of his suit, pulling at the cuff of each sleeve, and watching the man in the mirror critically.

He looked like success. The expensive suit was tailored to fit perfectly on his powerful build. The watch had a ring of diamonds glinting from its face. He looked exactly like the image he had worked two decades to create. Strong. Fierce. Successful.

He looked in the mirror and didn't see any of the fear that gripped his heart. Fear that, decades ago, he had sworn to destroy. Fear that, pre-Bell, didn't exist.

He swallowed, placing his hands on either side of the marble sink, and leaned toward the mirror, staring into his own eyes.

"He'll kill me." Gwen had believed the words, her face pinching in a way he hadn't seen in a long time.

He was supposed to protect women, not endanger them. But right now, if he kept moving forward, he'd put them both in danger. The only two women he'd ever loved, at risk because he couldn't control his dick and his heart.

He should give up. Step back into his role. Ship Bell off to fucking Alaska and set her up with an apartment and job there. Send her money every month and beg her to ignore his calls.

Because he would call. He would visit. He would drop to his knees in front of her Alaskan apartment and beg her to marry him. There was no way, with her somewhere on this earth, that he'd be able to stay away.

He was fucked any way he turned. Killing himself if he ended things with Bell. Endangering both her and Gwen if he chose Bell. There was no scenario where this wouldn't end badly.

Give me a few hours. He needed a few lifetimes to figure this out, but would barely last a few hours without seeing her.

He opened the door to the bathroom and stepped back into the restaurant. Gwen stood by the entrance, her Ferrari visible through the glass, a white-gloved attendant pulling open the door.

A few hours. She smiled at him, and he could see the thin veneer of her composure.

Fuck Robert Hawk. Fuck his callous and ruthless soul. Fuck his barbaric need for control.

Gwen didn't deserve this. None of them did.

✦

The steam filled the shower, a thousand individual streams of water hitting his skin and scalding his muscles. He pressed a hand against the tile wall, hanging his head, the water running down his face. Rolling his neck, he felt the bones crack into place.

The shower door opened and he lifted his head to see Gwen step in, her hair loose, expression quiet. He turned, facing her, and she closed the door, moving forward and into the spray.

"Gwen..." His voice cracked, and it was a plea more than a name. *Please don't make me tell you no. Please don't press this. Please don't cry and beg and break my heart.* She moved closer, pressing her body against his, and he slid his hands down the side of her body, closing them around her waist. She lifted her chin, her face free of the spray, and he watched as her hair grew damp, water splattering across her shoulders, rivulets running down her breasts, the brush of her nipples against his chest.

He hadn't seen her naked in years, the passing time softening her curves and edges. She was a beautiful woman. She deserved to be admired, to be lusted after, to be pleased. But not by him. Now, as she lifted onto her toes, her lips pressing against his neck, her body sliding along his, he felt nothing but sadness for her effort. He said her name softly, stepping away, and she pressed on, her leg slipping in between his, her thigh hard against his cock. She noticed his lack of arousal and lifted her chin, looking up into his eyes, and asking the question with her stare.

"I'm sorry."

She tried to kiss him and he pulled away from her mouth but brought her into his body, his arms wrapping around her, hugging her frame against his chest. "I'll always love you."

She clung to him, her head against his heart, nails digging into his back, and said nothing.

After the shower, she dressed in jeans, a silk sweater and tennis shoes. He stood on the upper level of their suite and watched her move to the door, grabbing her keys off the hook.

He didn't ask her where she was going. He watched her leave and walked down the hall, turning on the light in the closet, illuminating the neat rows of pressed and starched clothing.

Give me a few hours. He thought of Bell's text and glanced at the clock, the time growing late. Reaching for a pair of workout shorts and a T-shirt, he dressed. Eyed his phone. Stood on the balcony and wondered where, or to whom, Gwen had gone. He wasted a half hour with emails, checked in with department heads, and finally, just before midnight, got a text from Bell.

—on my way

Relief washed over him, and he willed himself to be patient. No point in rushing downstairs to her suite. He needed to show restraint, to learn some fucking patience. He poured a hard drink, his first in years, and carried it into the media room. He turned on sports, listened to late night commentators discuss playoff system changes and sipped it slowly, the bourbon lingering on his tongue, each swallow a burst of fire down his throat. He had a thought, pulled out his phone, and sent her a text.

Go in, get undressed and wait on the bed.

He closed his eyes and sank lower on the leather couch. Took another sip and imagined the look of her, laid out on that bed, waiting for him.

THE KILLER

Claudia had a cramp in her upper back. Lifting her arms slightly, she shifted, rolling her shoulders and rounding her spine, then arched it, trying to work the muscles. *Fuck*. With her luck, Bell would walk in the suite, and Claudia would be in the middle of a spasm.

It was the small space of this closet. She should have gone under the bed instead. Laid down on that plush rug and waited there. She tried twisting in place, and one elbow bumped painfully against the wall of the coat closet. She debated about moving, but this was, after touring the entire apartment, the best bet. With the door opened just a small crack, she would be able to see Bell's movements. Not in the kitchen, but as soon as she walked into the living room or headed to the bedroom, she'd have a clear view. She could lift the gun and finish this all.

And, if Bell Hartley wasn't alone ... if Dario Capece was with her? Claudia could just stay in place. She'd spent ten months in Robert Hawk's cell. That had taught her how to sit tight and wait. Eventually, the man would go to the bathroom, or take a shower, or fall asleep. Eventually, there *would* be an opening.

Besides, that second scenario wasn't likely. Dario had taken Gwen to dinner. They'd be back in their suite. He'd be telling her lies and pretending to love her.

Claudia heard something and stopped, mid-stretch of her neck. She cocked her ear toward the door, listening.

There was the soft swoosh of a door against the tile. Shoes slapped quietly across the floor. The front door closed. It was the quiet movements of a single individual. She smiled and carefully leaned forward, looking through the crack, unable to see her.

A drawer slammed. Silverware rattled, and she raised her gun, a bullet already in the chamber. Footsteps moved, and then Bell was passing by the closet, coming into view. The girl stopped, facing away from Claudia, and pulled a phone from her back pocket. Easing the door open, she tightened her grip on the pistol, lifting the gun and lining up the glossy brunette head in its sights.

An obsession with her cell phone would be her demise. A fitting end to a girl determined to ruin the Hawk dynasty. Claudia exhaled, paused, and tightened her trigger finger, following the training of Robert Hawk.

She had a moment of guilt, a moment of gratitude that the woman was facing away from her, the damage unseen, and then the gun snapped back in a clean, perfect shot. The back of Bell's head exploded, and it was all over for her.

THIRTY-TWO

THE WINNER

Bell Hartley slumped, the majority of her head destroyed by the bullet, and fell forward, her body sprawling.

Claudia had done it. She had killed. Saved Gwen's marriage. Pleased Robert Hawk. Secured her spot in their family. She turned her head toward the front of the suite, listening to see if there was any aftermath, any rush of feet, or shouts. Silence. *Dead* silence. She stepped from the closet and carefully closed it with one gloved hand.

Reaching into her back pocket, she pulled out the thin paper bag and dropped the gun inside, her mind working through all of the instructions from Robert Hawk.

Leave the gun. She placed the bag in the middle of the foyer, in a place it wouldn't be missed. *Done.* Steps quick, she pulled the front door open, her exit from the suite completed in less than a minute. Claudia used the code for the exterior stairwell and jogged down six flights of stairs, exiting onto the main parking garage and unlocking her car.

Less than a minute later, she was on the Strip and gunning the engine, heading toward Robert.

She smiled at the thought of his reaction and how happy and proud he would be.

"Pass this test, and I'll set up a dinner, just the two of my girls. How would you like that?"

Just the two of my girls. Just the way it always should have been.

BELL

My phone dinged as I pulled into the garage. Putting the car into park, I let it idle, digging through my purse and pulling out my cell. Dario's name was on the display, and I opened his text.

—***Go in, get undressed and wait on the bed.***

I smirked. Bossy man. I read the instructions a second time, my body already tightening in anticipation. I shot back a response.

walking in now

I turned off the car and opened the door, grabbing my bag and stepping out, the garage eerily cool and quiet. Locking the doors, I glanced around for a moment, feeling the same crawl of unease that had hit me in the Taco Bell. There, it was ridiculous, the restaurant crowded, no danger in sight. But here .... I listened for the echo of shoes against the floor, but only heard a squeak of tires, a few floors down. Taking a last look around, I entered my code and unlocked the door, moving through the hall and into the suite.

The lights were on, and I almost tripped over the bag, one left in the middle of the floor, just inside the front door. Picking it up, I reached inside, surprised to feel something hard. I stepped into the kitchen, where the light was better and looked inside. It was a gun, *my* gun. I reached inside and pulled it out, confused. In the light, I saw the differences. It was an S&W, not a Glock, this one a bit beefier than mine. I lifted my purse and placed it on the counter, my curiosity causing me to open the neck of it and verify that my own gun was inside. Yep. I looked back at the new weapon and grabbed my phone to text Dario. Maybe it was his. Though... why had he left it in the middle of the foyer?

I turned, stepping on the back of one shoe and lifting my heel, working off the tennis shoe. I flipped my foot forward and the Nike flew through the air and toward—

I stopped. The sole of a tennis shoe was exposed, a bit of an ankle showing before dark jeans began. It was all I could see, the wall hiding the rest of the scene. Someone was in the living room. Lying facedown. Unmoving. My tossed Nike hit the edge of the couch and the person didn't flinch or react in *any* way.

I choked back a scream as my brain warred between stepping backward or forward. In three steps, I could be at the door, twisting the handle and escaping. Three steps in the opposite direction and I would know what, or who, was attached to the rest of that shoe.

I glanced between the gun, the paper bag, and the shoe. My breaths shortened and panic flared.

The door clicked and I spun to face it.

DARIO

I pushed the door open, and she was in the foyer, her phone in hand, her face pale. I smiled, ready to chastise her for not being naked and waiting. But the look on her face, the panic that only intensified when she saw me ... I stepped forward and shut the door. "What's wrong?"

She didn't respond, didn't do anything but turn toward the kitchen, her hands gripping the edge of the counter, her weight heavy on it, her breathing hard. "The living room. I can't—"

She can't. She can't … what? He turned and saw the bottom of an Adidas cross-trainer. A shoe he knew. A shoe he jogged behind in Colorado, her legs pumping up a mountainside, her breath easy as he wheezed, her laugh floating down at him. A shoe he had kicked out of the way too many times, her messy habits the sort that leave clothes in the middle of hallways, and don't expect anyone to trip over them. A shoe that had been pulled on in stiff silence, laced up with short angry jerks, and all but stomped out of their home less than an hour ago.

Gwen.

He fell to his knees and crawled forward, calling her name, knowing, even as he rounded the corner, what he would find. Blood.

Blood, a coiled mess of it, drenching her dark brown hair. Specks of it on the grey sweater, the wood floor. He scrambled toward her, praying aloud, his hands clawing at her body, pulling her into his arms. She rolled toward him, her limbs limp, her features slack.

"Oh God. Gwen…"

He sobbed in a way he hadn't done since he was a child. He hurt in a way he never had in his life. He clung to her, hugged her to his chest, his hand cupping at the wet, damaged back of her head, and pressed a kiss, then a dozen kisses to her face.

She didn't move, didn't blink, didn't react. Her mouth didn't curve into the smile that he loved, her eyes didn't lift, and her chest stayed still.

BELL

I couldn't see what was happening in the living room, I couldn't will myself to move, to step forward, to know. But I didn't have to see. I could hear everything. I could hear the rustle, the scrape, the cry of his voice, the gasps, the shudder of syllables.

It was Gwen. He called her name over and over. Begged her to wake up. Told her he loved her. Told her he was sorry.

It was Gwen. *Dead*.

I lowered myself to the floor, my legs trembling, my knees pulling to my chest, my arms wrapping around them. I closed my eyes, blocking out the view of her foot, which now lay sideways, and moved a little in response to something that Dario was doing. I blocked out sight and thought, and only heard sounds.

The sounds of Dario breaking. The sounds of everything between us shattering.

It was ridiculous to think of myself right then. Crazy for me to have *any* thought in my head other than his grief and the realization that a woman was dead. A woman I didn't know, but one that Vegas had loved and respected. I shouldn't have been thinking of anything except her, and how I could help him.

I shouldn't have thought of us, but I did. I held my knees tightly, listened to him whisper her name, and felt tears leak down my cheeks.

I cried out of guilt.

I cried out of fear.

I cried because, with all of this, I didn't see a future for *us*.

He finally stopped. No more soft cries of Gwen's name. No more whispers of apologies. He stopped, and there was the creak of floorboards, and he came around the corner and stood there, looking at me. I lifted my head and wiped my fingers underneath my eyes.

"How long have you been here? Since you texted me?"

I nodded, mute. His voice was cold, a complete change from the man who had just broken into pieces at the sight of her body.

His eyes moved over the room, taking in details and zeroing in on the kitchen counter. The gun. I pushed off the floor and to my feet.

"Is that yours?"

He was terrifying in this moment. Not in his emotion, but in his calm fury, the controlled cadence of his speech, the emotionlessness of his words.

I shook my head. Wet my tongue. Found my speech. "No. It was in that bag..." I gestured to the paper bag, still sitting on the counter. "The bag was right inside the front door. I almost tripped over it. I picked it up."

"And you touched the gun."

"Yes."

"Don't touch anything else."

He walked over and looked at the gun. Looked back at the living room. "Fucking hell." He stared down at the gun, and I tried to figure out what he was thinking. I stepped closer and he held up his hand.

"Don't come near me."

I swallowed, panic welling at the curt tone and the way he moved, just a fraction of a step, away from me.

"This looks bad. This looks fucking bad."

I couldn't stop my head from turning, from looking at her shoe. Only now, in my new position, I saw more—her body, half-curled on its side. I closed my eyes and wondered if I would ever forget that image.

Is love worth a death? Is our love... this affair? I forced myself to look back at her, to understand the loss of life that I—*we*—caused.

Then, a second thought occurred to me. One I should have figured out the minute I saw her shoe. In 'my' suite. Her dark mess of bloody brunette hair.

"Did she... was I..." I couldn't find the words, form the thought, complete the question. Was that supposed to be *me*, slumped on the floor, one leg awkwardly bent?

Am I supposed to be dead right now instead of her?

Dario ignored me. He pulled out his cell phone, dialed a number and lifted the phone to his ear.

"This is Dario Capece." He spoke firmly, a man in control, a voice that gave me hope.

"I need an officer to Suite 908 of The Majestic. I'll have security meet you at the front desk and escort you up. There's been a murder."

His eyes met mine.

"The victim was Bell Hartley."

Want to know what happens next?
Continue with DOUBLE DOWN, available now.

STAY INFORMED

Did you enjoy EVEN MONEY?

Want to find out about Alessandra Torre's next novel?

Get her free monthly newsletter at www.nextnovel.com. Each newsletter contains stories, fun facts, writing updates and exclusive giveaways.

ACKNOWLEDGMENTS

With my first novel, I was alone on an island. Now, I have a tribe of many. While I don't use the same team on every novel, I would be remiss if I didn't reach out and thank the following individuals:

To Natasha, Marion and Madison - thank you for reading endless drafts, critiquing characters and plot points, and letting me pick and shift through your feedback. As you all know, I am a terrible first-drafter, and I appreciate you helping this baby to grow from its weak roots and into the beautiful creature it now is.

To Perla, Janice and Erik - thank you for combing every line, paragraph and page break and making this manuscript as error-free as possible. I wince and laugh every time I see the near-calamities that you catch.

To Tricia Crouch - Thank you for reading every single draft, for proofing endless Radish episodes, and for talking me through the rough spots and off the ledges. I love you!

To Joey - Thank you for the inspiration, the back rubs and advice. Thank you for distracting me when I needed it and supporting me when I holed up in my office and worked. I love you more than anything on this earth.

ABOUT THE AUTHOR

Alessandra Torre is an award-winning New York Times bestselling author of seventeen novels. Torre has been featured in such publications as Elle and Elle UK, as well as guest blogged for the Huffington Post and RT Book Reviews. She is also the Bedroom Blogger for Cosmopolitan.com. In addition to writing, Alessandra is the creator of Alessandra Torre Ink, a website, community, and online school for aspiring authors.

Learn more about Alessandra at alessandratorre.com or join 40,000 readers and sign up for her popular monthly newsletter at nextnovel.com.

facebook.com/alessandratorre0
twitter.com/readalessandra
instagram.com/alessandratorre4
amazon.com/Alessandra-Torre

Made in the USA
Columbia, SC
22 May 2018